**ABLE TEA**

MW00437076

## *ROSARIO BLANCANALES*
## *FIRED FROM THE HIP*

He swung the barrel of his weapon in a wide arc across the bow of the boat, firing for the waterline and then for the figure crouched behind the engines. The Able Team warrior fired again as another figure materialized at the stern, a man wielding a wide-barreled weapon. But in the same instant that he squeezed the trigger, he also saw the muzzle flash.

Blancanales knew immediately that given the range and its trajectory, the shell would pierce the Bayliner's hull.

Someone screamed as the muffled explosion from below sent shrapnel through the deck. The Bayliner lurched to port, and Blancanales felt himself thrown against the bulkhead. But as he scrambled to his knees, he jammed in another magazine and squeezed off six more useless rounds before a second explosion hurled him into the blackness.

## ABLE TEAM

### DICK STIVERS

# HOSTILE FIRE

## A GOLD EAGLE BOOK FROM
## WORLDWIDE.

TORONTO · NEW YORK · LONDON · PARIS
AMSTERDAM · STOCKHOLM · HAMBURG
ATHENS · MILAN · TOKYO · SYDNEY

First edition August 1990

ISBN 0-373-65402-2

Special thanks and acknowledgment to
Ken Rose for his contribution to this work.

# HOSTILE FIRE

## 1

The Black Ghosts came for Jackie Minh two days later than anyone expected. They pulled up just after midnight in a blue Toyota that had tinted windows and a customized grille. When Jackie attempted to resist, they hit him twice—first across the back of the head, then across the mouth. Traces of blood were later found on the staircase, still more on the gravel. Although there were at least a dozen witnesses from Gook Town, naturally no one was willing to talk....

JACKIE MINH'S FATE was sealed on a Thursday, a particularly bleak Thursday with scattered showers from the south and damp winds blowing along the coast. The low fog rising from San Pedro swirled around his crabbing boots as he waited for Detective Sam Vong on the finish docks below Westminster.

"You sure you want to go through with this?" Vong asked after he'd finally joined Minh.

Minh shrugged and gazed at the lean, dark detective. "Sure, why not?"

"Because once you make a statement, I'll have to file a report. And once I file a report, there's no telling where it'll end up."

Minh hesitated a moment, pondering the detective's dark eyes and studying his aquiline features. Then, nodding with a sigh, he said, "Yeah, I want to give a statement."

They withdrew to a concrete bench beside the Thoi-Trang Bait Shop. Beyond the wharf stood at least a dozen more shops with names liked Phoung Fashions and Thuy's Video...all testaments to Vietnamese fortitude and perseverance.

"All right," Vong said, "let's take it from the top. You were off the Oregon coast, right?"

Minh nodded. "That's right. I was fishing on one of Sonny Trang's boats off the Oregon coast."

"And was that unusual?"

"What do you mean?"

"To go all the way up to Oregon?"

"Sure, it was unusual. But when you fish for Sonny Trang, you don't ask questions, okay?"

"So then what happened?"

"Then out of nowhere comes this trawler. Very old, okay? Very old and rusty."

"And you'd never seen it before?"

"No, never."

"And then?"

"Then Skipper Huynh tells me and Bao Loi to help unload packages from the trawler and store them in the hold."

"What kind of packages?"

"Little packages of brown waterproof paper."

"How big?"

Minh held up his hands in order to indicate ten or twelve inches.

"And the weight?"

"About one kilo, okay? One kilo."

"What did you think was in the packages?"

Minh shrugged. "I didn't know."

"You mean until one of them broke open, right?"

"Yeah, I didn't know until one of them broke open."

"And then?"

Minh reached into the pocket of his raincoat and withdrew a two-inch square of cellophane filled with white powder. "And then this."

Vong unwrapped the cellophane, carefully removed a pinch of powder and put it to his lips.

"Okay," Minh said, smiling. "Now you going to arrest Sonny Trang, or what?"

Detective Vong stood and walked toward the end of the pier where he stared off at the two condominiums being developed by General Trang's consortium. He also took in the bronze monument dedicated to the Saigon dead that the general had erected eight months earlier.

"I suppose you realize that there are a number of people who won't consider you to be the most credible witness," Vong said at last, turning to face the man who had followed him to the end of the pier. "In fact, a lot of people might even think you concocted this story to get even with the general for stealing your girlfriend."

Minh frowned, jammed his hands into his coat pockets and gazed out at the skeletal condominiums rising above the south bay fog. "Okay, so maybe the general took Kim Kiet away from me," Minh replied. "So maybe I don't like him much because of that. But I know what I saw, and you also have evidence right in your hand."

"Tell me something," Vong began, "have you seen Kim lately?"

Minh shook his head, eyes still fixed on the towering frames above the gray skyline.

"Well, I've got to be honest with you, Jackie, she doesn't look too unhappy to me. In fact, she looks like she's doing pretty well. She's got a sixty-thousand-dollar sports car, a diamond the size of a knuckle and the sort of place you and I can't even dream about."

"Hey, those things don't mean anything to her. They don't mean anything at all to her. Besides, we're not talking about Kim Kiet. We're talking about Sonny Trang's heroin."

"Which brings me to another point," Vong said. "How do you know the smack belonged to the general? The fact that Sonny owned the boat doesn't prove he's guilty of possession."

Minh turned and clenched his fists. "Look, I bring you evidence and I make a statement. Now you go and file the report, okay? You file a report that says Sonny Trang is dealing heroin just like he did in Saigon, because that's the truth."

Vong lit a cigarette, rested his elbows on the railing and stared into the oily water below. He was the only Vietnamese cop on the Westminster Police Force, and he'd spent the better part of two years fighting the racial barrier that kept him from a legitimate beat in the city. In the end they had simply sent him back to Gook Town.

"I won't be able to protect you, Jackie," Vong said at last. "Once the district attorney gets wind of this, there's just no way I'll be able to protect you. It's not like in the movies. I don't have the budget and I don't have the manpower."

"Hey, I don't need the manpower. I supply my own manpower. You just file your report and start your investigation. Then we'll see just how big General Sonny Trang really is, okay?"

SIX DAYS PASSED, six days of menacing glances and suspicious looks. Jackie Minh soon noticed that people became quiet whenever he entered a room, that whispers followed him everywhere along the Little Saigon strip. Even the usually amiable Bao Loi had grown cold.

"So you think I'm bad news, huh?" Minh finally said one Tuesday morning when he and Loi found themselves alone on the dock. "So you think I got some kind of disease, huh? Well, I think you got some kind of disease, too. It's called cowarditis, okay? It's called real bad cowarditis.''

Loi glanced over his shoulder, probably to determine that no one was watching. A skinny man with fragments of Vietcong shrapnel still embedded in his hip, he had known Minh since his days in the refugee camp in Texas. On this particular bleak Tuesday morning, however, his eyes were the eyes of a stranger.

''Sonny Trang knows everything,'' he said. ''You understand what I'm saying? He knows everything. He knows when you been good and he knows when you been bad. He knows when you been telling the truth and he knows when you been lying. He also knows when you been getting the cops to snoop around his business, and he don't like it one little bit.''

''Well, maybe I don't like him taking Kim from me, okay?'' Minh countered. ''Maybe I don't like it one little bit, either.''

Loi turned again, once more meeting Minh's eyes. There was a look in them that Minh had never seen before. ''Hey, you listen to me. The general, he didn't take Kim from you. She went to him by choice. She went to him because she knows it's better to be with the general than with some stupid shrimper who doesn't know to keep his mouth shut. And even if she didn't go to him by choice, there's still nothing you can do about it because the general's the law around here, and that's just the way it is.''

It was also during those six days that Minh first felt the presence of the Black Ghosts. The Ghosts had been formed to protect the community from the roundeye attacks of 1977. By '78 or '79, however, the line between protection and extortion had grown thin.

*And if you have to ask who the Ghosts have come to watch, then surely they've come to watch you.*

MINH HAD BEEN DOZING in a chair by the window when the Black Ghosts finally arrived. On the table lay the remains of his dinner: a bowl of cold rice, dried fish sticks and a warm Coke. At his feet lay a dozen letters to Kim that he had never quite managed to mail. In the photograph on his knee she appeared as a fragile girl in gray silk and blue jeans. In the photograph clipped from a newspaper and tacked to the water-stained wall, she was completely dominated by the presence of Sonny Trang at her side.

When he heard the footsteps on the staircase, he assumed that it was only old Xuan returning from another night of mah-jongg. But when Xuan didn't shuffle past his door as he usually did, Minh finally eased the curtains back and saw them: four classic Ghosts with gel-slicked hair.

He slid his left hand across the table and switched off the light. He wasn't particularly frightened. In fact, after all the days of waiting, he was almost relieved at the prospect of a direct confrontation...a hard and direct confrontation with the darker side of Sonny Trang's world. He slipped on his shoes and dropped to a crouch. Then, hearing another footstep on the staircase, he eased into the shadows by the door.

He extended a leg to stretch the muscles at the sound of the squealing gate, then slipped deeper into the shadows as he heard the latch being lifted. For one or two decisive moments he contemplated moving to the drawer to get his fishing knife. But, in the end, he knew that his best defense was his faith in tradition, and tradition demanded that he have empty hands.

There were two locks on the door to Minh's home: a rusting Yale and a somewhat stronger dead bolt. But he knew that a lock was only as sound as the base that held it, and the wood that held these locks was virtually rotten to the core. When the first intruder thrust out his heel, both locks gave way as if hit with a battering ram.

Minh waited a full three seconds before making his move. He waited until both Ghosts had entered his room, until he could actually read the letter tattooed on their wrists, smell the bay rum and saki mix. Then, springing from the shadows, he struck with a quick kick to the first Ghost's knee.

The gang member was a lanky boy with greenish hair and a diamond stud in his left ear. When the edge of Minh's foot connected with the knee, the boy howled in pain and crumpled to the floor.

The second Ghost was a stocky boy, undoubtedly a boxer and obviously strong. But Minh didn't try to match the boy's strength. He merely stepped to the inside with a whipping "crane's head" to the temple.

This time the response was little more than an agonized groan, then a low sigh as the boy slid back against the wall. But when Minh stepped in to finish the job, he found himself facing a butterfly knife.

Minh hesitated, feinting with a hip and recalling his master's dictum: *when fighting an armed opponent, one must always control the weapon*. He feinted again, dropping his shoulder to draw the attack. Then, finally stepping in as the blade swung down, Minh grabbed the boy's wrist and snapped the arm across his knee.

His attack left the stocky Ghost gasping for air and virtually blinded with pain. Then, stepping in a second time with a double *shuto* to the neck, Minh easily dropped the ghost to the floor.

The first boy had risen by now and was also wielding a knife. But once more feinting at the shoulder, Minh spun with a circling rear kick and knocked the weapon away. In the end Minh was actually smiling into the boy's frightened eyes. But before he could deliver his last skipping kick, a third Ghost materialized out of nowhere.

Minh saw only the suggestion of the weapon—sixteen or seventeen inches of lead pipe. When it struck his skull, the world went went white, red, then black.

Minh fell to his knees, then finally to the cold linoleum. He regained consciousness as they dragged him down the stairs and out to their waiting Toyota. Using his last bit of strength, he tried to claw the stocky boy's eyes, but only succeeded in leaving traces of his own blood on the gravel.

THROUGH THE THROBBING PAIN at the base of his skull, Jackie Minh realized he was in a vast, poorly lit room. The massive crates along the far wall and the stench of tar and stagnant water led him to believe he was being held captive in one of Trang's warehouses.

"So, tough guy, you happy to be alive?"

The three Ghosts surrounded the chair he was tied to. One of them was still bleeding slightly from the mouth. Another clutched his ribs. The third wore wraparound sunglasses.

"'Cause if you're happy to be alive now, pretty soon you might feel differently. In fact, pretty soon you might give anything just to be dead."

Minh's attention was diverted by the faint odor of a rich cigar and the dim outline of heavy-lidded eyes watching behind the glowing tip. Was it Trang? he wondered.

"Okay, tough guy," Sunglasses said, "this is how we play. I ask questions, you give answers. When it's all over, we kill what's left. Okay?"

The stocky one stepped forward, carrying a *t'ieh-pien* or stiff bamboo whip in his left hand. In his right, he carried a length of silk cord.

"Question number one," Sunglasses said. "How come you been saying bad things about the general?"

Minh imagined the pain before he felt it, the stinging whip across his shins, then the burning agony from his ankles to his knees. But when the blow finally came, it was worse than what he'd anticipated.

Sunglasses moved a little closer, squatting on his haunches with an easy smile. He was a muscular boy with a thin scar running from his hairline to his jaw. The words *Hac Qui* were tattooed on his wrist.

"Okay, brother," Sunglasses continued, "why don't we try it a little differently? Like maybe this time we ask the question, you give the answer and then Little Li don't have to hit you. Now, how's that sound?"

But even before Minh had a chance to respond, the *t'ieh-pien* slammed against his shins again. The pain took his breath away; it wrenched the air right out of his lungs. But even before he could scream, the lanky boy hit him again.

"Look," Sunglasses said softly, "you think we enjoy this? You think we're having a good time? We're not. We're not having a good time, 'cause this isn't how Vietnamese should treat each other. You know what I'm saying here? If you're pissed off 'cause the general took your girl, then you should talk it over with the general. But you don't go to the cops, man, and tell them all kinds of lies, 'cause that's not good for anyone. That's not good for the general, that's not good for the general's people, and that's not good for you."

They must have hit him another four or five times before Minh finally blacked out, slipping into a soothing oblivion for at least three or four minutes.

"Come on, brother, let's be reasonable," Sunglasses murmured. "We already know you're a tough guy,
so what's the point of going on like this? If you don't
talk to us, then you're going to have to talk to the
Woman in White and, believe me, brother, you don't
want to talk to her."

Minh suffered through six more blows before he
lapsed into unconsciousness again. Then, for at least
a minute, he was only aware of vague impres-
sions . . . of spiked heels on the cold concrete, of a sea
breeze from the rafters, of the Ghosts withdrawing as
someone swore softly in Vietnamese. And, although
his eyes remained shut, he was completely conscious
when a woman stepped forward and said softly in
Vietnamese, "All right, prepare him."

THEY HAD INJECTED him with fire, he thought.
Someone had held his arm steady, and then they'd injected the vein with a ribbon of fire that shot to the
center of his brain. Moments later his heart began to
race and beads of perspiration dotted his face. The
woman's hands, however, couldn't have been colder.

She was very tall, with chiseled features and thin
lips. Her hair was drawn into a tight bun, accentuat-
ing her triangular face and tiny mouth. Her eyes were
virtually black, and the *ao dai* she wore buttoned to
the throat was white.

"Buckets and towels," she said under her breath.
"And the battery. Bring me the battery," she added in
Vietnamese.

He felt her fingers running deftly down the buttons of his shirt, then sliding lower to unzip his jeans. Then he felt the gentle shock of her nails on his testicles, and the equally soft shock of her voice as she said, "He's stronger than he looks."

There were faint whispers from across the room, then what sounded like the crackle of an electrical charge. The fire in his head was replaced with a numbing cold, and he couldn't seem to control his muscles.

"Look, maybe he doesn't really know anything," Sunglasses said. "Maybe he just..."

Minh chanced another quick look at the woman, another split-second glance at her face and black gaze. Then, as her fingers returned to his testicles in order to attach the electrode, he squeezed his eyes shut again.

"Okay," the woman whispered, "now we're ready."

IN THE END, he supposed he must have told them everything: what he had said to Detective Vong, what Vong had said in reply. He also might have told them things that hadn't been said...told them anything just to make the pain stop. And as each agonizing jolt had wrenched through his gut, he'd come a little closer to finally understanding that the woman actually enjoyed inflicting pain, actually loved every excruciating second of it.

Sunglasses untied him from the chair and the lanky boy hoisted him to his feet. The woman briefly inspected his testicles, gently cupping them in her hand.

Finally she turned toward the man smoking the cigar. "He's told us everything," she said.

"How can you be certain?" the man asked.

"Experience," she replied in Vietnamese.

The lanky boy withdrew the length of silk rope again and slipped it around Minh's throat. Then Sunglasses grabbed Minh's arms and jammed a knee into his back.

"Not here," the man smoking the cigar ordered. "Do it in the hills."

"But how do we—"

"Put him in the car and take him into the hills."

IT WAS ALMOST CHILLY on the docks, with another onshore breeze and a hint of rain in the air. Although Minh hadn't regained full consciousness, he was aware of little things: the water lapping against the pilings, the soft moan of mooring ropes and the cables of moonlight across the black water. He was also aware of the fact that in ten or twenty minutes he would probably be dead.

They draped him across the hood of the Toyota as the lanky one worked the key in the lock and Sunglasses scowled at the water. Minh realized the stocky one was probably also on the dock, although he sensed the man with the cigar and the woman had vanished.

"Why don't we put him in the trunk?" the lanky one asked, still struggling with the lock. "That way if we get stopped by the cops—"

"Shut up and open the door," Sunglasses replied.

"Hey, I'm just saying—"

"Just shut up and open the door."

There were sounds of squeaking hinges and someone banging a fist on the fender. "Hey, easy on the finish!" the lanky one yelled. "Okay, brother, time to go bye-bye,'' he continued, turning his attention to Minh.

But as Minh felt himself being hoisted to his feet again, felt the sickening stab of pain in his groin, he was also conscious of something else, something he hadn't felt since the night had begun—rage.

He stumbled as they dragged him to the door of the Toyota, then slipped to his knees as they tried to shove him into the back seat. But when they finally hoisted him to his feet again, he actually moved quite smoothly, virtually glided into the attack.

He went for the eyes, because he lacked the strength for a stronger blow. Using the *Erh-lung Chu*—twin dragons clutching a pearl—he struck with a quick flick of his wrist, actually feeling his fingers reach the back of the lanky boy's socket. Then, as part of the same phenomenally fast movement, he struck again with the ''tiger's claw.''

The lanky boy screamed, clutched his face and collapsed onto the dock. Sunglasses reached for Minh's arm, but suddenly he was also screaming, reeling back as Minh's fingers pierced the plastic lens and tore at the left eye.

Minh felt the blood and ocular fluid on his wrist, the howling scream in his ears. The lanky boy was now whimpering. Someone else shouted, ''Shoot him! Shoot him!''

But by now Minh had managed to reach the end of the dock, and although he'd never been a particularly strong swimmer, even death by water was better than death at the hands of the Ghosts.

The water was cold, and the shock of it sent crippling waves of pain from his groin. He knew there were sharks in the bay, and a strong undertow, but at least he would die on his own terms, he thought. At least he would die with his honor intact and a clean vision of Kim in his mind.

He saw her quite clearly in the end: lips parted in a shy smile, eyes moist from laughter. "Even when we're apart, we're together," she had once told him, and now more than ever it was true. She was with him for the first desperate breath beneath the pier, and the long plunge into blackness. She was with him when his arms turned to rubber and he felt he couldn't take another stroke... and she was still with him when he finally managed to reach the far shore.

## 2

Detective Sam Vong pulled out a pack of cigarettes, lit one and took a long draw. As he moved across the vomit-stained concrete, he also toyed with a key chain, a cheap brass thing he'd picked up at a law-enforcement convention in Cincinnati.

It was half past ten on a gray Friday morning. Although half a dozen uniforms still lingered on the Long Beach docks, Vong was alone in the warehouse. Among the clues now recorded in his well-used notebook were two notes concerning the blood on the gravel, and three buttons from Jackie Minh's shirt.

A beefy lieutenant named Lester Hogg peered through the doorway and shouted Vong's name. Although Vong was probably as close to Hogg as any man in the Long Beach station, they were hardly friends.

"You about ready to wrap this up, or what?" Hogg asked as he looked across the room at the crates along the far wall.

"Not really, no."

"Why the hell not?"

Vong knelt to examine another trace of blood beside the steel chair. Then, finally rising with a fragment of copper wire between his fingers, he said, "Because something happened here and I think we'd better find out what it was."

From the warehouse they moved back outside to the docks where the uniforms were either sipping from plastic cups of coffee or from tins of canned orange juice. Although three or four smirked as Vong passed, he ignored them. He was used to his colleagues' prejudices.

"You got any idea what it's going to cost this city to dredge the harbor?" Hogg asked as they gazed down at the oily water.

Vong ignored the question and knelt again to examine two star-shaped stains on the weathered planks. "Does this look like fish blood or human blood?"

Hogg shook his head with a tired sigh. "Sammy, I don't think you're listening to me. We don't have a murder here. In fact, we don't even have assault. All we got is a missing person, and frankly I just can't justify this kind of action."

Vong rose to his feet again, withdrew a penknife he'd picked up at a police officers' convention in Philadelphia and began to probe the splintered planks of a storage shed.

"There's also no evidence of any ethnic factor to consider," Hogg said. "I mean, let's face it, these people are always disappearing for one reason or another. Then two, three weeks later, surprise, it was all just a silly mistake.''

Vong turned, examined a shapeless wad of lead he had pried from the wood. ''Nine millimeter?''

Hogg merely shook his head again. ''Sammy. Sammy, listen to me for a moment. Even if you're right, even if something's going down around here, you think anyone's going to care? Shit, we're talking about the refugees. You got action here every night of the week. You start trying to make a federal case out of it and people are going to start complaining.''

Vong pocketed the slug and lit another cigarette. ''Story goes like this,'' he said. ''According to Minh, Sonny Trang's bringing in Asian smack via the Oregon coast. He's bringing in at least twenty or thirty keys per drop on trawlers manned by Vietnamese crews. When Minh tries to blow the whistle, Sonny has him whacked.''

''And the whole deal's run through Ho Chi Minh City, I suppose. Come on, Sammy, how many times have we heard this one before? Besides, way I heard it, Jackie Minh's had a problem with Trang ever since Trang shacked up with Minh's girl.''

Vong slipped the penknife back into his pocket and began to toy with the key chain again. ''It's not that simple, Lester.''

''I'm not saying it is. I'm just saying that everything cuts two ways. You got ten or fifteen cases on your desk. Now, you can either spend your time dicking around with the maybes, or you can start making some clean arrests. Anyway, I don't think you want to fool around with Sonny Trang. It ain't going to look right.''

"I don't have a problem with Trang."

"Maybe not, but that's not to say there isn't a certain political angle to consider. I mean, let's face it, the general's definitely a credit to the community."

Vong ran the back of his hand across his mouth and glanced down at what might have been another spot of dried blood. "So was Jackie Minh."

They reached a particularly foul stretch of wharf that was sometimes know as Ho Chi Minh Alley. At one time more than twenty Asian families had been crammed into cold-water hovels above the warehouse blocks—the men worked twelve hours a day on the shrimpers; the woman worked nine hours a day in the canneries; the children ran wild in the alleys.

"I want to write it up and send it to the Feds," Vong said as they moved along the refuse-strewn pavement, along passages that still reeked of spoiled plumb sauce and almonds. "I want to write a report and send it to the DEA."

"And tell them what?" Hogg countered. "Some nineteen-year-old dockhand with a chip on his shoulder claims Sonny Trang's dealing smack? Come on, Sammy, get serious. The DEA's got better things to do than run down rumors like that."

"Then what do you suggest?"

Hogg shrugged. "You want my honest opinion?"

Vong tapped another smoke from the pack. "Yeah, I want your honest opinion."

"Okay, then I think you should drop it. I mean, no offense intended, but we're talking about Gook Town here."

"Well, I don't think I can do that, Lester."

Hogg frowned. "Okay, it's your career." He turned to leave, then suddenly spun around again. "Oh, and, Sammy, just for your information, Sam Spade rolled his own."

Vong looked at him, the cigarette still drooping from the corner of his mouth. "What are you talking about, Lester?"

Hogg smiled again. "Sam Spade. He didn't smoke Lucky Strikes. He rolled his own."

VONG SPENT four days preparing the Jackie Minh report for the Drug Enforcement Administration, four gray days of intermittent rain and coastal fog. For the most part he worked at his kitchen table; he must have smoked at least six packs of cigarettes and belted down a fifth of Wild Turkey. As for his meals, he either grabbed a burger or threw a can of stew onto the hot plate.

Vong received a response to his report on Friday, a typically foul day with hordes of tourists wandering the beachfront and dozens of petty thefts. There were also the usual drunken brawls along the docks, and the usual complaints concerning the Gook Town gangs. Around noon, after processing at least four aggravated assaults and a possible attempted murder, Vong slipped out for lunch. When he returned to his office, he found a lean Texan named Houston Tide standing at his open window.

An intelligence aide during the war, Tide knew Vong from Saigon where they had tracked a Vietcong sapper who turned out to be a fifteen-year-old kid on a Honda. They had then spent three months together running down the ARVN drug rings. Since the fall of Saigon, their relationship was probably best described as "below the line," which meant they occasionally exchanged information on an unofficial basis.

"You want the good news first, or the bad news?" the DEA agent asked.

Between them on the cigarette-scarred desk lay Minh's report—well thumbed and marked with coffee rings. Vong sank into his swivel chair and began toying with his key chain. "Makes no difference to me."

"Okay, then the good news is that I think you may be onto something. The bad news is that I can't help you crack it."

Vong tapped out a cigarette. "You got any idea what twenty keys of number four horse brings on the street these days."

"Sure, I know. But I also know which way the wind blows, and believe me, this isn't the time to start mixing with Sonny Trang."

Vong slid his hand across the desk and withdrew a few scribbled sheets of paper. "What if I were to tell you that Jackie Minh isn't the only one who thinks the general may be dirty?"

"The verdict still stands, Sammy." Tide shrugged. "I'm just not in a position to pursue this one...not even informally."

"Why the hell not?"

"Because it crosses lines."

"What kind of lines?"

"Dark lines."

Tide moved away from the window and began to examine various objects on Vong's bookcase. Among the more telltale items were two ashtrays pilfered from hotels in Los Angeles and Chicago, a silver falcon in plaster of Paris and a cigarette lighter reputedly used in the Bogart-version of *The Big Sleep*.

"I like you, Sammy," Tide said at last. "You're one of the nuttiest cops I've ever met, but I like you. So when I tell you this is something you don't want to mess around with, you've got to believe it's coming from the heart. I mean, this isn't just the usual Washington bullshit. This is the truth—Sonny Trang's off-limits."

Vong casually flicked an ash to the floor. "Says who?"

"Come on, Sammy, you know how the game's played."

"Says who, Houston?"

"The Company."

Vong stabbed out his cigarette and moved to the window. "I thought the war was over."

"Look, you know how it is. Old links never die. They just go underground."

"So what's that supposed to mean?"

"It means the Company still has a little arrangement with Sonny."

"What kind of arrangement?"

"The usual. Sonny keeps his eye on the community, maybe runs a few operations back into Nam, and the Company keeps him out of trouble."

"Well, it stinks."

"Sure, it stinks, but it's also the name of the game, and you're asking for trouble if you try to bust it up."

"Yeah, well, maybe I could use a little trouble in my life right now."

Tide turned and moved toward the door, but Vong wasn't about to let the conversation end. He followed his old friend out of the building.

"Will you do me a favor?" Tide finally asked as they descended the shabby staircase to the parking lot. "Will you at least consider calling in a little professional help from the big boys?"

"I thought *you* were professional help."

"Come on, Sammy, you know what I'm talking about."

"No, I don't."

Tide withdrew a pencil stub and a spiral notebook. "There are some people I know," he said as he jotted down a telephone number. "I worked with them a couple of years back in Mexico City. If things start getting weird, I want you to call me at this number and give me a chance to talk to these people before you do anything else."

Vong took the piece of paper from Tide's notebook and studied it for a moment. "Able Team? What in hell is Able Team?"

"They're extralegal," Tide answered. "Under the table and extralegal. They're good, Sammy. They're good *and* they're clean."

"So?"

"So the CIA's got long arms, and you just might need a little backup."

"I already have backup."

Tide shook his head. "Not like this you don't."

ANOTHER THREE DAYS PASSED but for the most part, Vong only worked on the edges of the case. He returned to the Long Beach docks, where he questioned a couple of shrimpers who pretended they had hardly known Jackie Minh. He questioned Skipper Huynh, who practically claimed the same thing. He questioned a waitress from the Dak To Café whom he knew had served Minh fish and chips almost every night of the week. She claimed she didn't even recognize his photograph. Finally, he questioned Bao Loi.

Like Minh, Bao Loi was a wiry kid with muscular arms and a slightly concave chest. Vong found him at the Tai Loi Doughnut Shop in Saigon Plaza. The place was deserted, except for a couple of twelve-year-old boys from the Mother of Mercy Orphanage. Although the night sky was clear, he could hear thunder in the distance.

There was no preamble, no introduction. Vong simply slid into a booth opposite the boy and placed his pack of cigarettes on the table. Then, in Vietnamese, he said he wanted to talk about Jackie.

Loi smirked and pulled out his own pack. "English, man. You want to talk, you talk English."

"Fine, then how about telling me about Jackie in English?"

Loi shrugged. "I don't know anything, okay? Nothing."

"Well, that's not the way I heard it. In fact, the way I heard it, you and Jackie were pretty tight. You came out of the same camp in '78 when you were both only eight or nine. You went to the same school in the early eighties. You been working Skipper Huynh's boat every since."

"So talk to Huynh, okay?"

"I already did, but it seems he's got a little memory problem."

"Well, maybe I got a little memory problem, too. Maybe I can't remember what Jackie looks like, okay?"

Vong lit a smoke and lounged against the back of the booth, but didn't take his eyes off Loi for a moment. "Why don't you tell me about the last time you and Jackie saw each other?"

"It was a long time ago. I don't even remember."

"Couldn't have been that long ago. After all, the two of you were working Huynh's boat up until the night Jackie disappeared."

"So?"

"So, what did you talk about?"

"I don't know. Nothing."

"Nothing about Sonny Trang? Nothing about meeting a trawler off the coast of Oregon?"

Loi tapped a cigarette out of the pack, but couldn't seem to steady his hand enough to light a match.

"It's called sitting between a rock and a hard place," Vong added. "You know that expression?"

Loi screwed up his face and briefly shut his eyes. "Look, why pick on me? Why not pick on someone else?"

"Because you were his friend, Bao, and there was a time when that used to mean something."

"Well, maybe now all it means is a bullet in the back."

Vong withdrew his tarnished lighter and extended it to Loi's dangling cigarette. "You know, Sonny Trang's just another person. He may have a lot of clout around here, have a lot of money, but basically he's just another guy from Saigon."

Loi took a long drag, but otherwise remained still. "Look, maybe this isn't just about Sonny Trang, okay? Maybe this is also about certain people who are worse than Sonny Trang."

"What kind of people, Bao?"

Loi shrugged. "Just people, certain people."

"Vietnamese people?"

But this time the boy just shook his head. "Look, maybe Jackie Minh was a friend of mine, okay? But I also think he was sometimes pretty stupid. So the general steals Kim Kiet, but that don't mean you start giving problems to the general. You know what I'm saying? You don't start making trouble for the general and you don't make trouble for the general's friends."

"So where is he, Bao? Where's Jackie Minh?"

The boy shook his head again. "He's nowhere, man. Jackie Minh's nowhere."

IT WAS HALF PAST EIGHT in the evening when Vong finally returned to his apartment loft. By almost anyone's standards it was a shabby place.

For a long time he simply sat on his sofa, feet propped on the coffee table, eyes fixed on the slow-turning fan. He was still sitting there when the two CIA men knocked on his door.

They introduced themselves as Smith and Jones, although they might have been Mutt and Jeff. Smith was a tall, lean man with slightly graying hair swept back from his forehead. Jones was short, round and mostly bald. Their clothing was virtually identical: loud, ill-fitting but obviously expensive.

"Nice place you got here," Jones said, smirking as he ran his hand along the ratty sofa and inspected the grime on the windowsill. "Real nice place."

"You boys want to tell me what this is all about?" Vong asked.

The two men exchanged glances and smiled.

"Call it a courtesy visit," Smith said. "You're a hardworking law-enforcement official, and we of the federal government felt it was about time to pay you a little courtesy visit."

"In order to let you know just how much we appreciate your dedication," Jones added.

Vong moved to his makeshift bar in the corner and poured himself a rum. "I'd offer you one," he said, "but seeing how this is an *official* visit, I don't imagine you'd accept." Then, lifting his glass, he added, "Mud in your eye."

Smith had begun a slow tour of the room, first pausing at the bookshelf to examine a dog-eared copy of Duke's *Celebrated Criminal Cases*, then pausing again to examine a wall clock that probably hadn't ticked in years. Finally, turning with another easy smile, he said that maybe it was time to lay the cards on the table.

"Meaning that we'd like to talk to you about the Jackie Minh case," Jones added. "Meaning that we're not trying to move in on your territory. We just want to talk about it."

Vong sank back down on the sofa with his drink and lit another cigarette. "Okay, let's talk."

There was another exchange of glances as Smith also withdrew a cigarette and Jones pulled out a notebook and pen.

"More than a week ago," Jones began, "you followed up a fairly routine missing persons check with a twenty-two-page report concerning one General Sonny Trang, correct?''

Vong shrugged and took another sip of rum. "I don't know if I'd call Jackie Minh's case routine."

"Now, according to this report, you claim Sonny Trang's possibly involved with the clandestine importation of illegal substances. Also correct?''

Before Vong could answer, however, Smith interjected, "It's not that we think Trang's as pure as the driven snow. It's just that we think you might not have the whole story."

"Fine," Vong said, "so what's the whole story?''

"Sonny Trang happens to be a very important individual in the eyes of the U.S. government," Jones said.

"So's Jackie Minh," Vong replied. "So's everyone in my jurisdiction."

"Well, that's just it," Smith said, "what exactly *is* your jurisdiction? You see, we have it on very good authority that some of . . . well, *your* people are still walking both sides of the street. Now, I'm not talking about an occasional letter to the homeland. I'm talking about aiding and abetting honest-to-God Communist spies."

"That's not to say they're all necessarily willing," Jones put in. "But the effect is the same: Communist intelligence missions slipping in behind the Vietnamese refugee waves."

Vong butted his cigarette, put down his glass and moved from the couch to the window. He was sure they'd have men watching below.

"This isn't exactly a new story."

"Of course it isn't," Smith said. "But just last month we located two, count 'em two, six-cylinder Communist spies operating out of the Vietnamese community in New Orleans."

"They generally use the familial approach," Jones added. "They find a likely candidate and tell him, 'Hey, buddy, it just so happens your Uncle Sang's alive and well in Ho Chi Minh City. Now, if you want to keep him alive and well, you'll start passing us secrets from General Dynamics.' Of course, the variations are endless, but the effect's the same—nationalized Vietnamese serving a hostile power."

"And Sonny Trang's your man on the inside?" Vong asked.

"Well, your people respect him, don't they? They *trust* him. If one of those Red recruiters tries to put the squeeze on some guy in the community, that guy always knows he can turn to the general for help. All he has to say is, 'Hey, General, the Commies are trying to make a move on me. They're telling me that if I don't work for them, they're going to kill my uncle.' And the general's going to take care of it for him. Trang's got a thousand eyes and ears. He can go places we can't even find, talk to people who won't even give us the time of day."

"And naturally we also *trust* the general," Smith added, "which counts for a lot in this game. Believe me."

Vong lit another smoke and gazed down into the black streets below. Gook Town isn't a place, he reminded himself. It really *is* a state of mind.

"I think you might have the wrong idea about Sonny Trang," Vong said at last. "Vietnamese people don't trust him. They fear him."

"So what?" Jones countered. "The man's a buffer against Communist intrusion."

"Which is why we're going to have to insist that you leave him alone," Smith added.

Vong turned from the window, the cigarette dangling from the corner of his mouth again, his eyes reduced to slits. "No one's above the law. Not you. Not me. Not even Sonny Trang."

"Hey, we're not asking you to look the other way," Jones said. "We're just asking you to use a little discretion, to bear in mind that things aren't always what they seem. Like you think Sonny's dealing smack? Well, it just might be that we *want* people to think he's dealing smack. I mean, you can't run with scum unless you're covered with shit, right?"

"And who picks up the bill for Jackie Minh?" Vong asked.

"Jackie Minh's not a problem," Jones said. "You want us to help you find Minh? We'll be happy to help find him. But lay off the general."

Vong responded with a slow nod, but finally he said, "Sorry, but I don't think I can do that."

Smith rose to his feet, bit his lower lip and toyed with the change in his pant pocket. "Look, Vong, you got a pretty good thing going here. Good job. Nice little pension right around the corner. Why blow it?"

Vong looked at him. "Is that a threat, Mr. Smith?"

"It's a warning," Jones said from the opposite end of the room. "It's not a threat. It's a warning. See, we're just not prepared to let you step on Sonny's toes."

"Well, then tell him to keep his feet on the straight and narrow," Vong said. "Because if he crosses the line, I'm going to bust him same as anyone else. And that, gentlemen, isn't a threat *or* a warning. It's a fact."

VONG WOKE with a headache the next morning. Ignoring it, he dressed, left the apartment and, sliding behind the wheel of his '57 Chevy, moved out into the Long Beach streets. He drove at an easy pace, following the tourist buses to Leisure World, occasionally slowing to glance at women in doorways and half-naked kids flying kites from the rooftops. Although the rain had stopped, the air remained moist and heavy, reminding him of the winters in Saigon.

He must have gone about fifteen blocks before he noticed the blue Toyota on his tail—a late-model beige Corolla with tinted windows and a customized grille. When he turned suddenly below Beacon street, a Ford van with blacked-out windows and fog lights replaced it. Although he only caught a glimpse of the driver, he was fairly certain he'd seen the boy on at least three occasions—hanging out at the Saigon Center Pool-room, where the Black Ghosts often wasted their evenings.

He wasn't concerned, merely intrigued. Although the Ghosts could get pretty rowdy on occasion, he had never actually known them to take chances with the cops. He was also curious about how long they had been watching his apartment and whether or not they were armed. As he got closer to the waterfront, it suddenly occurred to him that all the kids had vanished, even the boys flying kites on the roof.

A number of things went through Sammy Vong's mind as he checked his rearview mirror and realized that both the van and the Toyota were still following him. He knew that this particular stretch of Long Beach was a virtual maze of narrow lanes and thus a perfect place for an ambush, and that it wouldn't make one bit of difference to the outcome even if the whole of Gook Town was watching from behind drawn blinds and fastened shutters. He knew that the barrel extending from the van looked as if it belonged to an AK-47.

Vong jerked the steering wheel to the left and drove back over the curb, but at least four slugs slammed into the windshield with a spray of glass and dust.

He pressed the accelerator to the floor, skidded past a warehouse block and slowed to a stop in the shadows of the cannery. He knew that he might have a better chance on foot, but it was obvious that he should have brought something a little larger than his snub-nosed .38 with him.

But when the Toyota roared toward him, there was no alternative. He withdrew the .38 and squeezed off four shots at the blackened silhouette behind the car's steering wheel. He saw the tinted glass dissolve, saw the dark head snap to the side in a spray of blood as the sunglasses slipped past the nose. He heard the scream above the squealing tires, and a second scream as the Toyota bounced off the warehouse wall.

There was a third scream as the van appeared, an enraged yell from a thin figure leveling another AK-47 from the passenger window. Then, although Vong slid down the seat, he couldn't escape the rain of lead.

At least four slugs tore into the dashboard, shredding the upholstery, two more shattering the radio. There was blood above his right eye, but he'd only been grazed. He jammed the gearshift into drive, stomped on the accelerator and felt the sixth or seventh shot rip into his left shoulder.

Vong felt a hard stab of pain in his ribs and wondered if the bullet had lodged in a bone. He caught another glimpse of the screaming boy behind the AK-47 and wondered how old he was. He heard another three or four slugs slam into the trunk, felt the Chevy lurching out of control and wondered if a tire had blown.

And, as the steering wheel collapsed in his hands and gray water covered the whole windshield, he finally wondered if a Chevy could float.

# 3

Whenever Rosario "Politician" Blancanales thought about Vietnam, he thought about the Ia Drang Valley in 1968. He thought about slipping into the mangroves to stand silent; about painting his face for the night patrol, then moving through elephant grass. He thought about quick firefights among the strangler vines, mutilated bodies in the lowlands and the raucous strains of rock and roll from the circling gunships. He also thought about the waste, and what it had felt like when he'd finally come home.

It was about ten o'clock on a Monday morning when all these thoughts came back to Blancanales, triggered by a briefing at Stony Man Farm in Virginia's Shenandoah Valley. Also present and obviously thinking about his tour in Vietnam was Hermann "Gadgets" Schwarz. And although Carl "Ironman" Lyons had never actually served in that Asian war, he had seen enough to imagine it.

"I guess you could call it our Vietnam legacy," Houston Tide said as he turned from the blackboard to face the three men who made up Able Team. "I guess you could say this is part of the price we pay for getting involved in the first place.''

Houston Tide was conducting the briefing at the request of Stony Man Chief Hal Brognola. Also seated at the oblong table in the briefing room was an administrative aide named Andrea Kline and a DEA attorney named Guy Phelps. Although the dark Virginia sky occasionally cracked with thunder, only the white noise of bafflers installed to inhibit audio surveillance interrupted the flow of conversation.

''Why don't you give them the demographic profile?'' Phelps suggested.

Tide turned back to the blackboard, scrawled the words *anchor people* in chalk, then turned again to face his audience.

''They're known as anchor people because emotionally and psychologically they're still tied to the homeland. They've still got family over there, and they haven't completely given up fighting the war. As far as the figures go, we're roughly talking about three hundred thousand in California, most of them in Orange County between Long Beach and the Westminster enclave. Officially the designation is RAV-COM, or Recently Arrived Vietnamese Community. And although we're actually talking about several separate settlements over a ten-mile area, most people think of it as one big suburb and simply call it Little Saigon or Gook Town.''

Tide pulled out photographs, beginning with an eight-by-ten glossy of Jackie Minh. It was a rather uninspired shot, probably taken at one of the immigration checkpoints outside San Diego.

"Typically sad case," Tide said as the photograph began to circulate the table. "Father took a VC rocket in the gut in 1969. His mother died in the Cambodian jungle. His sister threw herself into the South China Sea rather than face Philippine pirates. When he finally reached the States, they kept him in a camp for almost fifteen months. He wasn't even ten years old, weighed in at about forty-five pounds and his teeth were falling out. Jackie Minh still loves America, though."

"So what's his story now?" Lyons asked, gazing at the photograph.

"It's difficult to say," Tide replied. "On the surface it goes something like this. As of three weeks ago, Minh was just another fisherman. He mainly worked on a tub called *The Saigon Dream*, which is skippered by a man named Huynh but actually owned by Sonny Trang. During a trip up north off the Oregon coast, a tramp trawler pulled up to them during the night. Next thing Minh knows he's helping to unload about thirty-five keys of number four Chinese White."

The prim and oddly pretty Andrea Kline lifted her mechanical pencil and let her glasses slip down her nose. "Do we have a point of origin for the drugs?"

"According to the lab, it's probably from the heart of the Burmese poppy basket."

"What does thirty-five keys translate to on the street?" Kline asked.

"That's the point. We're talking about a major take here. *Major.*"

Tide next distributed the photograph of General Sonny Trang. Apparently posed with some care, the man—immaculately dressed—smiled down from the bridge of his custom-built yacht.

"Bao Trang," Tide said as the photograph began to circulate. "Sonny to his friends. Conservatively worth about five million, the bulk of it in Orange County property and those fishing boats. During the war he played it cute, doing a balancing act between the Corsican mob and the Chinese. He supposedly lost it all when Saigon fell and had to start from scratch when he arrived in the States. Trang likes to call himself a professional anti-Communist, but he never actually held an active command. He also likes young women. He's currently squiring a woman named Kim Kiet, whom he stole from Jackie Minh. Hence the theory that Jackie's lying about the smack and possibly even faked his own death."

"Which is a theory you don't necessarily subscribe to," Lyons said. "Right?"

"Well, let's just say I wouldn't put anything past a guy like Sonny Trang."

"Let's not forget, however, that he *is* highly respected within his own community," Phelps added. "I don't think we can entirely ignore that fact."

"Sure," Tide said with a sarcastic smile. "They just worship Sonny Trang in Gook Town."

The next photograph Tide circulated was an almost comical snapshot of Detective Sam Vong slouched against a lamppost in a ridiculous trench coat and gray fedora. "Vong happens to be a friend of mine. Thanks to Trang he nearly bought the farm."

"What kind of weapon was used in the ambush," Lyons asked.

"Ballistics is calling it an AK-47," Tide responded. "Apparently they caught him in his car, then forced him off the Long Beach docks."

"Any suspects?" Blancanales questioned.

"No one under lock and key, if that's what you mean."

Finally Tide showed them three or four mug shots of Black Ghost leaders, young but grim faces glaring out from behind identification plates. "Word is that Sonny Trang uses them for all his dirty work," he explained. "Extortion. Intimidation. Busting kneecaps and breaking heads."

"How many of them are there?" Schwarz asked.

"Hard to say. Fifty, maybe sixty. But they can generally only field about half that number at any given time."

"So why do you need us?" Blancanales asked.

"This is why," Tide answered as he tossed fifteen typewritten pages onto the table delineating Sonny Trang's relationship with the CIA.

"Now we're moving into very murky waters," Phelps said when Lyons and company had skimmed the report. "The Agency hasn't formally admitted anything, and I doubt they ever will."

"What about unofficially?" Lyons asked.

"Unofficially it's a proprietary skeleton from Nam," Tide answered. "The general's the Agency's eye on Gook Town. He makes sure the place isn't harboring Commie agents and that the RAVs are good Americans. I also imagine that a few boys in Langley still use the general as a talent scout to help stock the agent pools for the Southeast Asian Desk."

"So basically Sonny scratches Langley's back and Langley scratches Sonny's back? That the arrangement?" Lyons asked.

Tide nodded. "Roughly, yeah."

"So where does that leave the DEA?" Lyons questioned.

"Sitting here talking to you," Phelps said.

Houston Tide rose from his chair and walked to the end of the room with his fingers linked behind his back. "I'll be honest with you. What we got here is the worst kind of bureaucratic bullshit. The CIA claims Sonny Trang's a national asset, we, in the DEA, claim he's dealing smack. The FBI refuses to acknowledge the problem one way or another, and Justice doesn't even want to know about it."

"What about the White House?" Kline asked.

Phelps smirked. "The White House is sympathetic."

"Which means that, as usual, they want it both ways," Tide said. "If Trang's dirty, they want us to take him out. If he's clean, they'll give him a medal."

"So then basically you're asking us to operate between the cracks," Lyons said.

Tide nodded. "The DEA is just not in a position to mix it up with the CIA. We haven't got the authority, and we haven't got the muscle. Besides, we're not used to playing without a rule book."

"And you think we are?" Lyons asked.

Tide smiled. "I *know* you are."

As the meeting broke up, Tide managed to pull Lyons aside. "Mind if I give you a little supplemental advice?"

"You mean off the record?"

"Very off the record. You guys may think you're going to Southern California but, in fact, you're going to Vietnam. The other thing to keep in mind is that the Agency isn't fooling around on this. I don't know what kind of game they're playing, but they're definitely out for blood."

Lyons smiled. "Is that another way of telling us we can't trust the telephones?"

Tide shrugged. "Well, let's just say the bullets may be coming from a few unexpected directions."

"So how do we tell the good guys from the bad guys?" Lyons asked.

Tide shrugged. "Good question."

AT SIX O'CLOCK the following morning Able Team left for the West Coast, catching a military transport out of Virginia under randomly selected names. The flight was as rough as any Blancanales had experienced during the war, and the humidity and fog on land couldn't have been more reminiscent of the Ia Drang Valley. The smells and sounds in Orange County were the finishing touches needed to carry Blancanales back to Vietnam.

# 4

Sammy Vong has also returned to Vietnam. He returned through dim visions of windblown newspapers in Saigon's Lam Son Square, grim figures huddled on the terrace of the Continental Hotel. He returned through memories of mean children lounging in the milk bars and dazed soldiers staring out of brothel windows. Memories of pain and the stench of air conditioners took him back.

In all, Vong spent four hours reliving Vietnam while doctors at Long Beach Memorial Hospital struggled to remove the bullet from his chest. Then, although finally conscious, he still couldn't shake the feeling that Saigon lay just beyond the venetian blinds.

It wasn't until Friday that Vong began to pick up the threads of the Jackie Minh case from the confines of his hospital bed. Earlier that morning he had received a visit from Lieutenant Lester Hogg, a double-edged visit that had lasted about twenty-five minutes. It had begun on a predictable note as Hogg explained how everyone at the station was concerned about Vong's condition. Then, withdrawing a department-issue notebook, Hogg began to ask about the shooting.

Vong, in turn, recounted the incident from his first glimpse of the Toyota to the moment he had plunged into the water. After that, he said, he couldn't remember much of anything.

"Well, as soon as you're feeling up to it," Hogg replied, "I'll bring you some mug shots. Maybe you can pick out a face for us." He slipped the notebook into his sport coat and rose from the chair.

"That's it?" Vong asked. "That's your investigation?"

Hogg shrugged. "Well, what do you want?"

"You know what I want, Lester. I want you to tear this town apart until you find out what the hell's going on."

Hogg shrugged again; he might have even frowned sympathetically. "I'm sorry, Sammy, but I don't know what you're talking about."

ALTHOUGH STILL BANDAGED and largely immobile, Vong finally managed to convince the doctors to discharge him from the hospital the next day. He was alone in his loft apartment when Able Team appeared.

"Why don't you tell us about the community?" the man who'd introduced himself as Carl Lyons asked when he and the others had settled on the sofa.

"The community?" Vong smiled as he glanced past the frayed curtains at the peaked roofs of Saigon Plaza. "You don't have to beat around the bush with me, Mr. Lyons. Everyone here just calls it Gook Town."

For the most part these men were exactly what Vong had expected—lean, reticent "soldiers" who had obviously been around the block. The one named Blancanales wore a black nylon windbreaker, jeans and running shoes. The other two wore fairly subdued sport coats. Gadgets Schwarz carried a Delta Airlines flight bag. The other two carried nothing. On reflection, Vong supposed he had met quite a few men like them in Vietnam, although the majority of those were also dead.

"Gook Town," Vong said after a long silence, "isn't really a single place. It's anywhere that Vietnamese people have settled. It's Westminster, Long Beach, all along Bolsa Avenue. But mainly it's up here." He pressed a forefinger to his temple.

"And what's the story with Sonny Trang?" Lyons asked.

Vong smiled again. "I guess that depends on who you're talking to. If you're talking to the CIA, Sonny Trang's a pretty good guy. He keeps the Gook Town pinkos from playing footsie with Ho Chin Minh City. He helps them keep in touch with what's going on in Hanoi. But if you're talking to some fishing boy along the Gook Town docks or some shop girl in Saigon Plaza, then it gets a little more complicated."

"And if I'm talking to you?" Lyons asked.

"Then Sonny Trang is Sonny Trang."

There were sounds of children's laughter from below, and then the glimpse of a kite through the window. Blancanales rose from the sofa and began to examine a photograph on the wall: Vong on the steps of a Saigon pizzeria, high-gauge grilles in the windows, sandbags heaped along the doorway.

"You know, I remember him," Blancanales said softly as he smoothed the back of his hand across his mustache. "I think I remember hearing about Trang in '68 or '69."

"Those were his big years," Vong confirmed. "That's when he was posing for pictures with General Westmoreland and talking about the light at the end of the tunnel."

"According to the DEA, that's also when he started moving China White out of Burma," Schwarz added. "That's when he started playing pattycake with triads and the Corsican Mafia."

"Well, he doesn't play pattycake anymore," Vong said. "Believe me."

He withdrew a wad of handwritten notes from the pocket of his dressing gown and tossed them onto the coffee table. Among the papers was a snapshot of Trang clipped from a newspaper. Although the man appeared to be grinning, his eyes revealed nothing.

"Lesson number one," Vong began, "Sonny Trang's not just Gook Town's leading citizen. He's the unofficial law. If you're Vietnamese and you got a problem in this community, you go to the general. Some roundeye's giving you a hard time on Bolsa Avenue, you don't go to the cops. You go to General Sonny Trang. Someone's squeezing you for a mortgage payment, you don't go to the bank. You go to Sonny's underground savings and loan. Now, of course, Sonny doesn't just give. He also takes. Like that girl Kim Kiet, for example. Apparently she caught his eye one evening at the Pink Nightclub. He decided he wanted her and that was that, regardless of what Jackie Minh had to say. But by the same token, not too many people around here are going to argue that what Sonny did was unfair, because that's part of the price they pay for his protection. He wants something, he takes it. It's all part of the code. So regardless of whatever else you might hear about the general, don't forget he's still got a lot of friends here.''

''What about the Black Ghosts?'' Lyons asked. ''Do they also count as Sonny's friends?''

Vong smiled again and gingerly touched his bandaged shoulder. ''Look, I'm the last one to defend the Ghosts,'' he said, ''but by the same token you've got to keep the broad perspective in mind.''

''Which is?'' Lyons asked.

''When the Vietnamese people first settled here, they ran into a lot of trouble from the roundeyes. They also ran into a lot of trouble from the Mexican community, and even from some of the Koreans. So for a long time the Ghosts were our only salvation, and in certain respects they probably did a pretty good job...considering.''

''And then?'' Blancanales asked, still gazing out at the kite that had now been joined by others.

''And then they started feeding on their own kind. They started running extortion scams, stealing cars and dealing a little dope. They also started running errands for Sonny Trang, which is probably what this is all about," he added, touching his bandaged shoulder.

"What's their overall profile?" Schwarz asked.

Vong smiled again. "Pretty much what you'd expect. Most of them are under twenty-five. Half of them are functionally illiterate. And half of those can hardly speak English. But they're not all bad, just misguided. I mean, they come out here with dreams of a Mustang convertible and a penthouse above the marina, and the only job they can find is sweeping someone's floor. So they go for the easy money, and that generally means breaking the law."

"And if they get caught, Trang springs them. Is that pretty much the arrangement?" Lyons asked.

Vong nodded. "Pretty much."

"So then how would you suggest we approach them?" Blancanales asked.

"Very carefully," Vong said.

Upon that advice, Lyons and his team rose to leave. Although still obviously in pain, Vong insisted on getting to his feet in order to see his guests to the door. Then, for a moment, with a cigarette dangling from his mouth, something of his former self returned.

"Listen," he said as Lyons opened the door, "I may not be much help to you boys right now, but just give me a few more days. Then, if you need something done around this town, all you got to do is whistle."

Lyons nodded with a slow grin and glanced at a Bogart poster on the wall. "Yeah, well, we'll keep that in mind, Mr. Vong." Then he reached for the Delta Airlines flight bag and placed it on the floor. "But, in the meantime, maybe you'd like to hold on to this for us."

Vong waited until his guests had left before he unzipped the flight bag. Then, for a long time, he simply sat in his wing chair by the window and tried to make sense of it all. Inside the bag, neatly wrapped in greased brown paper, was the kind of weapon he'd heard about at trade shows in Philly and Frisco. It was a real killer's weapon: compact, light and capable of firing thirty rounds of NATO-specification shells faster than you could shout Gook Town.

# 5

"You feel it, too, don't you?" Blancanales asked.

"Yeah," Schwarz breathed, "I feel it."

They were standing on the seventh-floor balcony of a nondescript hotel. The setting sun had just left long shadows across Huntington Harbor. Also blanketed in shadows were the peaked roofs of the All-Asian Center, the plaster lions that graced the entrance to the Saigon Bank and the remaining subtle signposts marking the boundaries of Gook Town.

"It's just like it was in the war," Blancanales said after another long silence. "You know they're out there, but you don't know where."

"Yeah," Schwarz rasped.

Suddenly Lyons appeared in the opening of the sliding glass door behind them. Although it was a fairly warm evening, he wore a beige cotton jacket to conceal his side arm—a slightly modified .45 automatic. "You guys ready to take in the sights, or what?"

Blancanales turned from the wrought-iron railing, his eyes still fixed on distant places. "As a matter of fact," he began softly, "I sort of think Gadgets and I have already seen these sights."

Earlier that afternoon Lyons had rented a blue Ford van. He had also picked up another Heckler & Koch MP-5 to replace the one he had left at Vong's apartment. As the three men moved down to the hotel's garage, Lyons unzipped a nylon shoulder bag and withdrew the third item he had picked up earlier that day—a Nytech NVS 100 Starlite scope.

Blancanales took the scope, switched it on and scanned the far shadows beyond the mouth of the garage. What had previously appeared as dark and indistinct forms suddenly became exceptionally clear in the bright amber circle of the eyepiece. "Yeah," Politician sighed to himself, "just like in the war."

They climbed into the van: Lyons behind the wheel, Schwarz riding shotgun, Blancanales in the rear. As they pulled out onto Ocean Boulevard, heading south to the highway, Blancanales continued to scan the passing shadows with the night vision system. He generally focused on the nest of masts rising above the harbor. As they drew closer to Westminster, however, he began to focus on the pitch-black alleys.

They had traveled about seven miles before anyone actually spoke, and even then the conversation couldn't have been more clipped. "Are we going anywhere in particular, or are we just cruising?" Blancanales finally asked.

Lyons glanced at the rearview mirror. "Let's just call it recon. Let's just say we're going to poke around a little bit and see what comes out of the woodwork."

Blancanales switched off the scope and put it back into the shoulder bag. "During the war," he said, "we used to call it drawing fire."

It was half past six when they reached the outskirts of Gook Town. Although the side streets were empty, the boulevards were filled with Asians in Toyotas and Nissans. The dance beat of Milli Vanilli and Fine Young Cannibals blared from five-hundred-dollar stereo systems. Lean boys with gel-slicked hair gazed out through tinted windshields. Thin girls in short skirts and oversize blouses flirted from the curb. Around Little Saigon Plaza there were a number of more menacing kids who might easily belong to the Ghosts.

Lyons pulled the van into the plaza and eased between a chopped Celica and a cherry-red RX-7. Three, maybe four youths in balloon trousers and acetate T-shirts watched from the shadows of a plywood pagoda. Lyons, however, probably didn't even notice the youths. His eyes were fixed on the throbbing neon above the Saigon Center Poolroom.

The pool hall was a cavernous place with eight tables below a zinc bar and three ranks of video games against the green plaster walls. Suspended from the rafters were two clear statements of the owner's political leanings: an enormous South Vietnamese flag and the cross swords of the First ARVN Infantry. Hardly less conspicuous, however, were the Black Ghost signatures carved into the edges of the pool tables.

Lyons hesitated in the doorway, letting his eyes grow accustomed to the wavering shadows in the glow of purple lights. Although his hands were empty, he still carried the modified .45 beneath his windbreaker, while Blancanales carried the Heckler & Koch SMG in the nylon shoulder bag. For variety and a slight psychological edge, Schwarz also packed both his gun and his nine-inch knife.

"Why don't you guys just make yourself comfortable?" Lyons suggested as he gazed through curtains of blue cigarette smoke.

"You sure you know what you're doing?" Schwarz asked, smiling as he also scanned the interior.

In all there were at least fifty hunched forms at the video games and pool tables. Yet even from the doorway it was obvious there were no roundeyes.

"Like Pol said," Lyons said, grinning as he moved off into the gloom, "we're going to draw a little fire."

At least thirty pairs of eyes followed Lyons to the bar, where a rail-thin man known as Lucky Nam casually cleaned whiskey glasses. When Lyons paused to look back over his shoulder, however, the glances his way were quickly averted.

"What'll it be?" Nam asked as Ironman slid onto a stool.

Lyons met Nam's gaze with an easy smile. "How about a beer? And a little information?"

Nam reached for a glass, drew a pint of Miller from the tap and plunked it on the bar. "Three bucks."

Lyons pressed down a five-dollar bill. "And what about the information?"

Nam scooped up the bill and replaced it with two ones. "Check the yellow pages."

The jerky rhythm of a band called Joy began to echo from an adjoining room. A slender girl in a miniskirt swayed behind a curtain of glass beads. Nam had picked up a towel and another whiskey glass, but he couldn't ignore the hundred that Lyons suddenly slapped onto the bar.

"Why don't we try again?" Ironman suggested, sliding the bill across the bar but not lifting his finger from it. "See, I'm kind of looking for some people and I've got a feeling you might be able to help me find 'em."

Nam eyed the bill without turning his head, without stopping the motion of the rag along the rim of the glass. "I don't know too many people, mister."

"Oh, I think you know these people. In fact, I think you know them real well." Then sliding the bill a little closer to the edge of the bar, Ironman said, *"Hac Qui."*

Nam put down the glass, extended a finger and slid the bill back to Lyons. "You know what coffins cost these days? They cost lots more than a hundred dollars."

Lyons lifted his hand from the bill, slipped it into his pocket and withdrew another. "All right, how about you just pass them a little message?"

Nam couldn't seem to keep his gaze entirely off the money. "What kind of message?"

"You tell them I want to talk about Jackie Minh and Sammy Vong." Lyons raised his voice so that the nearest five or six boys along the bar could hear him say, "You tell the Ghosts I want to talk to them about what they did to Jackie Minh and Sammy Vong."

Nam's face split into a vaguely lopsided smile that revealed fanged incisors. "Okay, boss, I tell them."

All around the bar the air had suddenly grown alive with whispers in Vietnamese.

"And while you're at it," Lyons added, "you might also tell them they can find me right outside. You got that?"

Nam nodded with another slightly dangerous smile. But when he reached for the bills on the bar, Lyons's hand shot out and grabbed the slender wrist.

"For some reason I have the feeling they'll get the message whether I pay you or not," he said, slipping the money back into his jacket.

"Now what?" Schwarz asked once the three men had closed the door to the pool hall.

"Now we wait," Lyons said.

"For what?"

"You'll see."

Another fog had descended, a slow, drifting blanket from the bay. The breeze smelled faintly of fried pork and oil. Although three or four more pair of eyes had watched as Lyons made his way to the door, no one had actually followed. So they waited...slouched in the van, scanning the surrounding doorways and windows, basically just killing time.

"Dak To," Blancanales whispered after five or ten minutes of silence. "Kind of like Dak To."

"I believe you," Schwarz replied.

Lyons glanced at them both. "What are you guys talking about?"

"Dak To, 1967," Blancanales whispered again. "I was holding this post in the hills along with the 173rd and some Special Forces guys. Charlie was spread out in something like a thirty-mile arc. But every night he'd come in and suck a little blood. Finally Command started sending out patrols to draw the fire. One night we hit the trail about six or seven, snapped a couple of twigs, sang a couple of bars of 'The Big Bad Wolf' and then waited for all hell to break loose."

"Then what happened?" Lyons asked.

"They chewed us all to shit."

A midnight-blue Honda pulled into the parking lot, slowly cruised past the pool hall, then came to a stop at the end of the plaza. Moments later a gray Nissan also entered the lot. Headlights blinked. An engine revved. Then nothing.

"What do you think?" Schwarz asked.

Blancanales picked up the Starlite scope and focused on the Honda. "Two mean dudes just sitting there watching us." Then shifting his vision to the Nissan, he said, "Two more of the same."

"So what do you think?" Schwarz asked again.

Blancanales put down the scope, unzipped the nylon shoulder bag and withdrew the Heckler & Koch SMG. "I think it's just like Dak To," he said.

"Meaning?" Lyons asked.

"Meaning they probably want us to make the first move," Schwarz said.

Lyons put his .45 on the seat, inserted the ignition key and started the van. "What did you used to call trawling for action?" he asked as he shifted into drive.

Blancanales shrugged as he turned to watch the Honda pull out behind them. "I don't know. I think we just called it trawling for action."

Although the traffic was still fairly thick on Bolsa Avenue, Blancanales had no difficulty tracking the Honda on their tail. It wasn't until Lyons had turned down one of the quieter side streets, however, that he finally caught a glimpse of the Nissan.

"You notice anything funny?" Schwarz asked as they moved past ranks of low stucco houses to a block of storefronts closer to the docks.

"Kids," Blancanales said. "No kids."

Lyons drew to a stop at a rise above Huntington Harbor. Below lay two predominantly Vietnamese blocks sometimes called Dink Alley. "What about the kids?"

"Kids always used to vanish whenever the VC were about to make a strike," Blancanales said. "Never really figured it out myself, but somehow the kids always knew when to clear the streets."

They passed a rank of storefronts with names like Tuy Nha Cleaners and Bong Loi Alterations. Lyons started to say something about the Black Ghost graffiti on a gutted theater wall, but Blancanales cut him off.

"I lost the Nissan," he said suddenly. "Where's the goddamn Nissan?" he yelled as he lifted his SMG and released the safety.

Before either Lyons or Schwarz could answer, however, at least eight rounds from an AK-47 glanced off the pavement in front of the van.

Lyons swerved to the left, skidding across the center divider, and raced into a narrow lane between a cannery and the Bat Dat Seafood Company. Then, finally sliding into the shadows beneath a rusting crane, he cut the engine and picked up his .45 auto.

"This is the way they took out Sammy Vong, isn't it?" Schwarz asked. "A quick pinch on a quiet street?"

Blancanales shook his head. "They're not looking to take us out. They're just looking to scare us."

"So maybe it's time to give them a little piece of it back," Schwarz suggested.

"Exactly what I was thinking," Lyons said as he opened the door and stepped onto the pavement.

The fog was substantially thicker here, creeping up from the harbor and settling in pools all along the lane. The breeze, too, was stronger, stirring bits of newspapers along the pavement.

"How would you play it if this were Dak To?" Lyons whispered.

Blancanales glanced at Schwarz, then scanned the lane ahead until his eyes rested on a steel grate set into the concrete. "I'd dig in," he said. "Real deep."

He was again reminded of Vietnam: crouching in a fetid storm drain that might have been a foxhole, bracing himself against the slime-smeared wall that might have been the wall of a rice paddy, inhaling the stench of rotting vegetables that might have been the stench of corpses. And as the midnight-blue Honda rounded the corner with another AK-47 extending from the sunroof, he knew only that they were the enemy.

Blancanales shot at the tires because even in Dak To a live VC had been better than a dead one, assuming you could make them talk. He squeezed off two distinct bursts as the Honda came into view—three rounds to the left front tire, then three more to the right. Rubber shredded in long ribbons with a shower of sparks and screeching steel. The Honda skidded over the curb and bounced off the cannery wall before finally plowing into the loading dock.

Somebody, probably Lyons, shouted, *"Get them! Get them!"* But before Blancanales could react, the Nissan also appeared.

At least nine more rounds slammed into the brickwork behind Blancanales's head, another six or eight rounds into the doorway where Lyons and Schwarz had been crouching. Schwarz responded with a four-round burst from his SMG, but once again it was Blancanales who drove the point home.

This time he shot for the radiator, squeezing two quick bursts into the screaming engine as it bore down on top of him. Then, ducking back into the storm drain as the Nissan passed over him, he rose and let loose with another quick burst at the taillights.

The Nissan careered left, screeching off the curb and then vanishing down a side street. Schwarz fired another six or eight shots at its fading shadow, but Lyons shouted, "Just get the ones in the Honda!"

But even before Schwarz could turn or Blancanales could crawl out of the storm drain, the two dark forms had scrambled from the Honda and melted into the shadows.

There was blood on the Honda's dashboard and seat, strands of hair in the spiderwebbed glass of the shattered windshield. Lyons and his men also found the AK-47 lying on the floor of the car.

Ironman picked up the weapon, careful not to obliterate the fingerprints. "We can't assume they're not armed. And we can't assume they're hurt and that therefore they won't shoot back."

Blancanales released the spent magazine from his H&K and jammed in new rounds. "We also can't assume we're ever going to catch them if we don't start after them right now."

Schwarz glanced at Blancanales, then turned to Lyons. "He's right, Ironman. You might want to stay here and call in some of Vong's people, but Pol and I better get moving."

Lyons nodded. "All right, run 'em down."

TWO STREETS DIVERGED from the lane where the Honda had been abandoned. The first ran south, past rows of squat apartment buildings and a Mc-Donald's. The second ran west, past dark shops and a waterfront bar called Pho Dinh's. After a moment's hesitation, Schwarz and Blancanales decided to take the second street.

They moved at a moderate pace, half-crouched and keeping to the shadows along the north side of the lane. In addition to the Vietnamese notices plastered on the walls and the hand-painted signs in storefront windows, the odors seemed to have also been imported for old Saigon: rotting bean sprouts, shellfish, excrement and camphor. Then, along the pavement adjacent to Tu Do Cleaners, they found more blood.

Gadgets knelt to examine the stains—four star-shaped drops the size of quarters. "I'd say we're looking for a kid with a pretty nasty crack on the head."

"Yeah? Well, I've seen those people bleed for fifteen miles before they dropped," Blancanales replied.

Schwarz rose to his feet again and looked at Blancanales intently. "Those people, Pol? What do you mean, *those people*?"

"You know what I mean."

"No, I don't. See, I thought we were just tracking a couple of punks from the neighborhood. I had no idea we were going after Charlie again."

Blancanales returned the gaze for a moment, then let his eyes slide back to the darkness below. "Look, let's just get moving."

But Gadgets continued to stare at him. "The war's over, man. I know it's sometimes easy to forget that, but the war's been over for a long time."

There were more drops of blood in the alley below, then a shred of clothing on a chain-link fence. Beyond the fence lay a narrow path between rows of dwarfed palms and a small Buddhist shrine. Although nothing moved, nothing breathed, Blancanales released the safety on his SMG. "Cover me," he whispered to Schwarz.

"Pol, don't you think—"

"Just cover me."

Blancanales leaped the fence like a cat, then moved quickly on the balls of his feet until he reached the shadows of the palms. There were two bronze Buddhas in the courtyard ahead; they reminded Blancanales of a dozen shrines he had seen in Vietnam. Ultimately, however, his thoughts returned to a shrine at Hoc Bao, where he had pasted a fifteen-year-old VC sapper against the temple wall. And when that kid had finally died, half his stomach blown away, his smile had been only slightly less serene than the smile on the Buddha.

*What do you mean, those people?*

There were sounds of papers rustling in the breeze, prayer slips left by families still mourning the South Vietnamese dead. There were also sounds of wind chimes and the shivering willows along the banks of a reflecting pond. Then, as the wind suddenly died, there were even footsteps on the gravel—four uncertain footsteps less than ten yards away.

Blancanales dropped to a crouch, flipped the selector switch to single-burst mode and shifted his gaze to a lacquered footbridge above the pond. In addition to the footsteps there were also shadows now—two distinct shadows suggesting slender arms and shoulders.

*I had no idea we were going after Charlie again.*

Transferring his weapon from his right hand to his left, Blancanales scooped up a pebble from the path.

Then, counting off three seconds, he tossed the pebble into the willows and watched the shadows freeze.

*The war's over, man. I know it's sometimes easy to forget, but the war's been over for a long time.*

Yet when the shadows started moving again and Blancanales finally sprang from the darkness, he couldn't have been closer to it.

He struck at the first shadow with the butt of his weapon, struck for what appeared to be the stomach, and heard the kid's agonized groan. He struck at the second shadow with a quick jab, impacted with what may have been the jaw and heard another agonized cry. But, as he turned back to the first boy, the second was on him like a pit bull, leaping on his back and tearing at his face.

Blancanales twisted, trying to shake the boy loose as the kid's thin arms continued to squeeze like a vise around his throat. Finally, throwing his weight against the wall, he slammed the boy into the bricks and felt him slide off. Pol then stepped back and leveled the SMG as the first figure ran away.

He fired two warning shots into the air as the second shadow fled between the palms, then a third shot at the gravel. But even as he sighted down the barrel at the base of the fleeing figure, he knew it was pointless, that Gadgets had been right all along—the war *was* over.

Blancanales lowered his weapon and turned to the huddled form at his feet. In the faint light the kid looked like a lot of boys he'd seen in Saigon—fifteen or sixteen years old with at least four decades of hatred in their eyes. But when he finally grabbed the front of the boy's shirt and the cotton shredded in his hand, he found himself staring at a young girl's breasts.

She made no move to cover herself. She just kept glaring at him. Although there were traces of blood around her nose and mouth, she obviously wasn't the one who'd left the blood along the lanes.

Schwarz appeared, slipping out of the darkness and dangling a pair of handcuffs. When he realized the prisoner was a girl, he shook his head. Then, finally forcing her facedown on the gravel, he secured her wrists behind her back. "Where's the other one?" he asked.

Blancanales nodded at the girl, then at the rank of palms.

"So all we got is her?"

"Yeah," Blancanales breathed. "All we got is her."

Schwarz dropped to one knee, his lips only inches from her ear. "Looks like you got the short end of the stick, don't it, honey?"

The girl responded with a mute shiver, then turned and spat a mouthful of blood in Schwarz's face. Gadgets merely grinned and glanced up at Blancanales. "This is going to be fun."

"Let me talk to her alone."

Schwarz hesitated but finally rose to his feet with a silent shrug. "Okay, talk to her alone... for fifteen minutes. Then it's my turn."

Blancanales waited until Schwarz had moved back to the edge of the grounds surrounding the shrine, then knelt by the girl's side. He withdrew a handkerchief and dabbed at the blood around her mouth. In a different light, under different circumstances, he supposed she would have actually been extremely pretty—a slender girl with dark eyes and raven hair.

"I bet you're wondering why nobody bothered to read you your rights?" he asked softly. "Well, the fact is, we're not cops and you don't have any rights. So, unless you start talking to me real soon, my friend's going to come back here and start his own form of questioning. And, believe me, you don't want him to do that."

She turned her head away with another shiver, reminding him of at least a dozen kids he'd seen interrogated in Saigon. "Look, I don't know anything, okay?" she finally whispered.

"Well, you got a name, don't you? So why don't we start with that?"

She bit her lip, reminding him of a girl he'd once seen crying in the rain outside Qui Nhon, a girl they'd finally shot against the temple walls.

"My name's Lisa."

"And who told you to hit us, Lisa?"

She shook her head, whispered something inaudible, then shook her head again.

"Listen, honey, I'm not kidding. My friend comes back here and he—"

"Look, we were just trying to scare you because you were asking too many questions."

"Who told you to scare us?"

She tried to turn her head, but he grabbed a handful of hair and forced her to face him again. Then, catching a glimpse of the tears in her eyes, the cold terror etched on her face, he finally let her go and leaned against the wall. A fresh breeze had set the wind chimes tinkling again.

"Listen, baby, I'm not the bad guy," Blancanales said at last. "I realize you may not believe that right now, but I'm not really the bad guy. I just don't like being shot at."

She turned her head a fraction of an inch to meet his eyes briefly. "If I tell you anything, he'll kill me," she suddenly whispered.

He raised the handkerchief again to dab a fresh spot of blood from the corner of her mouth. "And who exactly are we talking about here? Are we talking about Sonny Trang?"

She let her head fall to one side with a tired nod. "It's not just the general. It's other people, and they're everywhere."

"Yeah, but there isn't anyone here right now. Right now it's just you and me. So how about you tell me about it, all right?"

Once again she shut her eyes and shook her head.

He withdrew his nine-inch Saburo blade and drove the tip into the damp ground. "Listen to me, honey, I wasn't kidding about my friend over there. He doesn't always play by the rules. In fact, most of the time he makes up his own. So why don't you start telling me about what's going on in this town?"

Although she might have whispered something, all he finally heard was "Please."

Blancanales removed the handcuffs and pulled her to her feet. "I don't know what you're going to tell your boyfriend. Hell, I don't even know what I'm going to tell my own people. But I guess we've done all we can do tonight, right?"

She looked at him, clutching her torn blouse with her right hand, wiping away a tear with the left. "You're letting me go?"

He shook his head with a tired smirk. "No, honey, I'm not letting you go. You're escaping. You're waiting until I turn my back and then you're running like a goddamn rabbit."

She glanced up the lane to where the palms dissolved in the gloom, then looked at him. "Why?"

"Because I've played this game before and I don't like the way it ends. Now, go on and get out of here."

She stared at him again, hesitating, wondering. Then, finally turning, she started down the path.

But before she had gone more than a dozen paces, he softly called her name. "Hey, Lisa!"

She stopped, waiting, but didn't turn around.

"If things get too hot for you, you can always give me a call. Know what I mean? Just contact Sammy Vong, and tell him you want to talk to Politician. You got that?"

Although she might have whispered something in response, all he finally heard was the wind through the tiny brass chimes.

"Do you want to say something, or should I just start shouting?" Schwarz asked.

Blancanales tugged on his earlobe with a faint smile. "Go screw yourself, Hermann."

They had returned to the rented van and a small mob of cops. Although it was nearly midnight, the earlier gunfire had drawn all sorts of local residents into the streets: old men and women in bathrobes, children in pajamas, teenagers in cheap leather and vinyl coats. There were also, undoubtedly, at least half a dozen Ghosts watching from the fringes of the crowd.

Lyons appeared, leaving a clearly irritated Lester Hogg glaring at the mess of oil and glass on the pavement. Among other things the police detective had wanted to know just who the hell had given Lyons and his men the authority to carry Heckler & Koch SMGs. Naturally Lyons hadn't exactly answered the question.

"You want to talk about this?" Lyons asked Blancanales when he slid back into the van.

"No," Schwarz answered. "He doesn't want to talk about it."

Lyons looked at Blancanales, then at Schwarz. "Hey, Gadgets, give us a couple of minutes, okay?"

Gadgets shrugged and stepped out of the van. In addition to the cops and curious residents, five or six reporters had also arrived, asking about bodies and suspects.

"Okay, let me get this straight," Lyons said. "You track two suspects to a local church. One gets away, the other one doesn't. You start asking questions, get no answers, and then finally let her walk. Now, is that roughly the way it happened?''

Blancanales pressed a hand against the dashboard. His eyes were fixed on the swarm of cops, the smashed Toyota and the gawking crowd beyond the crime scene tape. "It wasn't a church," he said at last. "It was a shrine. It was one of those little Buddhist shrines like they had in Nam."

Lyons let his weight fall on the steering wheel, then began to toy with the radio knob. "You know, you weren't the only one who spent time in Vietnam, Pol. Gadgets was there. Sammy Vong was there. Lots of guys were there."

Blancanales slid his hand off the dashboard and ran it through his hair. "Look," he said suddenly, "she wasn't going to tell us anything, anyway."

"How do you know?"

"Because I know. Because I saw it in her eyes. She was too damn scared."

"Well, maybe we could have helped her overcome her fear, Pol. Maybe we could have—"

"How? By throwing her out of a chopper? By chaining her feet to the back of a jeep and dragging her through the elephant grass? 'Cause I've played those games before, Ironman, and I'm fucking sick of them." He shook his head and gazed out the windshield again. "Besides, I don't think the Ghosts know what's going on. I don't even think Trang knows the whole story."

"What are you talking about?"

"Just something she said, something about people behind Sonny Trang."

"Any idea who these people are?"

Blancanales shook his head. "All I know is that she was terrified of them. I mean, really terrified."

"So you let her walk, is that it? She starts crying on your shoulder and you let her walk."

"Yeah, well, it comes with the territory, doesn't it?"

Lyons looked at him, the anger welling in his eyes again. "What the hell's that supposed to mean?"

"It means we're supposed to be the good guys, right? It means this ain't Vietnam and I don't scare the hell out of sixteen-year-old girls to make them talk."

It was nearly one o'clock in the morning when Able Team finally returned to their hotel rooms. Although Schwarz and Blancanales hadn't said more than five or six words to each other, the tension between them had finally subsided. The fog had also lifted, revealing the sort of things one would never have seen in Saigon: a Burger King, a Howard Johnson's and Sonny Trang's multimillion-dollar yacht.

## 6

At only eighty-six feet the *Asian Wind* wasn't the largest vessel in the marina. Yet given her fittings—the dark teak against polished brass and fiberglass, the long sweep of her gleaming hull—she was easily the most beautiful.

It was just after eleven o'clock in the morning and the sky was entirely clear. From their vantage point above the wharf, Lyons and Schwarz were even able to make out the gray silhouettes of Catalina and the lesser islands to the south. But, for the most part, they kept their eyes fixed on the *Asian Wind* and the reclining profile of Sonny Trang.

"Makes you think that maybe we're on the wrong side," Schwarz said as he scanned the planked deck with his binoculars. "Makes you think that maybe we should have cashed it in a long time ago and joined the opposition."

Lyons shrugged. "I don't know. I never liked boats much, anyway. They always make me seasick."

In white flannel trousers and a blue blazer, Trang was the stereotypical yachtsman entertaining guests on a Saturday afternoon. Yet even through the remote and narrow visions of binoculars, Lyons sensed the cruelty, the dark arrogance of every gesture.

"Any idea who the others are?" Schwarz asked, fixing his gaze on two lean men in gray slacks and polo shirts.

"I think the Asian's Trang's banker," Lyons said. "Calls himself Happy Thong. The white guy is Jay Meade, resident lawyer and smooth talker, according to Sammy."

"What about the woman?" Schwarz asked, focusing on a curvaceous Oriental woman in a revealing one-piece bathing suit.

Lyons glanced at the dashboard of the van, where he had laid out seven eight-by-ten glossies supplied by Vong. "Not sure," he said at last.

"Not Kim Kiet, though?"

Lyons hesitated, sweeping the deck until his vision settled on a second female, lounging by the railing in a simple white frock. "No," he said, "*that's* Kim Kiet. Over there by the railing."

Schwarz fixed his binoculars on the girl, then nodded with a slow smile. "Hmm, not too shabby, is she?"

A servant appeared, a squat but muscular man wearing white trousers and a black T-shirt. His arms were a tangle of tattoos and he was entirely bald.

"Tuy Xuan," Lyons whispered after glancing at the photographs again. "Sometimes also known as Chuckie Xuan, but don't let the name fool you."

"Looks like a creep," Schwarz replied, watching as the man in question deposited a tray of tonic water, gin and white wine.

"He is," Lyons replied. "Likes to break kneecaps. Likes to tear off fingers and stick them in ears."

The servant withdrew. Someone said something that Trang must have found amusing, because he nodded and grinned. Then, apparently growing bored again, he lifted an arm and snapped his fingers. Immediately Kim Kiet turned her head and nodded.

"She looks like she's having fun," Schwarz whispered as the girl slowly rose from her seat by the railing and approached Trang's little circle. "She looks like she's having one hell of a good time."

Trang delivered another command, this time with a flick of his wrist and a curt word. The girl seemed to hesitate, possibly a little embarrassed. But, finally responding with a shake of her head, she slipped off her dress and let it fall to the deck.

"Wow!" Schwarz breathed.

She was a slender girl with small breasts and narrow hips. Her bathing suit consisted of little more than three squares of silver Spandex, and her hair, lying in bangs across her forehead, emphasized her childish features and vaguely lost eyes.

"Looks like he's auctioning her off to the highest bidder," Schwarz said, watching as Trang directed the girl's movements, commanding her to turn, to lift her head and them turn again. "Looks like he's selling an expensive side of beef."

"Yeah, well, everybody's got their problems," Lyons muttered as he put down his binoculars. "Let's take a closer look."

TUY XUAN BENT at the waist to whisper into the general's ear. "Two men ask permission to board," he said in Vietnamese.

Trang smiled, glanced at his guests and adjusted his captain's cap. "What kind of men?"

Xuan shook his head and ran a hand across his hairless skull. "I've never seen them before, but they look like trouble."

Trang's smile grew marginally wider, and he glanced over his shoulder at the dock below. "Well, perhaps I'm in the mood for trouble. What do you think, Mr. Meade?" he asked, turning to his attorney. "Are we in the mood for trouble?"

"Why not?" the man responded.

"Very well, show them aboard, Xuan," Trang ordered.

"So," Trang said, smiling as Lyons and Schwarz quickly approached, "to what do I owe this honor?"

Lyons shifted his gaze from the banker to the attorney, then briefly to the woman and the girl. Finally resting his eyes on Trang again, he returned the thin smile. "Let's just say we've come to return something that belongs to you."

"Something that belongs to me? Whatever could that be?"

Lyons reached into the pocket of his windbreaker and withdrew a mushroomed slug from an AK-47.

"This," he said, and tossed the bullet onto a laquered tray.

Trang picked up the smashed slug, turned it over in his fingers and smiled again. "How interesting. How very, very interesting." Then, snapping his fingers, he ordered, "Come, Chuckie, what about some chairs for my newfound friends? Surely we can find a couple of chairs for these men."

"I'm Lyons. He's Schwarz," Lyons interjected.

Two more blue canvas deck chairs were placed around the little bamboo table. Another tray of drinks also appeared: gin and tonic, white wine and soda, frosted bottles of beer.

"So, I take it you gentlemen have a slight grievance with me," Trang said when Lyons and Schwarz had settled into their chairs. "A slight grievance over a very small piece of lead."

"That's right," Lyons replied.

"And may I ask how it was that this grievance supposedly occurred?"

Lyons shifted his gaze to the attorney, then took a casual sip of his drink. "Let's just say we happen to be friends of Jackie Minh."

It was difficult to tell whether Trang was smiling or merely squinting into the sun. But there was no mistake about his laugh. "Ah, yes, Jackie Minh. The young and persistent Jackie Minh. Well, *that* certainly clears things up. Yes, now suddenly everything is extremely clear." Then, shifting his gaze to Lyons, he continued, "Really, Mr. Lyons, you have no idea how glad I am that you're here."

The banker and the older woman were dismissed, leaving only Kim Kiet and the blond attorney. Also, presumably for the sake of intimacy, Trang removed his sunglasses.

"Permit me to tell you a small story concerning Mr. Vong, myself and the greater Vietnamese community," Trang began. "Once upon a time back in 1976 all Vietnamese refugees were brothers. All were very poor, very frightened and very much supportive of one another. Then, little by little, some of us began to make money. Some made money as bankers. Some made money as lawyers. I made money with my fishing boats and property. And then what do you think happened? Suddenly we were no longer brothers. Suddenly there was jealousy and petty feuds. Suddenly people like Jackie Minh began to blame me for all their misfortunes."

Trang withdrew a thin gold case from the jacket of his blazer and extracted a cigarette. Then, reaching for Kim Kiet's hand, he drew her to his side and began to caress her smooth thigh. "Look at her. Take a good look at her, gentlemen, and tell me, who wouldn't sympathize with poor Jackie Minh's loss?"

The girl lowered her gaze to the deck—a flawless possession on display.

"One evening I saw her in a popular nightclub," Trang continued. "Despite her extraordinary beauty, something told me she wasn't happy. So what did I do? I began to make inquiries. I began to investigate the source of her sadness. And what did I discover? I discovered that although she had a handsome young boyfriend, she didn't have anything else. She had to wait on tables for paltry tips. She had to give away all of her salary so that her cousins could attend school. She had to do all sorts of things that were unbecoming to such a beauty. So I made her a proposition. I told her I was smitten with her loveliness, and that I wanted her to come live with me. 'Of course, I'm a very ugly toad,' I told her, 'but turn me into a prince with your beauty and I shall give you anything you want.' So she thought about it. And spoke with her family and friends. Then, finally, she accepted the offer. But, of course, that made her boyfriend extremely angry and led to all sorts of complications.''

From the smooth hip, Trang slid his hand to the girl's left buttock, then watched Lyons's eyes for a reaction. Lyons, however, remained impassive.

"According to Minh, your boats have been bringing in more than fish," Ironman said.

"Exactly, Mr. Lyons. Exactly the sort of complications I was referring to. I take this beauty away from Jackie Minh, okay. So what does Minh do? He begins to tell terrible stories about me. He begins to slander my reputation within the community.''

"And then he disappears," Schwarz added, glancing hard at the attorney.

Trang smiled and slid a finger along the back of the girl's left thigh, then up again to the cleft of her buttocks. "Would you like to know what I personally think about this Minh business?" he asked. "Well, I'll tell you. I think Minh arranged his disappearance to create precisely the effect that it has had. He arranged his disappearance so that strange men would come around and ask me all kinds of improper questions. That's what I think, and frankly I consider it most unfair. After all, am I not a patriotic citizen? Haven't I contributed a good deal to local charities. Haven't I remained a staunch anti-Communist? And now all this trouble simply because I fell in love.''

Chuckie Xuan returned, this time with a platter of oysters on the half shell and baby squid.

''The sea is bountiful,'' Trang said. ''Property is also bountiful. So why can't I buy myself a little peace and quiet? Why can't I fall in love like other men and enjoy my prosperity?''

Lyons picked up an oyster but didn't eat it. ''The way I heard it, you had Minh pinched by the Ghosts.''

Trang fed an oyster to the girl, who now knelt by his side, then tossed a morsel of squid into his mouth with a broad grin. ''Ah, yes, the Ghosts. Well, allow me to tell you something about them, Mr. Lyons. Once upon a time, in about 1978, Vietnamese people were very much tormented and abused by roundeyes like yourself. They said we were Commie pigs. They said we took all the jobs. They said we got special treatment from the government even though we were bad people. Then they even beat us up, threw rocks through our windows and hurt our women. We formed the Black Ghosts as protection. Now, sometime later, maybe the Ghosts got a little out of hand. Maybe instead of just protecting Vietnamese people they also did improper things. But they were very much anti-Communist, and for this reason they were of benefit to people in government. If you want to know about the Ghosts, I suggest you ask the CIA. Don't ask people like me, because I don't know anything. I'm just an old man, and Ghosts don't listen to old men."

"And what if we wanted to know about Jackie Minh?" Gadgets asked.

"Then I suggest you consult the Missing Persons Bureau," the attorney interjected, "because my client has no information whatsoever on that subject. Moreover, should harassment on this subject continue, I'll have no other alternative but to seek a restraining order."

Trang smiled. "Which, of course, isn't to imply that you're not always welcome aboard my vessel. But you can see that all this talk of Jackie Minh upsets my little princess here." And then, running his fingernail along the perfect curve of her breast, he added, "Doesn't it, my darling?"

Trang rose, indicating he wished to end the visit. As he walked his guests to the gangplank, he offered them some parting words of advice. "I'm sure you're both extremely athletic and capable men, but I strongly advise that you drop this line of inquiry."

Lyons ran his hand along the varnished railing. "Is that a threat, General?"

Trang shook his head and smiled ingenuously. "Of course not. I merely think you gentlemen should realize that many of the young people in this community can be very emotional. They're not all like my Kim. And you've seen, she's extremely respectful and obedient. She's one of a kind. Not that one can blame

the others. After all, we're talking about war or-
phans. We're talking about young boys and girls who
suffered very greatly before the fall, and who continue to suffer. Still, I think sometimes they have a
tendency toward strong emotional reactions when
roundeyes like yourself ask too many questions."

"And is that what happened to Minh?" Lyons
asked. "Did he run into some people with strong
emotional reactions?"

Trang shrugged. "As I said, I believe Jackie made
himself disappear in order to embarrass me and to
cause me difficulty. But, of course, there are always
other possibilities."

"And among those possibilities one would have to
include what?"

"Look, Mr. Lyons. I've told you all I can tell you.
If Jackie Minh has suffered some terrible misfortune,
then I'm very much aggrieved. But if you continue to
make rash inquiries about him, then I'm afraid you
may also suffer some terrible misfortune. Do you understand?"

LYONS AND SCHWARZ didn't return to the hotel until
five o'clock that afternoon. There, they found Blancanales seated on the floor amid a pile of newspaper
clippings, handwritten notes and memoranda from
half a dozen Washington agencies. There was also a
map of Vietnam, another of the California-Oregon
coast and at least a dozen plastic coffee cups scattered across the carpet.

"Let me tell you a little story about General Sonny Trang," Blancanales said when Lyons and Schwarz entered the room. "Early '68, the DEA decides it's going to do something about all those eighteen-year-old Marines strung out on smack. So, in addition to organizing a few internal programs, they send in two guys from Washington named Barber and Bates. Now these guys are extremely determined investigators. They went up against the mob in New Jersey. They went up against the triads in Hong Kong. I mean, they'd really been around the block. So the first thing they do when they get to Saigon is start looking into rumors that maybe Sonny Trang is dealing with the opium clans out of Burma and Thailand. Well, Sonny, he doesn't like this too much. After all, he's got a pretty good thing going. He's got one of the softest commands in the ARVN. He's got a great relationship with Diem, and Lyndon Johnson always sends him Christmas cards. So he's not going to let a couple of DEA flatfeet bust him for running dope—no way."

From beneath a small mound of interagency correspondence, Blancanales withdrew a seven-page engagement report from 1969. Attached was a photo of two mutilated bodies. Although the definition was poor, it was enough to imagine what had been done, to imagine the heated bamboo stacks and the butterfly knives.

"Apparently it went down like this," Blancanales continued. "Barber and Bates had been snooping around the ARVN command for about two weeks when one day they got word that Trang was bringing in a shitload of opium to some little hamlet outside of Da Nang. All they had to do was drive down the road a piece, wait in the jungle and then catch Trang red-handed. There was one problem, though. It turned out the sector was swarming with Charlie. Now, no one was ever able to *prove* that Sonny Trang set up Bates and Barber to take a fall that night, but by the same token, no one could ever disprove it, either.''

"So who recovered the bodies?'' Schwarz asked, still examining the photographs.

"Ranger patrol.''

"And the final verdict?''

"They took one hell of a long time to die.''

Lyons squatted on the carpet and began to leaf through the papers around him. He'd noticed that many had been annotated with scribbled notes and cryptic diagrams. "Mind if I ask you a question, Pol?''

Blancanales glanced up from yet another yellowed newspaper clipping concerning Trang's stature in the community.

"Did you get all this stuff from Sammy Vong?''

"What if I did?''

Lyons shook his head. "No reason. I'm just wondering what the point of it is.''

Blancanales picked up another piece of paper, this one on Westminster Police Department stationery. "The point is,'' he said, "about forty-five minutes after you left Trang's boat, Narcotics got a phone call from one of their informants. The informant said that Sonny Trang was bringing in a shitload of smack on a couple of cigarette boats tomorrow night. He's supposedly bringing it right in to the beach at a little place called Sunset Cove. The only problem is that Sunset Cove is out of Westminster's jurisdiction. So, unless we want to bring in the Feds, we're going to be playing it alone.''

Lyons studied the handwritten report for a moment. ''What does Vong say?''

Blancanales swept a hand across the carpet to indicate the papers around him. ''Vong says that maybe we should remember what happened to Bates and Barber.''

That part of the conversation over, Lyons and Blancanales moved out to the balcony while Schwarz remained inside, slouched on the floor in front of the television.

''For whatever it's worth,'' Lyons said, ''I'm beginning to think Jackie Minh was telling the truth about the girl.''

Blancanales leaned against the wrought-iron railing. ''What do you mean?''

''She's not in love with the general. In fact, I don't even think she likes him. Maybe he made her an offer she couldn't refuse. Maybe she needed the money for her family. But she sure as hell doesn't love him.''

''So?''

''So it stands to reason that Jackie probably wasn't lying about the dope, either.''

Blancanales stared out at the whitecapped bay. ''Is this another way of saying that you want to go for it tomorrow night?''

"You got a problem with that?"

Blancanales looked at him. "Yeah, I got a problem with it. Look, maybe the tip about Trang bringing in dope is genuine, but I don't think so. I think it's just a little too neat. I think we're being set up the same way he set up those two DEA guys in Nam."

"Look, even if you're right, even if Trang is trying to set us up, I still think we can turn it to our advantage," Lyons argued. "I mean, after all, this isn't 1968 and we're not in Vietnam."

Blancanales looked at him again. "Yeah, well, I wouldn't be too sure about that."

## 7

Sunset Cove was a forgotten place, a tiny indentation set along the rocky coast below a line of unfinished housing tracts. Years before, when the south swells rolled up from Baja, the cove was almost always filled, with surfers. But the storms of 1980 had washed out the bottom and left nothing but a pitiful shore break.

It was six o'clock in the evening when Able Team accompanied Sammy Vong to the cove. Although the skies were still clear, another fog was mounting far out at sea. There was also a chill to the evening breeze, promising a long, cold night ahead.

"They'll most likely come from the north," Vong said, "hugging the coast from Seal Beach, then darting right into the shore."

"And this is the only approach?" Lyons asked.

"Yeah, this is the only approach."

"So what have we got to worry about?"

Vong rolled his eyes and shook his head. "Ever hear of Little Big Horn?"

They had rendezvoused on a narrow, half-paved road that wound through the unfinished housing tracts. In contrast to Lyons's field trousers and jacket,

Vong wore a cheap gabardine suit, brown shoes, white shirt and a black tie.

"I guess it's the timing that bothers me the most," Vong said after a moment's silence. "First you and Gadgets board the *Asian Wind* and obviously scare the hell out of Trang. Then, forty-five minutes later, Narcotics gets the call from their informant."

"So?" Lyons asked.

"So it looks pretty fishy."

"Just the same, I think either way we've got to go for it," Lyons countered. "I think we've got to try to steal the cheese without getting caught in the trap."

"You might also be interested to know that I did a little checking on the informant who made the call," Vong said.

"And?"

"Calls himself Andy Duck, and up until now he's been strictly nickel-and-dime. Gives us small-time pushers for small change."

"So?"

"So how come all of a sudden he's able to tell us where and when Sonny Trang's making a drop?"

Lyons shrugged. "Maybe he got lucky."

Vong smirked. "Yeah, and maybe Jackie Minh's just out of town visiting an aunt."

Schwarz and Blancanales emerged from the back of the van next to Vong's car. Like Lyons, they were also more or less dressed for a hard night.

"Want a little a suggestion?" Schwarz asked, gazing at the cove below. "I think we should get these vehicles out of sight. Maybe move them up behind those hills and climb down from there."

Lyons put his hand on Vong's shoulder. "How about it, Sammy? You feeling up to a hike?"

Vong shrugged. "Hey, I'm fine...just so long as the stitches don't pop."

There was something almost forbidding about the view of the cove from the hills. Sharp rocks gave way to a half-moon of dark sand, ragged chaparral and flowering Judas along the sandstone cliffs. "If there's a bad place to catch a cross fire," Blancanales began, "it's definitely Sunset Cove."

"Yeah? Well, look at it this way," Lyons countered. "If we can catch a few of Sonny's boys with some major weight, there's a good chance we can get at least one of them to turn state's evidence and testify against the boss. Now how does that sound?"

Blancanales glanced at Vong. Then Vong looked at Lyons. "I seem to recall that those two DEA guys had a similar plan...just before Sonny had them whacked in the woods outside Da Nang," Vong said.

Leaving their vehicles on an unpaved cul-de-sac beside a pickup truck and a heap of scrap lumber, Lyons led his little party to the edge of the cliff. From there, a narrow deer path led to the highway, then another steep trail to the beach. Although the sun had dropped below the line of fog on the horizon, there was still sufficient light to view the terrain.

"Tell me something, Sammy," Lyons said as he gazed down at the landscape below. "Those two DEA guys, Barber and Bates, what were they packing?"

"In what sense?"

"In the way of weapons."

Vong shook his head. "I don't know. Probably M-16s."

"Yeah, well, that's what I thought." Lyons eased an Assault System gear bag from his shoulder and placed it at his feet. In addition to their H&K MP-5s, Able Team now packed a six-shot 40 mm Armscor grenade launcher with an occluded-eye gunsight. "Ever see one of these, Sammy?"

Vong shouldered the weapon and sighted down the barrel. "Only in the movies."

"Yeah, well, this will blow the hell out of any action movie you care to name." He pointed at the revolving chamber. "Spring-activated. Feeds one per second." He pointed at the trigger. "Cocks the pin and releases the grenade in one action." He pointed at the safety. "Flip down and squeeze. That's all you have to do. Just flip and squeeze."

Vong examined the weapon for a few more seconds, then finally put it back into the bag. "I'm sure it's a good piece, but I think I'll just stick to this." With that, Vong drew his snub-nosed .38.

Turning back to examine the terrain, Lyons finally decided they would wait among the low dunes below the cliffs. He and Vong would take the sparse grass along the north end of the beach, Schwarz the sandstone hollows along the south end and Blancanales would half bury himself in the sand between them. Despite the wind, it wasn't that cold, and the sound of breaking waves on the shore was actually soothing.

IT WAS JUST after midnight when Blancanales heard the first distant throb of the boats. The breeze had grown stronger, and the fog was quite close, but the drone of the high-speed cigarettes was unmistakable.

He rolled onto his side, withdrew the Nytech NVS and scanned the rocky point. Okay, he thought, so this is just a clean little run-of-the-mill drug bust. This is just four guys in two cigarettes, and we're going to collar them, book them and then see if we can't persuade them to testify against Sonny Trang.

He withdrew a mini-Mag-Lite from his rear pocket, aimed it at Lyons, then rapidly switched it on and off. *Showtime?*

Lyons responded with three quick flashes from his own Mag-Lite. *Definitely showtime.*

Blancanales heard the faint click of steel as Schwarz jammed a magazine home. He heard the lower drone of the second cigarette apparently passing the first. Then, lifting the Starlite scope again and scanning the waterline ahead, he actually saw them: two lean, shallow-bottomed boats crewed by two wiry, dark Vietnamese boys.

Although obviously cautious, the boys didn't seem particularly nervous. After anchoring their boats outside the shore break, they slipped into the water with what looked like inflatable bags and slowly waded to the shore. Judging from the size of the bags, Blancanales estimated they were carrying about five or six keys each—not the largest haul on record, but definitely enough to put Trang away for a few years.

Upon reaching the shore, the boys rested. One of them lit what looked like a thin cigar. Another emptied his shoes of water. A third prepared the bags for the long climb up the cliffs. Then, obviously responding to the sound of Lyons slipping out of the dunes, all four suddenly froze.

"Federal agents!" Lyons shouted as he and Vong stepped onto the beach. "Place your hands on your heads and spread your legs." When the tallest of the boys seemed to hesitate, Ironman repeated, "Let's go! Hands on your heads and spread your legs. Now!"

There were quick whispers, and it seemed that a slightly chubby boy was weighing his chances of sprinting to the boats. But before the boy could even glance at the water, Schwarz appeared, the Armscor in his left hand and an H&K in his right.

"Let's go!" Lyons shouted again. "Let's go. Let's go!"

The boys obeyed with slow movements, lacing their fingers on top of their heads, spreading their legs and lowering their eyes. Then, as Schwarz and Vong kept them covered, Lyons withdrew four pairs of plastic handcuffs. "Why don't you take a look at what we've got there?" he suggested to Schwarz as he cuffed the chubby kid and then pushed him to his knees.

But Schwarz had already withdrawn his knife, already slit the first bag. Then, finally cocking the Armscor, he softly called Lyons's name. "Carl. Hey, Carl? I think we got a problem here."

Lyons cuffed the second boy, a skinny kid in a black T-shirt. "What are you talking about?"

Schwarz extended his left hand, then slowly spread his fingers until something began to trickle between his knuckles. "Sand. There ain't nothing here but sand."

Lyons stopped and looked at him. "What are you talking about?"

"Sand," Schwarz repeated. "These guys aren't holding anything but sand."

"Try the other bag," Lyons ordered.

But Vong was already shaking his head. "Also sand," he said.

Then it seemed as if everything grew very still as Lyons glanced up at the cliffs and whispered, "I think we'd better get the hell out of here right now."

FROM WHERE BLANCANALES LAY, still hidden in the dunes, it seemed as if a lot of things began to happen at once. The chubby boy began to scream as ten or twelve shots cracked from the cliffs above. Lyons, Vong and Schwarz broke into a sprint as a dozen tiny geysers of sand spewed up at their feet. Someone, probably Schwarz, shouted, "Incoming!" Then, following what sounded like a popping beer can, the entire beach was suddenly alive with orange light and billowing sand.

Lyons and Vong threw themselves into the shadow of the cliff as shrapnel rattled off the sandstone above their head. There were cries of pain, and Schwarz shouted out a stream of obscenities as he furiously scrambled beneath an overhanging ledge. Six more bursts of automatic fire raked the sand. Then, just as suddenly, the bombardment stopped.

Pol heard a moan and then another obscenity, followed by the sound of ripping cloth. "Gadgets?" he whispered, peering through the scope at the huddled form against the sandstone. "You all right, Gadgets?"

Schwarz shrugged with a hard smile, then gently extended a bloody left arm. "They've got a mortar, man. What the hell are they doing with a mortar?"

Lyons appeared, crawling silently out of the shadows between the dunes and the rocky walls of the cliff toward Blancanales. "Any idea where they are?"

Blancanales pressed a hand against the sandstone wall at their backs to indicate the ridge some sixty feet above. "How does right on top of us sound?"

"What about Gadgets?"

Blancanales nodded his head to the left, "Shoulder and arm. Could be serious."

There were sounds of movement on the beach, and Blancanales caught a glimpse of the four boys scampering into the water, then into the boats. When he finally raised his SMG, however, Lyons shook his head. "No point."

"All right, then, what do you suggest?"

Lyons glanced up at the overhanging wall of sandstone, then leaned out even farther for a quick look at the cliffs. "Well, as long as we keep our butts tight against these rocks..."

"And as long as they don't move that mortar..."

Schwarz appeared, sliding painfully on his belly, the wounded left arm at his side. Although his face was taut with pain and bathed in perspiration, his voice remained soft and calm. "Just in case you boys were worrying," he said, "it's mainly just rock fragments."

Lyons withdrew his Mag-Lite, switched it on and began to examine Schwarz's arm. "What about the elbow? Can you move it?"

Schwarz shifted his forearm to the right, then to the left. "Elbow's fine. Just tie it up and let's get the hell out of here."

But even before Lyons could remove his first-aid kit, the firing started again—half a dozen bursts from the cliffs, then the soft pop of a 60 mm mortar round.

Clouds of sand and fragments of seashells rose thirty feet into the air. A chunk of sandstone the size of a grapefruit slammed into Blancanales's shoulder. Lyons grunted with pain as a six-inch gash opened up on his left cheek and the blast of hot wind slammed him against the cliff.

"This isn't fun!" Schwarz shouted.

"Just give me the goddamn launcher," Blancanales hissed. He shouldered the Armscor and aimed for the ridge—a blind shot at which might have been a flashing AK-47. Running into a sandstone hollow twenty feet farther along the cliff wall, he squeezed off another three grenades.

Cones of white light erupted from the cliffs above, sending down another shower of rock and dust. Someone screamed, possibly in Vietnamese, while another four or five bursts raked the sand below the cliff wall.

Blancanales put the Armscor aside and picked up the Starlite scope. From this vantage point along the northern cliff, he was able to scan at least thirty feet of the ridge above. But apart from the suggestion of forms, he still couldn't see anything definite.

"Lyons was right," a muffled voice from the deeper shadows of the recess said. "The launcher's definitely a big help."

Blancanales shifted on his belly until his eyes spotted the huddled form of Sammy Vong. "Tell me something," Pol asked softly. "Who the hell are those guys up there?"

Vong scrambled forward, then eased to his belly next to Blancanales. "I'm not sure."

"But they're not Ghosts, are they?"

"I doubt it."

Blancanales picked up the scope again, first scanning the ends of the cove, then the far ridge. Finally shouldering the Armscor, he signaled to Lyons. Moments later, amid another blast of AK-47 fire, Lyons and Schwarz also reached the recess. Then, for at least another two or three minutes, there were only the sounds of the waves hitting the shore.

"Way I figure it," Lyons finally said, breaking the silence, "we've got two choices. We can either wait them out here, or we can try to make it around the point and back into the hills. Either way it's risky."

"I say we go for the point," Vong said.

Schwarz gazed out across the sand to where the cigarettes still lay bobbing in the water. "What about the boats? Maybe we can make it out to them."

Blancanales shook his head and scanned the cliffs with the scope again. "You guys still don't get it, do you?" Slowly he inched his finger from left to right in order to indicate the cliffs above. "We're not just dealing with a few punks on a ridge. These guys are pros."

Lyons slid to Blancanales's side, resting on his elbows and also gazing out at the dark beach ahead. "What are you talking about, Pol?"

Blancanales nodded at the cliffs and the ridge above. "They're trying to flush us out. They're trying to make us run so that they can hit us with a cross fire."

Lyons looked at him. "How do you know?"

"Because I've played this game before."

Schwarz also slid up to the mouth of the recess, his wounded arm still pressed to his side. "Pol may be right. Those guys out there definitely know what they're doing."

"So what do you suggest?" Lyons asked.

Blancanales handed the Starlite scope to Lyons, withdrew five 40 mm exploding shells and began to insert them into the launcher. "I suggest I crawl on up there and meet them on their own terms."

Lyons nodded, glanced at Schwarz, then shifted his gaze back to Blancanales. "All right," he finally breathed. "But if you run into anything you can't handle, give us a holler. Understand?"

Although Blancanales smiled, it wasn't the sort of smile Lyons had ever seen before. Not only was Pol's mouth twisted at an odd angle, but his eyes were at least six thousand miles away.

BLANCANALES MOVED slowly at first, sliding along the cliff wall in a half crouch beneath the overhang. Then, facing fifty feet of relatively open sand, he broke into a sprint. Although he thought he'd caught sight of something or someone moving through the dark chaparral above, when he looked again it was gone.

There were two trails leading to the ridge from where Blancanales finally came to a stop, two narrow trails between dark silhouettes of cactus and flowering Judas. After a five-minute deliberation, he finally chose the trail closest to the water where the echo of the crashing surf might help to mask the sound of his steps.

The trail was steep, and at times he had to drag himself from branch to branch. When he thought he heard a whispered command or a nervous question, he would stop—dead still, waiting just as he had waited through the worst moments in Vietnam.

The breeze shifted, bringing odors of skunk and cordite, but also bringing in the fog. I could make it with the fog, he told himself. Charlie may have the edge right now, but give me the fog and I might have a chance.

Emerging from a clump of tall weeds, however, he found himself confronting a dark figure on the ridge. Although the features were indistinguishable, the eyes behind the AK-47 couldn't have been more prominent. They were vacant eyes, almost like two plugs of glass, and just before the muzzle-flash, they reminded him of a rat's eyes.

A dozen slugs cut through the weeds above and to the left of where Blancanales lay. He flattened and waited for the impact, lips actually kissing the sandstone. Finally he flung himself off the trail and crashed into a pool of leaves below.

It became silent again, with only the sound of the wind through dry brush. He raised his head and scanned the ridge, but saw nothing. Gently he shifted his right knee and felt a quick stab of pain, then realized it was only the cactus.

Blancanales shut his eyes and recalled the distinct image of the face behind the AK-47, a face he had seen a thousand times in Vietnam. This is the real thing, he thought. These aren't just local kids; these guys are the real thing. Then, rolling onto his back and sucking in the foul night air, he found himself staring at the stars.

I should have brought the night scope and three or four flash grenades, he told himself. But then, letting his head rest on the sand, he supposed it wouldn't have made much difference. Could have brought a damn tank and it still wouldn't make any difference . . . because I'm past it. Over the hill, washed out and past it.

Blancanales heard something moving through the brush to his left and wondered if it was a coyote. He heard what he thought was the sliding bolt on another AK-47 and wondered if this was the end. Then, finally turning onto his belly and adjusting the Armscor on his shoulder, he simply started forward again.

He moved slowly but steadily, fixing his mind on the obvious problems. He worried about the dry leaves and brittle twigs. He worried about his footing in the soft soil and dislodging chunks of sandstone.

At forty yards below the ridge Pol flipped off the safety on his SMG. When he finally caught a glimpse of the enemy, he put the SMG aside and slowly drew his knife.

The figure stood on the high ridge, half crouching with an AK-47 resting on his hip. From where Blancanales lay, almost entirely obscured in chaparral, the figure might have been a boy. But as he slowly turned toward the light reflected off the sea below, Blancanales saw that he must have been at least thirty-five or forty, which meant that he had probably put in time with the South Vietnamese army or maybe the Cong.

Blancanales waited for the breeze to return before easing the Armscor off his shoulder and moving forward again. For the most part, sand lay between the clumps of chaparral, and in the sand he was absolutely noiseless. Although it finally gave way to dry soil, his approach still remained absolutely silent.

He paused as the wind subsided and the figure turned to the cove again. Finally rising into another half crouch and moving with the wind again, Blancanales crossed another ten or twelve feet until he could almost reach out and touch the man.

The Able Team warrior waited a full sixty seconds before finally crossing the last four feet. He waited until his heartbeat slowed and his breathing fell in time with the echo of the waves. When he was absolutely certain of himself, he gradually brought the knife up, bent slightly at the knees and let his instincts carry him into the kill.

Pol closed in with a single step, his left arm circling the man's head and twisting, his right hand bringing his knife up to the throat. Then, jamming his right knee into the spine, he arched the man back. He cut deeply, fixing his mind on the vocal cords first, then on the jugular vein. He felt the hot blood on his wrist and the blade working against the tissue. He felt the expiring breath in his ear, and the last desperate strain in the neck. Then he felt the deadweight and gently let the corpse fall.

He remained half-crouched above the body for another minute or two before moving on. Although the ridge above was clear, he was fairly certain they were still out there, either waiting in the hollows or deeper in the brush.

In all, he must have spent at least another ten to twenty minutes waiting below the ridge where the Vietnamese had placed the mortar. He waited among the stalks of another flowering Judas, waited on his feet, with his arms at his side and his back very straight. Although he only counted seven heads on the ridge, he imagined there were probably at least three or four more inching along the opposite ridge to nail Lyons and the others.

Blancanales dropped to one knee, put down the SMG and unslung the Armscor. He waited, once more vaguely conscious of the waves and the breeze through the dry chaparral. When he finally squeezed the trigger, however, he really wasn't conscious of anything.

He saw the blast before he heard it, saw the white light and a body lifting into the air. Then, as the echoing explosion tore through the surrounding shrub, he dropped to his belly and squeezed off a second grenade, aiming for the high rocks where two, possibly three figures had scrambled for cover. This time, when the shell hit, he actually caught a glimpse of a body under impact—back arched, eyes wide, a spray of blood where the chest had been.

Blancanales fired a third and forth grenade into the fury of shadows and screams. He fired blindly and closely enough to feel the concussion and rain of sand when the shells exploded. He saw another body twisting upon impact, a thin figure tossed into an impossible angle while portions of the skull dissolved in mist. Then, shouldering the Armscor and picking up the SMG, he started forward again.

Two slugs cut the air above his head as he pressed on through the brush. He responded with a short burst from his SMG, saw a dark-shirted man lurch from the branches, then let loose with a second burst. The man hung suspended, shivering for a moment before collapsing with a muffled sob. Then it seemed that everyone was sobbing, dozens of them sobbing out in pain from deep within the chaparral. Blancanales had to empty at least three more clips before the moaning finally stopped.

LYONS LOOKED at the bodies for twenty or thirty seconds, then shook his head and glanced at Blancanales again. Unlike Pol, he had moved up the trail very quickly, virtually at a sprint.

"Where are the others?" Blancanales asked finally.

Lyons jerked his head to the left, indicating the cliffs below.

"And Gadgets?"

"Still bleeding," Lyons said.

Blancanales shifted his gaze to the opposite ridge and the dark waves of brush beyond. "Yeah, well, if we try to move him now, they'll hit us from those trees."

"So?"

"So I think we'd better clear them out."

Lyons hesitated a moment, then finally nodded. But before they actually started moving, he placed his hand on Blancanales's shoulder and looked into the man's eyes. "Hey, Pol, are you all right?"

Blancanales returned the gaze with another genuinely crazed smile. "Never been better."

The breeze had returned, depositing layers of fog in the brush and a denser blanket over the water. There was also a new stench in the air—scorched wood. Every now and then their footsteps flushed small animals from the brush, undoubtedly rabbits and rats. Then, for a long time, there were hardly any sounds at all.

They paused where the deer path fell away to a shallow gully. There were trees beyond the gully, drooping eucalyptus and dying oaks. Although Lyons saw and heard nothing, Blancanales suddenly dragged him down into the brush.

"What's going on?" Ironman whispered.

Blancanales lifted a finger and pointed at the trees. "Out there."

"How do you know?"

Blancanales merely shook his head.

Another animal, possibly a coyote, bolted from the brush below. Lyons responded by cocking his SMG, but Blancanales pushed the barrel down again. "Just give me your Mag-Lite," the Able Team warrior said.

When Lyons tried to meet the man's eyes, he again saw something he'd never seen before. He finally looked away as he withdrew the tiny flashlight. Blancanales took it without a word, cupped his left hand over the bulb and switched it on.

"These guys are probably too good to start shooting right away, but we might be able to get them jerking, just like you did when you heard that coyote."

"Pol, don't you think we ought to—"

"Just watch the brush."

Blancanales counted, and Lyons watched him mouth the numbers. Then, cocking his arm, Pol hurled the glowing Mag-Lite into the brush ahead.

Something? Nothing? Lyons couldn't be sure.

But when Blancanales finally unslung the Armscor and sent another shell into the trees, there were definitely muffled cries.

Two figures darted from the trees, one of them possibly clutching a mangled hand. When Lyons raised his SMG, however, a third and fourth figure fired from the denser brush and nearly cut him in two.

"Give me a reading," Blancanales whispered as he rolled onto his side and hefted the Armscor again.

Lyons peered above the brush, but again saw nothing. "Sixty, seventy yards to the left ... maybe."

Blancanales cocked the Armscor, but couldn't squeeze the trigger before another burst of autofire cut through the brush around him. "Look's like they've got us in a squeeze," he whispered.

Lyons rose to one elbow and extended the H&K through the branches. "Yeah, well, maybe I can ease the pressure," he said.

Blancanales shot out a hand and eased Lyons's weapon back down. "That's exactly what they want us to do. They're trying to draw fire so that they can target our muzzle-flash."

"All right, then how do we play it?"

Blancanales slowly raised his head to peer out again across the waves of dark chaparral. "Quietly," he whispered. "Very quietly."

Two trails led from the deep brush to the shallow gully below. After another moment's hesitation, however, Blancanales led Lyons on the middle path, which consisted of a narrow tunnel through coils of dry thorns and cactus spears. They moved on their bellies, almost as if moving through water. Now and again there were more sounds, possibly made by rattlers, but neither man paid them any attention.

The ground was moist in the gully, and the leaves were damp from the fog. There were also pools of foul water, possibly sewage. The rocks, however, afforded some cover, and apparently Blancanales liked the view from the opposite rim.

"Tell you what we'll do," Pol whispered. "Give me fifteen minutes to reach that rise, then open up on those trees. When they return the fire, I'll pop 'em with the launcher."

"I want at least one of them alive," Lyons said.

Blancanales slowly shifted his gaze to the left until he encountered Lyons's eyes again. "You're never going to get one of these people to talk, Ironman. It's just not going to happen."

"Maybe, maybe not. But I still want one of them alive."

"Well, I'll see what I can do," Blancanales breathed. He then slung the launcher over his shoulder again, slithered out of the gully and was gone.

A BIRD BROKE from the spears of black brush as Blancanales continued sliding forward. For an instant he thought it was a parrot or a tropical crow. Then he remembered that he wasn't in an Asian jungle; it had probably been just a sparrow.

There were all sorts of vague reminders of the jungle now: the stench of foul water, arched palms and dangling vines. There were also mosquitoes, hundreds of them rising out of the marshland. *Forget about the Cong,* they had told him in Da Nang. *It's the jungle that kills you. It's the damn ground that eats you alive.* And after four months of night probes in the Highlands, Blancanales had come to realize it was true.

But, for the moment, he was glad that the ground was moist and yielding while the twigs bent instead of snapped. He was finally even glad about the mud that muffled his steps.

Pol paused again, peering out between two ranks of stunted palms at the denser growth of oaks. Beyond the trees lay another fairly barren stretch of ground, then virtually nothing until the highway. Either they're gone, Blancanales told himself, or else they're just waiting in those trees. Finally, withdrawing his Mag-Lite and cupping the bulb with his hand, he muttered, "Just waiting in those trees."

He signaled twice before Lyons responded—two quick flashes from the Mag-Lite, then another two. Moments later he heard Lyons firing with quick, raking bursts through the dry brush and into the trees. But it wasn't until he caught a glimpse of the return fire that he even unslung the launcher.

His next movements couldn't have been more precise. He released the safety with his left thumb and peered through the sight until a single aiming point appeared above the palms. Finally, holding his breath and squeezing, he released the first three shells.

Again he saw the explosion before he heard it— three balls of white light briefly leaving everything in black relief against the sky. Then came the blast, the trailing orange sparks and finally the agonized scream.

Blancanales sent another two shells into the brush below the trees, splintering the palms and cactus spears. He then picked up the H&K and started moving again in another half crouch, but faster now and with his finger welded to the trigger. When a gray figure staggered out of the oaks, he let loose with two quick bursts. He saw the figure collapse into a roll, then let loose with another long burst.

The gray figure rose from the brush and stumbled into the clearing. At first glimpse Blancanales thought he was an old man, deeply tanned and lame. When he came closer, Pol saw that the man was actually fairly young—thirty-five or so—and that the limp was probably caused by fragments of shrapnel in the thigh.

Lyons appeared, easing himself out of the gully to the left and ten yards behind Blancanales. In addition to his SMG, he was also carrying another pair of handcuffs. "Where are the others?"

Blancanales nodded to the prisoner, then to the trees beyond. "Looks like this one held us off till his pals could escape."

"So he's all we've got?"

Blancanales met the prisoner's gaze and held it for at least ten seconds. "Yeah," he finally said, "he's all we've got."

Another ten seconds passed while Blancanales and Lyons scrutinized the prisoner: his smiling eyes, his new boots and fatigues, his camouflaged jungle hat and his partially hidden hands. It crossed Blancanales mind that the prisoner looked a little too happy, particularly as he continued stumbling forward out of the line of splintered trees.

"That's far enough," Pol told him as the man continued forward. "I said that's far enough, pal," he repeated.

But the man kept moving, his smile growing slightly wider, his right hand gradually slipping from his head.

Again a lot of things happened at once. Lyons called out Blancanales's name. Pol grabbed Ironman's arm and pushed him into the brush. The prisoner's smile twisted into a grimace as he screamed out something in Vietnamese. Then, finally dropping onto his stomach, Blancanales squeezed off the last burst.

Three 9 mm rounds slammed into the prisoner's chest, sent him reeling in a spray of blood and tossed him onto the ground. A second later, however, the body rose again, bucking nearly a foot into the air with the blast from what was probably a stick grenade.

"How did you know he was holding a grenade?" Lyons asked, amazed.

Blancanales rose to his feet, picking out fragments of palm from his hair and brushing the dust from his sleeves. "Vietnam."

What was left of their prisoner lay ten yards deeper into the brush. Although the face was unmarked, the torso had been virtually shredded. Blancanales looked at the head, then knelt to examine the contents of the pockets: one crushed pack of cigarettes, one 9 mm clip, one book of matches from Pep Boys Automotive Supply, one silk scarf embroidered with a red star.

Farther along the trail Blancanales also found four mortar shells, while Lyons followed three pairs of footprints and a thin trail of blood to the highway.

"If we hustle," Ironman said, "we might be able to catch them."

But Pol shook his head. "Don't bet on it."

Lyons stooped to examine the tire tracks and what looked like a trace of vomit. He gazed out at the empty highway, and then at the hills where they had left the van. "All right," he finally said, "then just hike on up to the van, call the cops and tell them to send an ambulance for Gadgets."

Blancanales nodded, then flipped on the safety on his SMG. "I'll make the call, but I can tell you right now that the cops aren't going to be able to help us with this one."

# 8

It was nearly dawn when the police arrived. Although the fog had lifted from the hills, the beach and gullies still remained hidden. There were also threads of fog along the point, and it still clung to the trees along the highway where Lyons and Blancanales sat with Sammy Vong.

"You boys realize, of course, that they may ask you to sign statements," Vong said. "Maybe even take a little ride downtown."

Lyons glanced through the trees at the rotating dome lights. Apparently there were also three or four unmarked cars en route from the city, at least one of them carrying federal agents.

"I have no problem giving a statement," Lyons said. "Just so long as they don't get personal."

Vong smiled and worked a toothpick between two teeth. "I'll make sure they understand that."

There were sounds of Schwarz grunting with pain as a couple of paramedics attempted to examine his shoulder. They heard breaking glass, then another grunt through clenched teeth. "You touch me again with that thing and I'll make you eat it," Gadgets yelled.

A few moments later Schwarz limped into the trees along the highway, and collapsed onto the grass. After shutting his eyes, he whispered, "I hate needles."

Lyons shook his head and glanced at Schwarz's shoulder. Although the paramedics had managed to stop the bleeding, the lower arm was still pretty raw. There were also puncture wounds along the rib cage and two or three small cuts along the collarbone.

"If you think I'm going to take you home to meet the family looking like that," Lyons said, "you'd better think again."

Schwarz opened his eyes and gave Lyons a weak grin. "Don't worry. I'm not going to kiss anyone."

There were sounds of another approaching car, slowing to a stop on the gravel. Doors slammed with a muffled thump and then Able Team heard voices and a dark figure with a flashlight whispering, "Shit!"

A cop, pointing through the trees, said, "They're over there." Finally someone called out Vong's name.

In reponse, however, Vong simply spit out the toothpick and turned to Lyons. "Remember those two CIA guys I told you about who came to my house?"

Lyons nodded as he watched the two figures approach from the ring of parked cars and vans. "Yeah. What about them?"

"Well, I think you're about to be introduced."

Smith and Jones faced Lyons from the edge of the highway. Once again they were dressed almost identically: gray flannel slacks, herringbone jackets and brown suede shoes. After meeting Lyons's tired gaze for three or four seconds, they turned their eyes to Blancanales and Schwarz.

Finally, after running a hand through his steel-gray hair, Smith shook his head and said, "Hello, Sammy. How are you?"

Ignoring the comment, Vong turned to Lyons. "That's Smith," he said. "The other one calls himself Jones."

Lyons looked at the two men again, then nodded. "Well, it's a real pleasure to make your aquaintance, gentlemen."

"You may not feel that way when you've heard what we have to say." Jones replied. "And tell that man to get himself to a hospital," he added, glancing at Schwarz. "We've already got enough dead bodies around here."

Schwarz just smiled at Blancanales and shut his eyes again.

Then, following another three or four minutes of taut silence, Smith suddenly dropped to his haunches and whispered into Lyons's ear, "Look, we just want to talk. That's all. We've got nothing against your people here, but we'd be real grateful if you'd give us just a few minutes alone."

Lyons worked his jaw for a moment, then finally spit out a blade of grass and rose to his feet. "All right, let's talk alone."

The three men walked toward a rocky point where the highway gently curved to the east. There was a long panorama of the cove as well as a view of the cliffs where at least a dozen cops were examining the bodies that Blancanales had left in his wake.

"Looks like you boys really did a number here tonight," Smith began. "I mean, I've seen some bad action the past few weeks, but this really takes the cake."

"Yeah, we tend to get a little excited when people start dropping mortar rounds on us," Lyons said. "Don't know what it is. Some nut starts trying to shell us, and for some reason we just get pissed off. Now, what did you want to talk about?"

Smith glanced at Jones and sighed. "I guess basically it's a question of jurisdiction. Now I realize that you people have a pretty broad license, but by the same token you're still encroaching on Company ground."

Lyons glanced back over his shoulder at the circle of trees and the rotating lights of the ambulance and patrol cars. Although he couldn't be certain, it looked as if Blancanales was watching from the shadows... still armed and still furious. "Since when has Langley started working domestically?"

Jones started to speak, possibly in anger, but Smith shut him up with a glance. Smith smiled. "Well, that's just it. We're not talking domestic."

Lyons looked up at the highway ahead to a billboard advertising Disneyland and another touting Sea World. "Could have fooled me."

They moved to the edge of the point, and for a moment all three just stared at the remnants of the chaos below: the bodies laid out in bags along the sand, the splintered palms and scorched oaks.

"Look, I'm not saying there isn't drug action around here," Smith said. "All I'm saying is that there are also a few things you don't know about."

"And what you don't know can definitely hurt you," Jones added with a scowl. "It can hurt you real bad."

Lyons smiled again while he examined an empty shell casing. "Look, if you boys have something to say, then why don't you just say it?"

"All right," Smith said with sigh. "You want it straight? We'll give it to you straight. The fact of the matter is that some, and I repeat *some*, of Trang's people may be dealing a little dope. Now that doesn't mean Trang himself approves, and it certainly doesn't mean the Company approves. It simply means that we're aware of the problem and intend to take action in due time."

Lyons smirked. "Which will be when? Sometime in the year 2000?"

Once again Jones started to say something, but Smith shut him up with a glance. "Hey, I know how you feel about us," Smith said. "I know we may not have the best reputation in terms of law enforcement, but I want you to know that we've got just as much at stake in a drug-free America as anyone on your side of the street. The only difference is that we're not in a position to act on impulse. We have to take the broader view."

"So what's the broader view?" Lyons asked, his eyes still fixed on the dim outline of the body bags lined up neatly on the cliffs.

"Let me put it like this," Smith began. "Yes, there are some nasty people on Sonny Trang's team, but by the same token there are nastier people on the opposing team. Now I'm not just talking about the local criminal element. I'm talking about six-cylinder commie hoods. I'm talking a full-fledged Vietnamese Communist intrusion."

"He's also talking ultrasensitive information," Jones added with a growl.

Lyons grinned. "Well, in that case I'll try to keep my mouth ultrashut."

"I'm afraid we're going to have ask you to do more than that," Jones said. "I'm afraid we're going to have to ask you to lay off Sonny Trang."

"See, it's like this," Smith interjected. "Trang may not be the sweetest apple in the barrel, but he's tough and he's dedicated. He also enjoys the support of this community, and we need that support right now. In fact, we need it real bad."

"Hey, I don't have a problem with Trang," Lyons said. "I've got a problem with the guys who popped Jackie Minh. I've also got a problem with the guys who tried to pop my men. Now if that creates problems for you, I'm sorry, but there's not a whole lot I can do about it."

"All right," Smith said, "how about we try a different tack? How about we really lay our cards on the table? Now, what I'm about to tell you is strictly top-secret. That means you don't discuss it with Sammy Vong. You don't even discuss it with your girl-friend."

"It also means," Jones threatened, "that if you talk, we go to your boss with a *formal* complaint."

"But seeing as how we're basically on the same side," Smith continued, spearing Jones with a hostile glare, "I'm going to tell you the following. As we speak, the Hanoi government is nurturing no less than four, count 'em four, major intelligence probes into this area. Now, for the most part, we're talking about low-grade stuff. Maybe a little skinny on ship move-ments. Maybe a few rumors from the Marine base. But recently we've also begun to notice some leaks out of Lockheed, and frankly that's just not okay."

"So how come I'm not talking to the FBI right now?" Lyons asked skeptically. "How come I'm not talking to a couple of flatfeet in cheap suits?"

"Come on, Lyons, you know how it is. The Bureau steps in, arrests the first suspect they see and the real brains slip back into the woodwork. Besides, with any luck, we might just be able to run it right back down their throats."

"But in order to do that we need Sonny Trang's people," Jones said.

"And in order to ensure that," Smith added, "we need your cooperation."

Lyons bent and picked up a spent shell casing from the mortar that had nearly cut Able Team in two. There were at least a dozen shells from AK-47s scattered at his feet. "Tell me something. Who were those guys we hit tonight?"

Smith responded with a casual shrug, then shook his head. "Probably just a little local talent with mail-order weapons."

"Yeah, well, they sure didn't move like any local talent I've ever seen," Lyons said.

"Well, that's the whole point. Some of these people have received a little training through one of our programs."

"What kind of training?"

"Anti-insurgency, anti-sapper, anti-Communist."

"And so now they're using their talents to protect the drug links? Is that the bottom line here?" Lyons asked.

"Absolutely not," Jones cut in. "For one thing you didn't find dope. You found sand. For another thing you were snooping on their ground, asking all kinds of dangerous questions and generally causing trouble. Sure, their response might have been a little exaggerated, but after what these people have been through in their homeland, can you honestly blame them?"

"Who's blaming them?" Lyons gazed down at the cliffs, where the paramedics were dragging yet another mangled body out of the brush.

"Look, we're not condoning what happened here tonight," Smith said suddenly. "We're not saying that it was all just some terrible mistake that your boys crossed the line with our boys. We're just saying that nothing's black or white, that there's no such thing as a good guy and a bad guy anymore. Everybody's a little gray. Okay, so maybe some of Sonny's people tried to hit your team tonight. And maybe you got lucky and kicked their butts. But the next time you might not be so lucky. In fact, next time I might be standing here talking to some guy named Hue while the paramedics zip you up in a bag. Know what I mean?"

"Sure," Lyons said, "I know what you mean."

"So then you'll lay off Sonny Trang?" Jones asked.

Lyons nodded with an easy shrug. "Sure, I'll lay off Trang, as soon as I find out where he's getting the dope and what he did to Jackie Minh."

IT WAS NEARLY six o'clock when the last body was dragged from the brush and the last patrol car returned to the city. Although Smith and Jones had claimed they were actually en route to Washington, Lyons was fairly certain they had been lying and that they would simply go underground in Gook Town. As for the others, Vong had eventually left with a couple of inspectors from Internal Affairs, while Lyons had finally convinced Gadgets to at least spend a couple of hours getting patched up in the hospital.

"You think I've flipped, don't you?" Blancanales asked. "You think I've finally turned the corner and entered that little black room that's always been waiting for me."

They were sitting in the van, gazing out at the gray dawn. Lyons was sipping a cup of rank coffee that one of the cops had given him. Blancanales was still picking thorns out of his forearms.

"You think I've crossed the double yellow line right into oncoming traffic, don't you?" he added.

Lyons shook his head. "All I think is that maybe you're shooting a little close."

Blancanales ran his hand along the inside of his forearm, examining the specks of blood. "Want me to guess what those two characters from the Company told you?"

"Pol, listen to me."

"No, you listen to me. They told you that what happened here tonight was all just a big mistake, didn't they? They told you that basically we just ran into a few local drug dealers who may have an affiliation with Trang but are nonetheless needed to bust Commie subversion in the neighborhood. Now, am I right? Isn't that pretty much what they told you?"

Lyons took another sip of coffee, then nodded. "Yeah, that's pretty much what they told me."

"Now, do you want me to tell you how I know?"

"Pol..."

"I know because I've heard it all before. See, in Saigon there were guys like Smith and Jones all over the place. They'd call you into their stinking little offices and tell you all about how this or that operation was classified so that you'd just damn well better look the other way. And why? Because in reality they were playing games with the NVA, the ARVN and the Hong Kong mob, pulling down maybe fifteen million a year in heroin profits all in the name of Anti-communism."

Lyons took another sip of coffee, then finally tossed the cup into the garbage. Although more than three hours had now passed since the last shots had been fired, he still kept smelling hints of cordite on the breeze. "All I can tell you," he finally said, "is that this isn't Vietnam."

"Maybe you're right, but those guys we tagged a few hours ago weren't just local dealers, either. They were grade A regulars from Hanoi. And I'll tell you something else. Sonny Trang isn't just dirty. He's black right down to the core."

# 9

Sonny Trang sat in the shadows in the far south corner of the room. It was a large room, primarily decorated in brown tones with paneled walls and teak trim. It was also vaguely menacing, with a high, coffered ceiling and two massive jade serpents standing guard. Although the view through latticed windows was actually quite stunning, more often than not the shutters remained closed and the shades remained drawn.

It had been about four o'clock in the morning when Trang had received word of what had gone down at the cove. He had then slipped out of bed and gone downstairs to the sitting room to stare at the night sky. It was now nearly eight in the morning, and he had hardly moved at all. When Kim Kiet had appeared, inquiring if there was anything he needed, he pointed to his feet and told her to sit down and be quiet. Then, although he occasionally touched her, occasionally ran a finger along her bare shoulder, he still didn't speak.

She must have sat there for about an hour before she heard cars pull into the courtyard and the ominous thump of slamming doors. Finally there was a knock on the door.

Trang slowly turned his head to the left and snapped his fingers. A moment later the doors slid back, revealing four figures in the darkened hall: two slender men in khaki uniforms and the massive outline of Chuckie Xuan. There was also an angular woman in white whom Kim had seen only once or twice before. Before acknowledging his guests, Trang dismissed Kim to the tiny walled garden where she could only see shadows and hear fragments of the conversation.

"Am I to have an explanation?" Trang immediately demanded when he knew Kim was out of earshot.

"Keep your voice down," the woman said. "There's no reason to shout."

Trang returned to his chair by the window and calmly replied, "Very well, then, who's going to tell me what happened?"

Chuckie Xuan spoke next, but softly so that Kim could only guess at what he said—something about how the three strangers were a lot more experienced than previously thought.

"Which is another way of saying what?" Trang asked. "That you failed? That nine of your so-called finest were unable to stop three unsuspecting round-eyes?"

"They had a grenade launcher," one of the slender men in khaki said in Vietnamese. "No one told us they would have a grenade launcher."

"They also had knowledge of jungle fighting," the second man in khaki added. "At least one of them had keen knowledge of jungle fighting."

"Oh, well, that explains it," Trang said. "Yes, now I can see perfectly how three surprised roundeyes were able to kill seven of your—"

He broke off, and then for a moment let loose with a furious stream of Vietnamese obscenities.

Then, at last, the woman calmly spoke. "What is done is done," she said softly. "Now, I think it's simply question of ensuring that it doesn't happen again. I invite you," the woman said to Trang. She indicated the two men in khaki now standing in the center of the room. "Come. I invite you."

The general hesitated uncertain about what the woman was suggesting. Then, either glancing into her eyes or finally catching a glimpse of the tiny pistol in her hand, he recoiled. "What is the point, madam?" he demanded.

She smiled, mumbled something in Vietnamese, then reverted to English again. "The point is that it's easy. An easy solution to your frustration."

"Well, I don't see it."

"Don't you?" She smiled again, this time reducing her eyes to thin slits. "You've expressed unhappiness with the performance of my soldiers. Very well, then, you must ensure that such a poor performance is never repeated. You must ensure that a lesson is learned from last night's failure, a lesson that will never be forgotten. So I invite you. Take the pistol and give them a lesson they'll never forget."

The general also smiled, then dabbing a handkerchief to his lips, he shook his head. "Okay, you've made your point."

But the woman continued to stare at him, the nickel-plated automatic in her open palm. "On the contrary, General. The point is not made until the point is made. These men betrayed their comrades. They chose to run instead of die. They chose to save themselves instead of giving their last full measure of determination. Now, is that acceptable? I don't think it's acceptable. I think it's disgusting. I think it's the sort of behavior that finally led to the defeat of your side and the victory of mine, and consequently I don't think it's something we can tolerate. So, I invite you, General. I invite you make an example of them, an example the others will always remember."

Trang rose from his chair, moved slowly across the gleaming tiles and took the pistol from her hand. "This is barbarous," he said, reverting once again to his native tongue. "I won't do it. I simply won't do it."

"Barbarous, General? This isn't barbarous. This is expedient." Snatching the pistol from his hand, she stepped behind the two men in khaki.

Although badly perspiring and clearly terrified, the two men still hadn't moved. Their eyes remained fixed on the far wall, on a delicate watercolor of cranes among willows. Their arms remained stiffly at their sides. The younger of the two, a smooth-faced boy of about twenty, winced as the woman ran her fingers along his shoulder. His eyes, however, didn't waver.

"I know what you're thinking, General," the woman said softly. "You're wondering if I'm merely testing you. You're wondering if I'm...how do you say—bluffing? Well, I'm not bluffing, General. These two young men failed to uphold our standards. They watched their comrades die but failed to make the same sacrifice. Where would we be today if their fathers had behaved like that?''

She slowly ran her fingers down the young man's back until they reached the base of his spine. Then she replaced her fingers with the muzzle of the pistol. ''Well, I'll tell you where we would be. We'd be right here!''

The young man's face contorted as the bullet shattered the bone and he dropped to the floor.

''There,'' the woman said calmly, turning to the second young man. ''There's the lesson for today. Now return to your comrades and tell them how I deal with cowards.''

After another five minutes of silence, the woman finally said, ''You think I'm a barbarian, don't you? You think only a barbarian would do such a thing to her own men.''

The general responded with an unintelligible grunt and tossed another ice cube into his glass.

''Well, I'll tell you something,'' the woman continued. ''I'm not a barbarian. A barbarian would have shot both men. But, as you see, I only shot one in order to make a vital tactical point. Now that young man will return to his comrades, explain to them the price of failure, and we'll never have another night like the last. It's all really quite logical. Or do you still disagree?''

The general responded with another unintelligible grunt, then very clearly he said, "I leave these matters in your hands."

"Exactly," she replied. "You leave these matters in my hands because you haven't the stomach to deal with them yourself." She sighed, letting the air hiss out between clenched teeth. "Although, in the final analysis, I suppose it's all for the best. Because not only have you no stomach, you also have no sense of security."

Trang turned and looked at her. "What are you talking about?"

The woman smiled, slowly turned her gaze to the window and extended a finger. "That," she said. "I'm talking about that little bitch of yours in the garden. I'm talking about the fact that she's been watching us since I entered the room. Now, are you going to tell her to come in here, or shall I go out and get her?"

Trang frowned and called Kim into the room. She entered slowly, hesitating in the doorway until Trang nodded. Then she moved to the center of the room. Although she tried to keep her eyes fixed on the tiles, she managed at least a sideways glance at the hostile woman's face.

"Come here," the woman demanded. "Come over here and let me look at you."

Kim hesitated again, then briefly fixed her gaze on the body that had been dragged into the corner.

"Don't worry," the woman cooed. "I'm not going to shoot you. I just want to look at you." When Kim moved closer, the woman ran her finger along the girl's bare shoulder while the others in the room watched in silence. "Like silk," the woman whispered. Then, turning to Trang, but still not removing her hand from Kim's shoulder, she repeated herself. "Like the very finest silk."

The general mumbled a protest but was ignored. Kim tried to avert her face, but by now the woman's fingers were coiled in her hair.

She gradually wrenched back Kim's head to expose her neck. "Unfortunately silk is such a fragile material," the woman whispered, "such a very fragile substance. One foolish slip with a knife, one careless gesture with a cigarette...and suddenly all is ruined." The woman's left hand appeared, the knuckles lifting Kim's chin until their eyes met again. "Now, you wouldn't want that to happen to you, would you?" she whispered. "Hmm? You wouldn't want someone to ruin this lovely face?"

Kim shut her eyes, squeezing out a tear and whispering, "No, madam."

"No, is right. So that's why you must never, never spy on me again. Do you understand?"

"Yes, madam," Kim moaned.

"Yes, what?"

"Yes, I understand."

Then, although the fingers finally released Kim's hair, the eyes still held her gaze. "Not that I wouldn't mind teaching you a lesson one day," she cooed. "Not that I wouldn't mind driving the point home to such a lovely little girl..."

Dismissed with a curt nod of the head, Kim moved past the body and slowly up the staircase to the general's den.

KIM WAS STILL SEATED in the den when the general finally came to her. As always he entered without knocking, and as always he addressed her in English.

"I don't suppose I have to tell you," he said, "that you're to forget everything you witnessed just now."

She nodded but remained facing the oval window above the courtyard.

"I also don't suppose I need to tell you that things aren't exactly as they seem. That woman is an associate, nothing more. I allow her to play boss because she seems to enjoy it. But ultimately I'm in charge, and she knows it."

Kim nodded again, fixing her eyes on one of the general's favorite paintings, an ornately framed oil suggestively entitled *The Tribute*. The work portrayed a young girl kneeling at the feet of an obviously severe monarch. Her clinging dress was partially torn at the shoulder. Her face was half hidden by her hair.

"Why did you let her touch me?" Kim finally asked.

Trang stepped to the bed and gently placed his hand on the back of her neck. "What was the harm in it?"

She shook her head. "It frightened me, that's all."

He lifted her hair and began to massage her shoulders. "Well, you know sometimes it's good to be frightened. Sometimes fear can teach us things that are good for us. Besides, didn't you find it just a little bit exciting? Yes? No? Not even a little bit?"

When she tried to respond, he pressed his hand to her mouth. When she tried to turn away, he grabbed hold of her hair and gently pulled her head back to expose her neck.

"Because I'll tell you a little secret," he whispered. "That woman wasn't so concerned about your having peeked through the window as she was about your beauty. Yes, she pretended to be outraged that you were spying on her, but, in fact, the outrage was false, an excuse to turn her attention to you. Because that's the effect you have on people, even on other women. They can't keep themselves from looking at you. You should be pleased."

He let go of her hair, grabbed her left wrist and lifted her to her feet. "Now, why don't you run along and change your dress?" He smiled. "Put on your blue dress that we like so much. Then tell the cook to prepare us eggs and I'll join you in the garden."

IN CONTRAST to either the sitting room or den, Kim's bedroom was an airy place. The windows offered an expansive view of the sea through a rank of palms. The furniture, in pale rattan, further added to the tropical motif. Although she rarely slept in this room, she almost always spent at least part of her day here...resting, thinking, entering passages into her diary.

It wasn't really her diary, not at least in the usual sense. Yes, now and again she recorded subjective observations of day-to-day events. But, for the most part, the passages were devoid of emotion and entirely objective. On this particular morning, for example, she recorded only that an unidentified woman in white had shot and killed a Vietnamese male. The woman, also Vietnamese, was perhaps forty or forty-five years old with shoulder-length black hair and a pale complexion. Her accent suggested North Vietnam, while her bearing suggest a military background. Although the general may not have been complicit in the murder, he had clearly permitted it to happen. Also present during the murder was Tuy Xuan and another unidentified Vietnamese male.

After recording this passage, she replaced the diary behind the filter of the air-conditioning unit and moved into the bathroom. Although fairly certain she was going to be sick, the feeling finally passed and she stepped back into the bedroom and put on the blue dress.

# 10

"Why don't I just give you the facts?" Vong suggested.

It was eleven o'clock in the morning, a windless and sultry day with a solid cap of gray clouds and patches of darker fog. After telephoning the hotel at half past ten, Vong had met Lyons and Blancanales in a classically dreary café called Peaches. There, they sat in a vinyl booth while a bleached blonde in a candy-striped dress poured coffee and dropped plates of french fries on the tables. The jukebox only played fifties stuff: Elvis Presley, Bobby Darin, Jerry Lee Lewis and Little Richard. The cherry Cokes weren't premixed.

"Fact one," Vong continued. "Hanoi may do a lot of cheering about their new workers' paradise, but I'll take Social Security any day. Fact two, since the fall of Saigon ten to fifteen percent of the medical professionals have either fled the country or gone out of practice. Fact three, you go to a state-approved dentist in Vietnam and you're virtually putting your life on the line."

Lyons took a bite of his burger, then pushed it aside, along with his grease-drenched fries and watered-down coffee. "So what's the point?"

Vong withdrew a tiny plug of steel from his pocket and put it on the tabletop. "This is the point."

Blancanales picked up the steel plug and examined it in the palm of his hand. "Pretty neat, Sammy. What the hell is it?"

"Filling. It's a filling that was extracted from the molar of the guy you wasted on the cliff. It's a filling that was implanted in the poor bastard's mouth ten to twelve months ago and almost certainly by a dentist currently residing in Vietnam."

Lyons plucked the piece of steel out of Blancanales's palm and examined it for a few more seconds. "Okay, Sammy, bottom line?" he asked, dropping it onto his plate.

"Bottom line? We're either talking about someone who travels to Ho Chi Minh City to get his cavities fixed or else we're talking about a full-fledged Communist agent. Because this little piece of steel didn't come from an American-made mouth."

The waitress appeared and asked if anyone wanted pie. Blancanales started to order a slice of the apple, but Vong cut him short with a quick shake of his head. Everything on the counter was at least four days old.

"But you're certain this filling isn't something the guy could have picked up before the fall?" Lyons asked.

Vong nodded. "Lab went over it three times. Even brought in a little outside help from the university.

We're definitely looking at a man who was in Vietnam within the past year or so.''

"Well, people do go back, don't they?" Lyons suggested. "I mean, the country isn't entirely closed."

Vong merely smiled again. "That's right, and Santa Claus is going to bring me a Cadillac for Christmas. Anyway, there's more."

"You mean about the teeth?" Blancanales asked.

"No, about the fingerprints. Every Vietnamese man, woman and child who entered this country after the fall gave a full set of fingerprints to Uncle Sam. Now, obviously there were a few who slipped in illegally, but we're talking about no more than a couple of hundred."

"So?" Lyons asked.

"So how come not one single print taken from those bodies on the cliff can be matched with a known Vietnamese immigrant? I mean, as far as the fingerprints go, not one of those guys we faced last night even existed."

"You checked with the Bureau?" Blancanales asked.

"Hell, I even checked with the DMV. Those boys simply don't have a record in this country, and I mean nothing."

"What does your department say?" Lyons asked.

Vong shrugged with yet another quick grin. "My department says you're on your own. My department says they don't even want to know you anymore."

Lyons nodded, then picked up the filling for another thoughtful look. "And what about you, Sammy? What do you say?"

Vong shook his head. "I say you should learn a little more about who and what you're dealing with. I think maybe you should talk to the Kite Man."

THE KITE MAN LIVED on the southeast edge of what was sometimes called the Huntington Marsh. It was a poor piece of land cluttered with abandoned oil derricks, storage tanks and rusting automobiles. Although apparently devoid of life, a number of stray cats actually lived in these fields. Some were supposedly fierce and were said to have never known the touch of a human hand . . . except that of Nguyen Hy, otherwise known as the Kite Man.

The Kite Man was old and frail with blue eyes and a trailing white beard. According to local legend, he was said to be at least ninety years old and possessed memories of the homeland from a time when there had been no war. He was said to have served as an oracle in the court of Khai Dinh and walked with the emperor along the Perfumed River. Legend said he predicted the French defeat at Dien Bien Phu and the American withdrawal from the South. Although no one within the community could call him a friend, they all knew of him—the pale man who lived like a ghost in a shack behind the eucalyptus groves.

It was three o'clock in the afternoon when Lyons and Blancanales reached the Kite Man's house. From the edge of the highway the house was merely a shack.

As they moved closer, the men smelled the rose water, the joss sticks and the cats.

There must have a dozen cats perched on the low stone walls that bordered the entrance to the garden, and still more stretched out on the flagstones. As Lyons and Blancanales made their way between the walls, several animals lifted their heads to watch. None, however, seemed particularly concerned.

"You may place gifts at my feet if you want," a voice said from the shadows.

Lyons and Blancanales spun on their heels, but initially saw nothing. Then, shifting their gazes to the corner of the garden, they found themselves staring at a thin figure seated on a straw mat among the bamboo. He wore a gray sweater, unraveling at the shoulder, gray trousers and a baseball cap. In his left hand he held a pocketknife and a bit of string. In his right hand he held the makings of a newspaper kite.

"But, of course, if you have no gifts, that's okay, too," he said. "We don't stand on tradition here."

Lyons and Blancanales lowered themselves to the flagstones and sat. Despite the cats, the branches above were filled with sparrows.

"Sometimes they get eaten," the old man said, noticing Lyons's glance at the trees. "Then I have to talk to the cats."

Lyons turned to Blancanales, then returned his gaze to the Kite Man. "I don't suppose you know why we're here?" he asked.

The old man picked up two sticks that would form the crossbars of his kite. He smiled. "Let's see. It wouldn't have anything to do with Jackie Minh, would it?''

Lyons glanced at Blancanales again, then out across the garden at the lounging cats.

"We'd like to find out what happened to him," Blancanales said. "We'd like to find out who did what to him and why."

The old man shook his head. "Do you know what Tao says about mysteries? Tao says that mystery is like honey to a fly. It smells sweet and tastes good, but almost always becomes a trap."

"According to Sammy Vong, Jackie Minh used to come here quite a lot," Lyons said. "In fact, according to Vong, he came here at least once a week."

The old man nodded, but not necessarily in agreement. "Lots of people come here. Sometimes they come to ask questions like yourself. Sometimes they come for advice regarding their love life or maybe their family. Sometimes they come just to be quiet."

"And why did Jackie come here?"

"To cry."

Although the old man's eyes never left his guests, his hands continued to work on the kite, snapping bits of stick, cutting bits of string, tearing bits of paper in clean, even strips.

"I'll tell you the story of Gook Town, okay? I'll tell you because Sammy Vong is a pretty good man, and if Sammy says you're okay, then probably you're okay. But don't expect me to do anything. Because I don't do. I just talk."

He picked up a small bottle of glue and applied eight tiny dabs to the edges of the paper. "Love is also pretty sticky, okay? Take Jackie, for example. Once upon a time he was like lots of young men in Gook Town. He fished. He drank beer. He played sports. He dreamed. Then one day he met Kim Kiet, who was very pretty and sweet. Next thing they knew, their hearts were intertwined. Their thoughts were like one and they suffered whenever they were apart. But what was the point if in the end it left them blind?"

"Blind?" Lyons asked.

The old man nodded. "Blind to dangers."

"What kind of dangers?"

"The kind that follow Sonny Trang like a shadow at his heels."

A cat slipped through the stalks of bamboo, sank to the old man's side and idly extended a claw.

"Kim Kiet was a boat person," the old man said. "When she was a very little girl, she had to flee Saigon on a boat with her brother and maybe her father. I can't remember. She was a boat person and she had a very bad time. Boat people got on the boats, sailed into the green sea and then found out there was no clothing and no protection against pirates. Sometimes they ate seaweed. Sometimes they even ate rats. To keep warm they huddled together and wrapped themselves in whatever they could find. But against the pirates there was nothing they could do. Against pirates all they could do was pray."

The old man picked up a stick and began smoothing the rough edges with his pocketknife. His eyes, however, still remained fixed on his guests.

"You, *monsieurs*, are probably pretty tough guys. You probably had some hard times, but in the end you always give the bad guys an even harder time. Well, on the boat it wasn't like that. One night Kim Kiet was sleeping with her brother on the boat, then all of a sudden there were cries and maybe gunshots. Next thing she knew, pirates were boarding the boat. Now these were maybe Malay pirates, the worst kind, and they climbed onto the deck and shot all the men. They raped all the women. Then they took all the little children like Kim Kiet and sold them into slavery."

The old man put down the knife, picked up another bit of string and began to loop it around his index finger. Then, applying another dab of glue, he told them that slavery was also very sticky.

"You must, of course, imagine the circumstances," he continued. "They were put into cages and then sold to the highest bidder. Ten- or twelve-year-old girls, with no clothes, were left to the mercy of cruel masters. So, naturally, when she was finally rescued by an American navy ship, she was very grateful to Uncle Sam. Then, when Uncle Sam found her mother's sister and arranged for her to live with cousins, she was even more grateful. But sometimes gratitude can lead to sacrifice, and sacrifice isn't such a good a thing...especially when the sacrifice is made to someone like Sonny Trang."

Having finished with the glue, the old man picked up a stick and began to notch the ends. Another cat, a mangy Siamese, had begun to toy with the loose bits of string.

"Sonny Trang is a very rich man," the Kite Man said. "He can afford to fill his house with all kinds of beautiful things. He can afford to buy precious scrolls from big importers in San Diego. He can afford to buy gold and silver from little shops in Gook Town. He can afford to buy anything he wants, even young, beautiful girls like Kim Kiet. So, when Sonny Trang told Kim Kiet that he would support her aunt, give money for the education of her cousins and money for other family benefits, then she had no choice but to take the offer. She had no choice but to say goodbye to Jackie Minh and go live with the general. And that is the story of Kim Kiet and Jackie Minh."

"But Jackie Minh didn't give up, did he?" Lyons asked quietly. "Jackie Minh wouldn't turn his back and say goodbye, would he?"

The Kite Man shrugged as he gently looped bits of string around his thumb. "Jackie Minh is an orphan, okay? During the war he also had a pretty hard time. Even after the war he had a pretty hard time. Then, all of a sudden, he had the most beautiful girl in Gook Town, and suddenly everything was wonderful for him. So, naturally, he didn't want to give that up without a fight. He didn't want his sweet *chérie* to live with some old man named Sonny Trang. Especially when that old man is maybe not so good, when that old man is maybe a crook."

Before fitting the newspaper to the frame, the Kite Man spent a long time examining the joints, ensuring that the glue had dried and that the knots were secure. Then, finally laying down the frame and retrieving the pocketknife, he began to cut the paper.

"I'm a simple person, okay?" he said at last. "I don't read newspapers. I make kites out of the newspapers. But even so I know one or two things about Sonny Trang. I know, for example, that he's not necessarily what he appears to be."

"Meaning politically?" Lyons asked.

"Politically, yes. But also ethically and morally. For example, he appears to be a great blessing to the Vietnamese community, a great blessing and a great anti-Communist. But I don't think he's such a great anti-Communist...especially when dealing with Communists who are also capitalists."

Blancanales, who up until now had remained virtually motionless, slowly extended his hand and touched the old man's sleeve. At least two or three cats, intrigued by the gesture, suddenly lifted their eyes to watch. "Tell us about the Communists. Tell us about those Communists who are really capitalists."

The old man smiled vaguely. "This is just a rumor, okay? This isn't something I saw with my own eyes."

"Sure," Blancanales said. "A rumor."

"But maybe something's happening in Gook Town that's never happened before. Maybe that's why everyone is so afraid. Because maybe Sonny gets a little too greedy for his own good and starts making deals with certain very greedy Communists."

"What kind of deals?" Lyons asked. "Political deals? Terrorist deals?"

The old man shook his head. "You have to understand something. Communism is just a word, okay. Communism isn't always ideology. So maybe there are certain Communists in Hanoi, and these Communists get the idea in their heads to make lots of money just like the Americans and the South Vietnamese who were friends of the Americans. So what are they going to do? They're going to talk to a guy like Sonny Trang, who's an expert in making money by dealing with Americans. They're going to tell him they want to make lots of money. They're going to tell him to forget about ideology for a minute and think about business."

"You mean drug business?" Blancanales asked.

"Sure, why not? First you have the French in control of the Burma opium fields. Then you have the Americans. Now you have the Vietnamese Communists. And why shouldn't they also want to make money? You understand? Some people will tell you that maybe Sonny Trang and the Black Ghosts are the main anti-Communist force in the community and that drugs are just the unfortunate consequence of having to deal with a certain bad element in the Black Ghosts. But the Black Ghosts aren't responsible for bringing in the drugs. Sonny Trang and the Communists are responsible."

Having completed the construction of his kite, the old man slowly rose to his feet. The leaves, however, were still motionless. "Maybe I tell you one more

thing, okay?'' the old man said as Lyons and Blancanales also got up. ''Maybe I tell you one thing I never
tell anyone before.''

''You mean about Sonny Trang?'' Lyons asked.

The old man shook his head again, his eyes still
fixed on the motionless branches above, a damp finger testing the dead air. ''No, not just about Sonny.
About everyone. About everyone who is still fighting
the war.''

''What do you mean, still fighting the war?'' Lyons
asked.

''I mean, they are still fighting the war, okay? I
mean, that the Vietnam War may be over in Asia and
America, but it's not over in Gook Town. In Gook
Town the war is still being fought...except now it's
underground.''

Lyons and Blancanales were halfway back to their
van when the old man's kite began to rise above the
walls. It rose slowly, hovering for three of four minutes between the trees. Then, apparently catching an
unfelt breeze, it finally vanished into the fog.

IT WAS HALF PAST THREE when Lyons and Blancanales returned to the hotel. Although Schwarz wasn't
supposed to be released from the hospital for another
day at the earliest, he was waiting on the balcony when
Lyons and Blancanales appeared. He was seated on a
folding chair amid more stacks of intelligence briefs
from the DEA and a few selected files concerning the
CIA's involvement with the opium lords, circa 1966.
Despite the fact that his wounds had been classified as

superficial, there were still traces of blood seeping from the bandages. His eyes also looked bad.

"You get anything interesting?" he asked as Lyons moved out to the balcony.

Lyons looked at his friend's shoulder, looked at the six or seven circles of blood that had soaked through the gauze. All he finally said, however, was, "Maybe."

"Well, I've got something," Schwarz said. "Can't promise it's going to lead to the family jewels, but it may be a step in the right direction."

"What are you talking about?"

"Remember that little girl we caught in the temple the night the Ghosts tried to hit us? The girl Pol let go?"

Lyons nodded. "What about her?"

"Well, apparently she just got in touch with Vong. Says she wants to talk. Says she's got something important to say about what's been going down in Gook Town."

Lyons glanced at Gadgets's shoulder again, then over the railing at the fog-matted boulevards below. "Could be another trap," he said.

"It's not," Blancanales replied from the sliding glass door. He was carrying three bottles of beer in his left hand and a bag of honeyed peanuts in his right. "She might be a little devious, but she's not setting us up."

Lyons turned to face his partner. "How do you know?"

"Because she's basically just another Gook Town kid, and basically the Gook Town kids want to see this thing stopped as much as we do...maybe even more."

"Yeah, well, they didn't seem too eager to stop it the other night," Gadgets countered, tapping his bandaged shoulder.

"I'm not talking about the Ghosts," Blancanales said. "I'm talking about your average kid on the street. I'm talking about the kid who carries your luggage and parks your car. I'm talking about the people who really *live* here."

"All right," Lyons finally said, "so what do you want to do about it?"

"I want to talk to her. I want to hear what she has to say."

"You mean alone?"

Blancanales shrugged. "You got an objection?"

"Well, I've got an objection," Schwarz said. "You meet her alone and her boyfriends are likely to chew you into little pieces."

"Gadgets is right," Lyons said. "We can't take any more chances until we know what the hell's going on out there."

Blancanales shifted his gaze to the fog-bound streets below, to the nest of masts rising from the harbor mist and the maze of alleys behind the docks. "But we do know what's going on out there. It's just like what the old man said. It's 1968 and we're back in the war again."

# 11

There were actually two Gook Towns. There was the
Gook Town where tourists posed for photographs on
the steps of plywood pagodas and there was the Gook
Town the tourists never even dreamed existed. It was
a Gook Town of flyblown basements, shuttered lofts
and unlit passages between laundries. It was the Gook
Town where Lisa Hoa had chosen to meet the roundeye.

"What made you come?" she asked.

Blancanales sought out her eyes in the sticky gloom,
then shrugged with a slow smile. "You said you
wanted to talk, didn't you?"

"Yeah, but how do you know you can trust me?
How do you know I didn't bring the Ghosts?"

He shrugged again. "I don't."

It was nearly midnight, but still warm and windless. There was still the fog, a vaguely yellow creeping
fog that stank of the canneries. The room, an anonymous crash pad, also stank; although Blancanales
couldn't identify the smell—maybe more joss sticks,
maybe some sort of ointment.

"So what is it you wanted to tell me?" he asked.

She shook her head and settled into a beanbag chair. Although she appeared fairly relaxed, he suspected it was only an act, that, in fact, she was as nervous as hell. He also suspected she had spent a lot of time selecting her clothes: a short black skirt, a skintight tank top, spiked heels and silver bangles.

"I heard you got pretty tough with some guys at Sunset Cove the other night," she said.

He nodded. "I guess you could say that."

"You have fun?"

He ignored the question and shifted his gaze to the far wall where someone had spray-painted Good Love for Bad Girls.

"I also heard you went to see the Kite Man," she said.

He nodded again. "Word gets around fast, doesn't it?"

She shrugged. "It's a small town."

He glanced around the room. In addition to the beanbag chair there was a well-worn sofa and a mattress on the floor. The walls were disfigured with water stains, one of them in the shape of a mushroom cloud or a dog's head. There was also graffiti, but only in Vietnamese.

"So what did you talk about?" she asked.

He shook his head, searching out her dark eyes again.

"I mean, with the Kite Man. What did he tell you?"

"He said the war never ended. He said it just went underground."

She let her chin fall to one bare shoulder and sighed. "Well, he's right."

He moved to the sofa and eased himself down onto the bulging springs. Among the debris at his feet were dozens of rat pellets and numerous tiny bones.

"First thing you've got to know," she said suddenly. "I'm not a Ghost, okay? I've got friends who are Ghosts. Sometimes maybe I party with the Ghosts, but I'm not a Ghost myself. Understood?"

He nodded. "Sure."

"Second thing you've got to know. The Ghosts aren't the real problem here. Okay, so maybe sometimes some Ghosts get into a little trouble. Maybe sometimes they steal cars or rob a store. Maybe sometimes they even do jobs for the general, but they're not the real problem. Like the guys you creamed at Sunset Cove, for instance—they weren't Ghosts. They were something else."

"What kind of something?"

She shook her head, biting her lower lip. "This is just something people say, okay? This is just a rumor."

"Sure, a rumor."

"The general, he had a pretty good thing going in Saigon during the war, right? He was making lots of money through the sale and distribution of opium. Also he had lots of power. Then the war ended and suddenly he no longer had all that money and power. Not that he was doing all that bad, because he had all that land and those boats, but it wasn't the same thing. It wasn't like being able to control all that opium. So one day he got a visit from a Vietnamese, and this Vietnamese person told him that certain other Vietnamese persons would like him to distribute dope just like he did in the war. Only this time he wouldn't be distributing dope for the CIA or CIA allies in the Golden Triangle. This time he would be distributing dope for Communists.''

''Is anyone willing to say exactly who these suppliers are?''

She bit her lower lip again and shook her head. ''Everyone has a different theory, okay? Some people say it's now the official Hanoi plan to make money and continue the war against United States by selling dope to American youth. Others say it's mainly the plan of the Hong Kong triads, who convinced the Communists that it was stupid not to make a profit with the poppy fields. Then there are others who say it's something even worse than all that.''

''Like what?''

''Like maybe it's much bigger than anyone can imagine. Like maybe it even involves certain people in the CIA and a certain Communist colonel who was especially famous during the war for doing horrible things to people. Anyway, that's what some people say.''

''And what do you say, Lisa?''

''I think maybe you need to bust some of the inside guys. I think maybe you need to catch one of the guys who really knows what's going on, and then make him talk.''

She ended up speaking to the floor, her knees pressed together, her arms folded across her breasts, her eyes fixed on the litter of paper and rat droppings. "You don't have to believe me. You can think that maybe I'm just setting you up, just like you got set up on Sunset Cove. But what I'm going to tell you is true."

"Lisa, if you—"

"No, listen. You did me a favor, okay? You let me go so that your friends wouldn't hurt me. All right, so now I'm going to do you a favor so that you can stop the trouble in Gook Town. There's going to be a shipment of dope, okay? Not a shipment of sand like at Sunset Cove, but real dope. It's coming down from the Oregon coast, just like Jackie Minh said. It'll come down on one of General Trang's fishing boats and will be transferred to a speedboat and taken to the docks. This will happen tomorrow night, probably at one or two o'clock in the morning."

"Where did you get this information?"

She shook her head, although it might have been a shiver. "I overheard it from friends who work on the fishing boats. Friends who aren't directly involved but who are in a position to know certain things."

"And these friends are—"

"Never mind my friends. My friends are just little fish. My friends are just guys who work the fishing boats, who like to play cards and maybe get drunk on a Saturday night. You don't want my friends. You want to get the big fish. You want to get the guys who drive the speedboats. You want to get guys who are not from around here, but who are maybe from Hanoi or someplace like that. You want to get the guys who are still fighting the Vietnam War.''

Blancanales figured the talk was over and headed for the door. Before leaving, though, he turned and called out her name. But when he couldn't think of anything to say, he left her on the beanbag chair, her eyes still fixed on the floor, her arms folded across her breasts, her body still faintly shivering.

KIM KIET WAS SEATED in the darkness, and she was afraid. Her eyes, however, were fixed on the general's reflection in the mirror, an enormous gilded affair that had been strategically placed against the far wall. It was one o'clock in the morning, and although the wind had picked up, the fog still hung above the water.

"What's the matter?" the general asked.

She shrugged and shifted her gaze to the window and a blue vision of the city below. "Nothing," she finally breathed. "Nothing's the matter."

He rose from the bed, crossed the room and moved to her side. In gray silk pajamas and a burgundy robe he resembled an Oriental Hugh Hefner. "You think I'm heading for a little trouble, don't you? You think I'm in over my head with all this so-called import business. Well, let me tell you something. I've been through far worse storms than this, my dear. Far, far worse.''

He extended a finger to her neck and slowly slid the strap off her shoulder to expose her left breast. Then, lowering his head, he gently followed the curve of her throat with his lips. As always, he smelled faintly of rose water. "I'll tell you something else," he whispered. "I actually enjoy the storms."

The telephone rang—once, twice, three times before he finally broke away and answered it. At first he kept his voice low, and she only heard fragments of what was said—something about another shipment of produce from Oregon, something else about ensuring that the sailors were well armed and that guards were posted on the docks. Then, very plainly in Vietnamese, he said, "On the contrary. I think it would be most amusing if you were to send them in to see me now."

He put down the receiver, moved back to her side and placed his hand on her bare shoulder. "It seems that I have a small degree of business to conduct with some people in my employ. But there's really no reason for you to leave. In fact, I think I might prefer it if you were to stay."

She looked into his eyes, then glanced at her own reflection in the mirror. Earlier that evening, possibly in anticipation of this moment, he had insisted that she wear a particularly revealing negligee, consisting of little more than a thin bit of silk across her thighs. When she attempted to hide her breast, he gently grabbed her wrist and shook his head. "But you look so lovely just as you are."

He told her to kneel in the corner, to read a magazine if she liked or simply gaze out the window, but to remain kneeling until he told her otherwise. Then, pouring himself a cognac, he sat on the sofa and waited for his associates.

The associates turned out to be two young men she had vaguely known from her first days with the general. One was a stocky Chinese boy called Charlie Fang. The other was a thin, mean Vietnamese boy named Hoop. Occasionally she had seen them watching her from a distance, but she had never spoken to them.

They entered the room slowly, probably not even aware of Kim's presence in the corner. The stocky one was still wearing jeans and fishing boots. Hoop was dressed in an oversize shirt and pleated trousers. He wore two diamond studs in his left earlobe, and his hair had been gelled. There may have been a brief, awkward silence when their eyes finally fell on Kim, but the general pretended not to notice.

"So what's the problem?" Trang asked in Vietnamese.

Although still somewhat stunned by the vision of the half-naked woman in the corner, Hoop managed to reply that there was no problem really. It was simply a matter of confirming a few last details.

"And what details are those?" the general asked.

Hoop shrugged with a nervous smile, his gaze flicking back to Kim. "Details regarding security of the northern shipment," he said.

By now the Chinese boy was also staring at Kim, virtually devouring her naked hip with his eyes. Apart from a very faint smile, however, the general still appeared not to notice.

"It's just that there has been a lot of talk," Hoop added in English. "A lot of talk about how someone may try something tomorrow night. The colonel wanted us to tell you that we should increase the number of guards, that maybe we should have a few more guys on the docks . . . just to be on the safe side, you understand."

The general's smile grew more pronounced as he glanced at the gawking Chinese boy. "Then, by all means, increase the number of guards."

Hoop said something else about increasing the escort, but by now it seemed that the conversation had grown entirely superfluous, an absurd excuse to examine Kim's half-naked form. She heard the general inquire about weapons, and in the brief pause that followed she suddenly became conscious of their eyes on her breasts, on the slope of her shoulder and her exposed right thigh. She was also now acutely conscious that the boys were roughly her own age, that she had probably seen them a dozen times in the dance clubs and record shops and that by tomorrow afternoon every kid in Gook Town would be talking about her.

Yet the worst of it came later when the boys had departed and the general called her to his side again. By this time he was drunk on cognac and exhausted. But before he dismissed her he felt it necessary to drive the point home.

"You found that embarrassing, didn't you?" he asked in Vietnamese.

She nodded, her face still burning with shame. "Yes. It was embarrassing."

"Well, there was no need to be embarrassed. In fact, you should have actually felt proud. Yes, proud that you're able to create such an effect on men. Because not every woman possesses such beauty, and those that don't would kill for it."

Although she had finally managed to cover her breasts, he once again insisted that she lower the strap from her shoulder. Then, guiding her to the mirror, he ordered her to look. "That's right, look. Take a good look at yourself and rejoice in your beauty, because it's a rare thing."

He placed his hand on the small of her back and turned her to the left, then to the right.

"You see," he whispered, "you're beautiful from every angle, from every conceivable perspective."

He lifted her hair, then let it fall in strands to her shoulders. He ran his knuckles across her left nipple, then pressed his palm to her belly.

"And now I'll tell you another little secret," he whispered. "You see, although I'm basically a jealous man, I actually find it quite exciting when other men look at you... when I know they're desiring you more than they've desired any woman they've ever seen. Take those two young men, for instance. They would have done anything to have you, anything at all. I think they would have even killed to have you, and that's just one small example of your power over men."

Slowly he removed her panties so that soon she finally had to face him with nothing on at all. "You must never be ashamed of your body," he told her. "Because your body represents perfect beauty, and beauty is just another form of power. And that's the main lesson for tonight. Yes, you possess great beauty, but at the same time you also possess power, which is something you must always remember. Do you understand?"

Yet, ultimately, she told herself, it was the details of what had been discussed with the boys, the references to a shipment from the north, the information concerning the guards along the docks and the escort of speedboats that she had to remember. It was also, of course, important to remember the names and dates and to record them accurately in her diary.

## 12

"What we have here," Lyons confirmed, "is a belt-fed M-16 conversion fitted with a variable-intensity Aim-point sight. We also have three standard M-16s complete with flash suppressors. Now, these weapons aren't exactly state-of-the-art, but they'll beat the hell out of the H&Ks for distance. And if they try to hit us with unaltered AK-47s, I think we can cancel their tickets right then and there."

Vong ran his hand along the barrel of the modified M-16 and squinted through the sight. "Very nice," he said. But, shaking his head, he wondered out loud, "Although I can't help thinking there's only one thing worse than falling into a trap."

Lyons looked at him. "Yeah? And what's that?"

"Falling into two traps."

It was just after nightfall, and the same fog that had blanketed the streets two days earlier now lay suspended above the marina. It was particularly thick along the jetty and even thicker in the bay. In addition to Vong and Able Team, two others sat huddled on the dock: Wiley, a beefy detective from Narcotics, and a thin kid named Bobby Cole from the SWAT team. Although there had previously been a lot of discussion regarding the additional personnel, Wiley and Cole had primarily been chosen because they had been available.

A detailed map of the coast that Vong had picked up from a friend in the Coast Guard was being examined. Vong had also purchased nautical maps, although Lyons said they wouldn't be necessary.

"It's going to be an offshore strike," he said. "We're going to hit them just inside the jetty."

"And if they try to bolt?" Vong asked.

Lyons jabbed a finger at a thin black line across the harbor's mouth on the map. "Then you and your boys will hit them at the breakwater."

Vong glanced at the map, then out at the gray stretch of sea beyond the gently shifting boats. "You make it sound so easy."

"It is easy... as long as we keep our cool and stick to the plan. The main thing is to catch them by surprise. Hit them fast and hard before they get the chance even to think about it. Then you boys can come in and pick them up in the second boat."

"Just like scooping up fish from a pond," Schwarz added from the end of the dock.

"Exactly," Lyons said.

Vong shook his head again. "Only problem," he said softly, "is that we won't be able to see a damn thing in all that fog, and the fish may turn out to be sharks."

Although there had also been a lot of talk about what sort of boats would be needed, Vong had only been able to requisition a couple of twenty-one-foot Bayliners that had been impounded by the police department the previous October. Essentially weekend craft, they would be no match for the sleek speedboats the runners would use. There was also a stench to them that had nothing to do with the sea.

"We should probably split ourselves up," Lyons said to Schwarz and Blancanales as they neared the end of the dock. "Gadgets and I can go with Vong. You can take the launcher and go with the others, Pol."

Blancanales glanced back over his shoulder at Wiley and Cole. Although Cole seemed fairly relaxed, Wiley was clearly nervous. After a few seconds, however, Pol finally nodded. "Sure, I'll go with the cops." Although he didn't say anything, he also didn't much care for the name of his craft—The Bozo.

They cruised out at an easy speed—Lyons behind the wheel with Vong and Schwarz astern, Blancanales and the two cops some thirty feet behind in *The Bozo*. Closer to the jetty, the fog became a virtual wall, a single gray sheet from the breakwater to the horizon. There was a penetrating chill to the air that reminded Blancanales of river patrols in and around the Mekong Delta.

"You were over there, weren't you?" Cole asked. He had been watching Blancanales for a long time while Wiley manned the wheel.

Blancanales looked at him, then nodded. "Yeah, I was over there."

"Where?"

"Lots of places."

"Da Nang?"

"Yeah, Da Nang."

"Wiley was in Da Nang. But he didn't see any action. All he did was suck eggs and chase pussy. Ain't that right, Wiley?"

The beefy cop turned with a lopsided grin. "Yeah, well, I'm still in one piece, ain't I?"

For a while they simply sat in silence. Cole watched Blancanales from the corner of his eye, Blancanales watched the shifting fog banks to their left, and Wiley watched the running lights of the first boat. Now and again they heard horns from unseen craft passing in the distance, and once or twice a fish jumped. For the most part, though, there was nothing except the drone of the engines and the occasional crackle of the radios.

The anchors were dropped about four hundred yards beyond the mouth of the breakwater. Although only fifty yards separated the two boats, the fog was so heavy that visual contact was lost. The water was calm, the mist like a gray cocoon. There were no lights and no sounds apart from the clanging buoys.

"So what happens now?" Cole asked.

"Now we wait," Blancanales answered.

"What happens if they don't show?"

"Then we go home."

Another fish broke the water to their right. Responding to the sudden splash, Wiley spun from the wheel and cocked his M-16. Then, shaking his head with an embarrassed grin, he put down the weapon and turned back to the wheel. "Damn fish!"

"Mind if I ask you something else?" Cole said after another few minutes of silence.

Blancanales looked at the eager young face, the vaguely scared eyes, the knuckles white as he gripped the railing.

"How come you do this kind of work? I mean, you're not CIA, right? And you're not DEA. So what makes you want to do this kind of job?"

Blancanales ran a hand across his mouth. "Does it matter?"

"Not really, but I was just wondering if it . . . well, was some kind of personal thing with you. I mean, are you like one of those vets who . . . well, kind of got messed up in the war?"

Blancanales shifted his gaze back to the wall of mist beyond the jetty. Although he briefly thought about telling the kid to go to hell, he finally said, "Yeah, I'm one of those vets who kind of got messed up in the war."

THEY WAITED almost two hours before they heard the sound of approaching boats. By this time the fog had become a solid wall and even the harbor patrol had retired. Although Blancanales again tried to keep his mind on simple things—on the echo of the engines drawing closer, on the softer slap of the swells against the hull—it wasn't long before he realized that the kid had been right. For the first time in many years he was letting his memories of the war affect him.

He picked up the radio mike and whispered Lyons's name. "You hear that?"

"Roger, Pol, we hear."

"Any idea where it's coming from?"

"That's a negative."

He put down the mike, picked up the Starlite scope and began to scan the open water off the bow.

"This is crazy," Wiley said. "You can't see anything out there."

"He's right," Cole added. "We can't see ten feet in this shit. How are we going to collar a couple of cigarettes?"

Again Blancanales just looked at the kid, and shook his head.

There were sounds of a second engine, then the sound of the first shifting to low. Blancanales swung the scope back to the left.

"Look, maybe we should contact Vong," Cole whispered. "Maybe they don't—"

"Shut up," Blancanales hissed.

The second engine dropped to an idle, and there may have been the echo of a frantic voice less than thirty feet away.

"Sounds like they're looking for the channel," Wiley whispered. "But either way they're close. Real close."

Cole picked up his M-16, jammed in a magazine and flipped off the safety.

"Keep it on," Blancanales ordered. "Keep it on until I tell you otherwise."

A second and third voice broke from the fog not twenty feet to port, a half-whispered name followed by a soft reply in Vietnamese. But it wasn't until the cigarette was virtually on top of them, actually close enough to touch, that Blancanales finally saw it.

"Holy shit!" Cole shouted as he flipped off the safety and swung his M-16 around.

Equally frantic shouts came from the cigarette where three Vietnamese scrambled for their weapons. Then there was the metallic bark of a bullhorn as Lyons attempted to identify himself and order a surrender. That was followed by the sudden roar of twin Mercurys, then another frantic shout broken by the crack of an AK-47.

Four bullets slammed into the Bayliner's hull as the cigarette veered off into the fog. Fragments of wood and fiberglass flew across the deck, peppering Blancanales's shins. Chilled spray from the wake stung his face, and another two-second burst nearly hit him.

"Punch it!" Blancanales shouted. "Punch it now! Hard!"

Wiley revved the Bayliner's engine and spun the wheel to port. Blancanales fell back into his seat with the acceleration, but still managed to reach for the radio mike.

"Ironman, do you read?"

"Roger, Pol."

"We're in pursuit. Suggest you hold your position and lock them in."

"Roger."

They could hear the second boat now, cruising slowly somewhere off their port side. Blancanales put down his rifle and picked up the Starlite scope, but still couldn't pierce the wall of fog. "Any idea where we are?" he asked.

Wiley smirked. "Hey, do I look like Popeye?"

There were also echoes of another clanging buoy, and what sounded like a block of gulls circling above the gray blanket. But beyond the dim outline of the breakwater nothing was visible.

"We might as well be in a cotton ball," Cole whispered. "Might as well be blind." But even as he whispered these words, something began to take shape in the swirling mist off the starboard side.

"You see what I see?" Wiley whispered.

Blancanales nodded, put down the scope and reached for his weapon. "Cut the engine."

There were no sounds at all except for the clanging buoys, unseen gulls and the slap of water against the hull.

"Turn to port," Blancanales whispered.

"To what?" Wiley asked.

"Left. Turn left."

There were voices again, someone calling a one-syllable name, someone else responding in Vietnamese. Cole began swearing under his breath, but Blancanales told him to be quiet. Then, less than fifteen feet into the grayness, came the definite outline of a sleek bow.

Cole gently swung his M-16 over the railing, while Wiley withdrew a .38 Police Special. Blancanales raised an arm, the palm flat and the fingers together. There were suggestions of figures now: a head and shoulders bent over the wheel, another head above the stern. Then, very suddenly, like some hulking phantom, a third figure materialized out of the mist—a lean face squinting from behind another AK, a hunched shoulder and cocked arm.

Blancanales dropped his arm and shouted, "Now!" He heard three shots explode from Wiley's gun, saw a simultaneous muzzle-flash from the AK, then heard Cole collapse with a cry.

"Oh, God!" the kid moaned. "Oh, God, help me!"

Two more AKs flashed through the fog as the cigarette's engines roared to life. Blancanales fell to the deck, felt something warm and moist under his hand and realized that it was probably a hunk of Cole's left thigh.

"We have contact!" Wiley shouted into the radio mike as another six or seven slugs slammed into the hull. "Do you read me? We have contact!"

As the cigarette banked hard to starboard and the twin Mercurys screamed with the strain, Blancanales finally managed to let loose with a burst. He fired from the hip, swinging the barrel in a wide arc across the bow, aiming first for the waterline, then for the figure crouched behind the engines. His target stiffened as the bullet penetrated his shoulder, and Blancanales heard a muffled curse in Vietnamese. The Mercury engines also whined in metallic agony as four rounds burst into the engine block. The Able Team warrior fired a third burst as another figure materialized on the stern, a thin boy in a life jacket, hefting some sort of wide-barreled weapon. But in the same instant that Blancanales squeezed the trigger, he also saw the other muzzle-flash.

It instantly passed through his mind that what he had undoubtedly seen was the flash of a Soviet grenade launcher, probably one of the AGS series. Pol knew that given the range and trajectory there was a good chance the shell would actually pierce the Bayliner's hull.

Cole screamed as the muffled explosion from below sent a rain of shrapnel through the deck. The Bayliner lurched to port, and Blancanales was thrown against the bulkhead. He heard Wiley shout, "We're taking water!" as another half-dozen slugs slammed into the hull. Blancanales skidded toward starboard, where Cole lay huddled in a pool of blood. Then, finally scrambling to his knees and jamming in another magazine, he managed to squeeze off six more useless rounds before a second explosion hurled him into blackness.

A single thought seemed to dominate Blancanales's consciousness: *dead in the water*. Not far away from where he had fallen, Cole lay weeping while Wiley pleaded into the radio mike.

Blancanales raised himself to his knees, glanced warily over the side and then peered through a ragged hole in the deck. At least three feet of churning water had filled the lower cabin. He peered over the stern, but still saw nothing. Finally, rummaging through a storage compartment behind the bulkhead, he withdrew the first-aid kit.

"I can't believe this," Cole muttered.

Blancanales lifted the young man's hand from what initially looked like a fairly modest puncture wound below his rib cage. He discovered a hole the size of an orange. There was also a lot of blood pouring from the left thigh, and pieces of shredded flesh hanging from the hip.

Blancanales tore the plastic sealing from a dressing patch, applied it to the wound beneath Cole's rib cage, then yanked off his belt to tie the leg.

"We have casualties," Wiley yelled into the mike. "We have casualties, we're taking on water and our engines are down. Please respond."

There were sounds of cracking fiberglass as the Bayliner listed to starboard. Then Blancanales heard nothing except the clanging of the buoys.

"I'm dying, aren't I?" Cole moaned.

Blancanales pressed a third dressing to Cole's shoulder and shook his head. "I don't think so."

"Yes, I am. I come out on this damn boat in the middle of the night, I get blown to hell by a hand grenade and now I'm dying. And for what?"

Blancanales glanced over his shoulder at Wiley, called the man's name three or four times, then finally shouted, "Wiley, get me a life jacket."

Wiley put down the microphone and gazed stupidly at the knee-high water around him. "Life jacket?"

There were faint sounds of a straining engine off the port side, but Blancanales told Wiley to ignore it. "Just get me the life jacket."

"We're sinking, aren't we?" Cole whispered. "I'm filled with shrapnel and now we're going to sink."

Wiley passed Blancanales the life jacket, and he gently slipped it over Cole's head. Then, slowly dragging the man to the stern, he told him to lie still and be quiet.

"They're circling back to nail us," Wiley screamed. "We're sinking and I can't even swim. What the hell are we going to do?"

Blancanales picked up an M-16, inserted a fresh magazine, and aimed into the fog where the noise of the straining engine grew closer.

"You might try shutting your mouth for starters," he said.

As the cigarette materialized, they could see black smoke trailing from the crippled engines. Blancanales also made out a figure crouching behind the wheel and another slouched across the starboard railing. As the throbbing engines revved to a howl and the cigarette swung to port, a third figure rose with the AGS grenade launcher.

Blancanales fired at the muzzle-flash because it was the obvious target. He fired with both eyes wide open and his back to the bulkhead. The enemy reeled with the impact, but Pol lost his balance as another grenade exploded somewhere below him.

Shrapnel shredded the fiberglass around him, leaving him peppered with tiny cuts, and more water poured across the deck, sweeping him back to the listing stern. He felt Cole's clawing hands at his shoulders, then the young cop's breath in his ear. "We're sinking!"

Blancanales scrambled to his feet, then fell to his knees again as the Bayliner lurched. There must have been at least two feet of water swirling across the deck, leaving the craft entirely swamped. He heard Cole scream again as more water gushed up from below, and he caught a glimpse of Wiley struggling to prevent himself from being washed overboard. Dragging himself to the bulkhead again and frantically reaching for an M-16, Politician saw two faces peer down from the cigarette that was now virtually on top of them.

"They're going to ram us!" Wiley shouted.

But Blancanales only registered that the muzzles of the AK-47s and the glazed eyes behind them had targeted him. A full two seconds passed before the AK-47 opened up, time in which a lot of things suddenly became very clear. The Able Team warrior realized that a boat was a lot like a tank, and he knew there was nothing worse than sitting in a crippled tank. He sensed that the enemy's strategy was similar to the strategy the NVA had employed at Hue, and he knew that he should at least try to get off a burst or two before they cut him down.

But even before he could squeeze the trigger, it seemed that the bullets were flying out of his gun and that the figures aboard the cigarette were disintegrating in a rain of lead.

Another second passed before Blancanales realized what was happening, before he actually saw Lyons at the bow of the second Bayliner, squatting behind the machine gun while Gadgets fed in the belt. The effects of the weapon were immediately obvious: the cigarette rocked in boiling water, the pilot shivered with impact behind the wheel and bits of flesh and a spray of blood rose from the stern. Before it ended, Pol even heard screams in Vietnamese—a high-pitched sound not unlike the screams he had heard when clearing out hootches in Hue.

He watched from the deck of the second Bayliner as the first sank from view. For a long time, eight or nine minutes, it seemed as if the craft would simply remain half-submerged. Then, listing again to port, it disappeared. Although also swamped and dead in the water, the cigarette remained afloat.

"Any idea where the second boat is?" Blancanales asked. He was soaked to the bone, still breathing hard from having dragged Cole out of the sinking boat.

Lyons shook his head and scanned the fog banks around them. "Probably long gone."

"So basically we got nothing again. Nothing except a boat full of dead Vietnamese and a seriously wounded man."

Lyons shook his head. "Cole isn't wounded. He's dead."

Blancanales took a step or two forward until he caught a glimpse of Cole's body stretched out on the bunk below. When they had transferred him from the sinking Bayliner, he had screamed his head off. Now, however, he looked remarkably peaceful.

"Well, I guess that means there's no reason why we shouldn't pursue the second cigarette," Blancanales said. He stared down at the young cop's body, at the left hand dangling from the bunk, at the shadows of Vong and Gadgets and the tracks of blood across the deck. "I mean, now that there's no reason to take Cole to a hospital, we might as well go after that second boat."

Wiley appeared, clutching a bottle of Wild Turkey he must have picked up from the tiny galley below. "You're joking, right? Going after that second boat . . . you've got to be crazy."

Blancanales ignored Wiley and turned to Lyons. "So how about it? Do we move or what?"

Lyons gazed into the fog again, to the forty or fifty yards of visible water and the gray mass beyond. "I don't know, Pol. It doesn't look good."

"What are you talking about, Ironman? We came out here to collar a couple of boats. We sustain a casualty, and then we go home? What the hell kind of operation is that?"

Lyons pressed his hands to the railing, his eyes still fixed on the wall of fog. "Fact is, Pol, that second boat's probably long gone by now. They've probably docked, unloaded and gone."

Gadgets appeared, slipping down from the bow where he had been stringing a line to the bullet-riddled cigarette so that they could tow it in. "Ironman's right, Pol. That second boat's probably long gone."

Blancanales shook his head with a furious smirk. "Yeah, well, we won't know that until we go look for it, will we?"

But Gadgets shook his head. "I don't think so, Pol. For one thing, there's no dope aboard the one we tagged."

"So?"

"So it probably means that it was just the escort, that it was just there to draw fire while the second one ran the goods in."

Blancanales shook his head again. "Yeah, well, I still say we can find them. I think we've got them trapped inside the jetty, and that means we've still got a chance."

Finally Vong also appeared, his hands and clothing covered with Cole's blood, his eyes fixed on the deck. "I just took a call from the Coast Guard. They want to know what the hell's going on out here."

Wiley, roused from his silence, took another swig of whiskey and slammed his hand against the bulkhead. "What does it take to get through to you people? A good man's dead. There's nothing more we can do here."

Lyons nodded to Gadgets while Vong slipped behind the wheel, until suddenly everyone grew very still at the faint drown of engines on their starboard side.

"You hear that?" Blancanales whispered.

"Yeah," Lyons replied. "I hear it."

"Then what the hell are we waiting for?"

Lyons glances out into the swirling fog again, then back at the waiting faces around him.

"This is crazy," Wiley whispered. "I'm telling you, this is really crazy."

Lyons simply nodded again. "All right," he sighed. "Let's go get them."

Gadgets set a slow, tacking course east toward shore. At three-minute intervals he cut the engines and everyone listened. Once, drifting into a relatively clear stretch of the channel, he and Blancanales thought they caught a glimpse of the second cigarette two-thirds of a mile off the bow. By the time they had alerted Lyons and Vong, it was once again a wall of fog.

"Let me tell you how I see it," Blancanales said to Lyons as they sank to a crouch on the bow. "You're one of those runners, okay? Two hours ago you picked up twenty or thirty keys from a shrimper. You speed in past the jetty and all of a sudden someone blows away your escort. What are you going to do?"

Lyons extended a hand to the gunwale. "I'd high-tail it to the docks," he said. "I'd make for the drop point, unload the keys and get the hell out of there."

Blancanales ran a hand across his mouth. Looking down, he realized there was a lot of Cole's blood on his clothing, as well. "Yeah, well, I don't think so. I think you'd have to figure the docks were also covered, which means you'd want to drop at an alternate spot. Maybe a little to the south. Only problem is, you can't see shit in this fog. So you cruise a little. You skirt the marina, then head for shallow water and pray for a clearing."

Gadgets had cut the engines again, but the only sounds now were the clanging buoys and a distant foghorn to the north.

"All I'm saying," Blancanales continued, "is that maybe we should head for the beach. Forget about trying to catch them at the marina. They're not going to be there."

"Kind of seems like a long shot to me," Lyons said. "Besides, Gadgets isn't exactly Sinbad. What happens if we run aground?"

"Then we swim, but at least we'll have a chance to catch them."

Lyons still shook his head. "I don't know, Pol. I mean, intuition is one thing, but we're—"

"Look, it's not intuition. I'm telling you they're heading for the south beach right now."

"And you base this on—"

"On the fact that I've played hide-and-seek with these sort of guys before."

"In Nam?"

"That's right, in Nam."

After a five-second hesitation, Lyons finally glanced back at Schwarz on the bridge and extended a hand to the south. Although the fog still lay fairly thick in that direction, there were brief glimpses of the coast now: a rocky point below the cliffs, a dark cove below white dunes, rotting pilings and the remnants of a pier. They also saw signs of shoals.

Vong reappeared, moving unsteadily up from the cabin where he had wrapped Cole's body in a blanket. There was fresh blood on his hands. "I suppose you realize the Department's not going to let this slide."

Lyons glanced back at the stern where Wiley was still seated with his bottle. We could all use a drink about now, he thought. Finally he said only, "Why don't we cross that bridge when the time comes, Sammy?"

"Well, you're going to have to think about it sooner or later, because there are definitely going to be questions when we get back. I mean, we just lost an officer, and the Force doesn't take that kind of thing lightly."

Lyons glanced at Blancanales, but Pol just shook his head. "It's an acceptable casualty rate. Given the degree of exchange, we're lucky the count wasn't higher."

Vong took a moment to digest Blancanales's words, then slumped against the gunwale. "An acceptable casualty rate?" he whispered.

Lyons placed his hand on Vong's shoulder. "I think what Pol means—"

"I know what he means," Vong replied. "I know exactly what he means. But let me just say that we're not at war and this isn't Vietnam."

They were less than a mile from shore when Schwarz suddenly cut the engines again and called to Lyons. "It's a possibility. Nothing we can bank on, but there just may be something out there."

Lyons picked up the Starlite scope and began to scan the misty shore off the port side. Although he saw nothing, he definitely heard it—the dull throb of idling twin Mercurys. "Start her up again and bring her to starboard.

Schwarz complied, and the silence was broken by the rumble of the Bayliner's engines.

"Now give her some gas," Lyons ordered. "Give her everything she's got. Go! Go!" he yelled as he caught a glimpse of a shape just inside the reef.

The Bayliner lurched forward, throwing Vong and Wiley toward the stern, leaving Blancanales hanging on to the gunwale.

"What the hell?" Wiley shouted.

As if in response, at least four bursts cracked out of the fog, spitting up water off their bow.

"Looks like we've got a live one," Gadgets said, grinning as he eased the wheel to starboard.

Another nine shots kicked up spray as Gadgets ran the Bayliner into another patch of clotted fog, but by now Blancanales had seated himself behind the machine gun with at least a hundred rounds on the belt. As a third hail of slugs from the AKs tore into the Bayliner's hull, Gadgets squeezed off a two-second burst at the fleeing stern of the cigarette.

"We've got to take them alive!" Lyons shouted.

"Yeah? Well, first we've got to catch them," Schwarz replied. "And at the moment that doesn't look promising."

"All right, then just try to keep her steady," Lyons said as he reached behind him for the M-16 fitted with that Aimpoint sight.

There were two distinct masses of fog off their bow, two low clouds between a narrow channel toward shore. For the first few seconds Lyons saw nothing. Then, as the cigarette materialized out of the mist, he slowly squeezed the trigger.

He fired the first three shots in rapid succession, saw two spouts of water rise off the cigarette's stern and a third slam into the hull. Then, sighting on the boat's engines, he squeezed off another four rounds.

There were echoes of what might have been a ricochet, then a brief glimpse of flame and black smoke. The cigarette veered sharply to the left, faded into the mist again, then swung back into view. Lyons squeezed off six more rounds into the engines, saw another tongue of flame and black smoke, then heard what sounded like the whine of a dying piston.

The cigarette banked hard to the right, an AK-47 flashing from the stern. Lyons responded with another two rounds, this time apparently shattering the engine block, letting loose long jets of flame. Then, suddenly the cigarette was gone, veering back to starboard and into the mist. It was silent now, possibly dead in the water, possibly just waiting.

Gadgets cut the engines again and let the Bayliner drift. Lyons put down the M-16 and picked up the Starlite scope. Wiley rose from the stern and joined Lyons and Blancanales on the bow. Then, for a while, they simply listened, scanning the gray stretch of fog ahead.

"Doesn't anybody think it's about time to call the Coast Guard?" Wiley whispered.

But not even Vong acknowledged the man at this point.

"Why don't you start her up again?" Lyons said to Schwarz. "Move her in a little closer and see if we can't draw some fire."

Before Gadgets could respond, however, Vong placed a hand over the ignition. "I wouldn't get any closer if I were you," he said, pointing at a buoy fifteen yards off port. "Sandbar."

"How about we try to skirt it?" Blancanales suggested.

Lyons glanced at Blancanales, then at Schwarz. "What do you think, Gadgets? Can we maneuver this tub between the sandbars?"

Schwarz shrugged. "Only one way to find out."

He started the Bayliner's engines again, eased the throttle forward and slowly turned the wheel to port. There were groans from the bullet-shattered fiberglass and a squeal from the nylon rope attached to the cigarette in tow. And then, briefly, the awful sound of the hull scraping bottom.

"Easy," Lyons breathed. "Take it real easy."

More gulls screamed now, and waves crashed on the rocks off starboard. As they slid deeper into the fog, they could also hear the cries of pelicans.

"Do you see anything?" Schwarz whispered.

Lyons shook his head. "Negative."

"Pol?"

"Nothing."

"That's because there ain't nothing out there," Wiley grunted. "Except maybe sand and rocks." But as he tossed his head back for another swig of Wild Turkey, he lost the left half of his face.

"What the—" Vong yelled as a piece of bloody flesh slapped him across the cheek.

Wiley pitched forward, spewing more blood from his nose and mouth. Then, hanging for a moment on the gunwale, three more slugs ripped into his chest and sent him crashing into the sea.

"Get us out of here!" Lyons shouted as another burst from an AK-47 slammed through the hull. "Right now, Gadgets! Go!" he yelled as he reached for his M-16 and let loose with a quick, blind burst.

Gadgets jammed the wheel to starboard, then threw himself down into a spray of Plexiglas and teak. The Bayliner's engines screamed with the strain. Lyons, bracing himself against the bulkhead, caught a fading glimpse of a muzzle-flash and squeezed off another three rounds.

"Circle around and hit him from the other side!" Ironman shouted.

But by this time Blancanales had slipped off the bow and was crouched next to Lyons. "Look, this isn't going to work. We can either blow them out of the water or get ourselves shot all to hell. But we're not going to take them alive from out here."

"So?"

Blancanales glanced at the fog, then up at Schwarz. "Do you think you can take us just inside that buoy?"

Schwarz nodded. "I can try."

"Well, then let's do it."

Gadgets eased the throttle forward, banked to starboard and cruised back into the fog.

"Hold her here," Blancanales whispered. "Right here." The Able Team warrior then kicked off his boots, stripped to the waist and withdrew his double-edged knife.

Before anyone could protest, Politician slid down the Bayliner's hull and eased into the water. Although it was cold, at least it was cleaner than the Central Highland swamps or the paddies at Ia Drang. And there were no leeches.

He swam silently, propelling himself forward with an easy breaststroke. At one point, crossing the sandbar, his feet even touched bottom, allowing him to rest for a moment. But feeling the cold penetrate his muscles, he finally pushed off into the fog again.

He must have swum about thirty yards before he caught sight of the cigarette, gently bobbing with the swells. Then, as the fog briefly parted and the boat dropped with a swell, he was able to see two men sitting low in their seats, anxiously peering over the gunwale.

There were faint echos of metal against metal, then a muffled word or two in Vietnamese. I should have brought the .45, Pol thought. Could have wrapped it in cellophane, and strapped it to my hip. But then, pushing gently off the bottom again and gliding forward another four yards, he found himself almost touching the cigarette's stern, with his knife set quite comfortably in his teeth.

He waited, legs gently kicking to keep himself afloat, left hand actually clutching the propeller shaft. Despite the chill, he felt quite calm, quite confident, almost glad that it finally had come down to a solitary confrontation. The only problem was that if he didn't move soon, the cold would cramp him badly.

He heard the men in the cigarette talking, nervous whispers in the dark. Although his Vietnamese had never been particularly good, he was still able to pick up words—something about an ally on the loading dock, something else about the price of failure and a calculated sacrifice with a grenade.

And then he made his move, reacting to an opportunity. It began with a low throb from the Bayliner's engines and the cocking of a machine gun. Straining for a better view, one of the Vietnamese rose to his feet while the other got to his knees. In response, Blancanales slowly lifted his legs until his feet were braced on the hull. Then, grasping the knife in his right hand and pushing off with his legs and left hand, he finally let the blade fly.

The knife took a full turn before it hit, plunging between the kneeling man's shoulder blades. There was an odd cry as the body arched in death and the hands groped blindingly in the air before the corpse slumped to the floor of the boat.

Blancanales flung his arm over the gunwale and grabbed for the second man, throwing every ounce of strength into a sudden jerk. The gunman wavered, desperately trying to maintain his balance while the boat tripped violently toward port. He stumbled, screamed as the weapon flew out of his hands and plunged into the water.

Blancanales was on him immediately, locking an arm around his neck and forcing his head below the surface. He felt the dull pain of a boot heel against his shins, the sharp pain of fingernails across his face. Pol took a deep breath of cold air, then let himself sink into the colder water, dragging the man down with him.

Fifteen seconds. Twenty seconds. Thirty seconds. A full minute.

In a last desperate effort to break free, the man twisted in Blancanales's grip, twisted until their faces were only inches apart, eyes locked together, lips almost touching, escaping bubbles merging and breaking together. Then, as the dark eyes rolled back and the jaw grew slack, Blancanales finally yanked the man up to the surface for a violent, gasping breath. For a long time they simply rested, clinging to the side of the cigarette, sucking in air. When at last the Bayliner appeared, looming out of the fog with a searchlight darting across the water, Blancanales lifted an exhausted arm and shouted one word in a cracked voice: *"Vietnam!"*

# 13

"Let me talk to him for a while, Carl," Blancanales requested as the three Able Team warriors looked down at their prisoner.

Lyons exchanged glances with Schwarz, a long and solemn glance. It was just after four in the morning and the Bayliner had just pulled into its slip. "Okay, Pol," Ironman said finally. "Sit down and talk to him."

Blancanales glanced around the cabin, then squatted beside the cot and ripped off the electrical tape that covered the prisoner's eyes and mouth. For the first minute or two the man still remained silent, keeping his eyes shut. Then, finally meeting Blancanales's gaze, he clenched his right hand into a fist.

"You got a name, Comrade?" Blancanales asked, bending a little closer.

"Maybe he doesn't speak English." Lyons suggested.

"Maybe we should find out," Schwarz added, gently running his thumb along the edge of his fishing knife.

The threat was more than the man could take. "I speak English," he whispered.

Blancanales glanced at Schwarz, shook his head with a disgusted smirk and returned his attention to the prisoner. "So what's your name?"

The prisoner closed his eyes. "My name is Hanh."

"And where are you from, Hanh?" Pol asked.

"Southern California."

"Shit," Schwarz breathed. "He's lying through his teeth."

"Tell him we're not fooling around here, Pol," Lyons whispered as he leaned closer to Blancanales. "Tell him if he doesn't start speaking soon, we're going to help him along."

But Blancanales just shook his head and sighed. "All right, let's try another tack. Let's talk about who you're scared of, okay? I know you're not scared of us, so who is it?"

Although the prisoner said nothing, each Able Team warrior recognized something in his eyes, some fleeting shadow of admission.

"Who is it?" Blancanales asked again.

But this time the prisoner merely turned his head to the wall and fixed his gaze on the corner.

"Oh, to hell with it," Schwarz sighed. "This is getting us nowhere." Withdrawing his fishing knife again, he moved to the opposite side of the cot.

Blancanales extended a retraining hand. "Look, will you just wait a minute, Gadgets? I think I'm onto something here."

"Pol's right," Lyons interjected. "I think we may be getting somewhere."

But in that moment of indecision, when both Lyons and Schwarz were watching Blancanales and Blancanales was watching Schwarz, the prisoner suddenly made his move. He rose with a violent lurch, ripping through the electrical tape that bound both his wrists and his left ankle to the cot. Schwarz reacted with his elbow and brought the fishing knife into play. But the prisoner had no intention of avoiding the knife. In fact, he wanted it, actually drove himself toward it. Before anyone could stop him, he'd grasped Schwarz's wrist and plunged the blade deep into his belly.

It seemed to take forever before Schwarz and Blancanales managed to pull the man off the knife—ten, maybe fifteen seconds. He kept wrenching Schwarz's wrist from the left to the right, letting the blade rip up to his ribs and deep into his organs. Then, for another ten seconds, the man simply continued to sit on the cot, arms laced across his lacerated stomach, his lips spread in a oddly silly grin.

Schwarz tossed the knife away and looked for the first-aid kit. Lyons said something about tearing up the bed sheets, but Schwarz said to forget it. When Blancanales attempted to intercede, the prisoner simply collapsed into his arms.

"Why?" Blancanales whispered, his ear only inches from the dying man's lips. "Why?"

The prisoner shook his head, then spit up a mouthful of blood. "Palm," he breathed. "Palm."

Schwarz found the first-aid kit and fished out a dressing. But when he attempted to lift the prisoner's arm, Blancanales yelled for him to get away.

"Palm what?" Blancanales asked, once more pressing his ear to the prisoner's lips. "What's palm?"

"Doe," the prisoner whispered. "Palm doe."

"Palm doe? What about palm doe? Come on, say it. What's palm doe?"

But although the prisoner may have whispered something else, he was dead before anyone could make sense of it.

Blancanales rose from the cot slowly, first glancing at Schwarz, then at Lyons. Although his hands and forearms were covered with blood, he didn't seem to notice.

"So that's it?" Schwarz asked wearily. "Palm doe? That's our fucking clue?"

"Maybe it's an acronym," Lyons suggested. "Or maybe a place."

"No," Vong said, suddenly making his presence known. "Phom-do isn't a place. It's a name. It's the name of a certain female colonel who's also known as the Woman in White."

IT WAS NEARLY DAWN, but there was no clear demarcation between the light and the darkness. Lyons and Blancanales had joined Vong on deck, while Schwarz remained below. Although Vong had telephoned the police station, there was still no sign of either the patrol cars or the ambulance. In fact, apart from the circling gulls and the clanging buoys, there were no sounds at all.

"So who is she?" Lyons asked. "Who's this Woman in White?"

Vong shrugged, glanced at Blancanales, then shook his head.

"She's a legend," Blancanales finally said. "She's a bad myth from the war."

"But neither of you have ever actually met her?" Lyons asked.

Vong shook his head. "Few have met her and lived to talk about it."

"According to the boys at S-2, she was counterintel for the First NVA," Blancanales said. "But that doesn't even begin to describe what she did. Guys out of I Corps called her the Vampire. Down in Ia Drang they called her the Blood Bitch."

"Yeah, but who *was* she?" Lyons asked again. "*What* did she do?"

"She interrogated people," Vong said. "By the most horrible means imaginable."

Blancanales moved to the gunwale and gazed out at the fog-shrouded dawn. Although he had managed to clean the blood off his hands, his clothing was still a mess. "Story goes like this," he said after a long silence. "In early '66 or '67 reports started coming down from the Highlands about this woman that Charlie used to bring in to to crack difficult cases. They'd pick up some grunt or maybe one of the ARVNs, and if the regulars couldn't make him talk, they'd give him to this woman, who always wore white."

"Which is the Vietnamese color of death," Vong added softly.

"Yeah," Blancanales breathed.

"So what happened to her?" Lyons asked.

Blancanales shrugged. "No one knows. Some say she bought it during Tet. Others say she melted back into the woodwork and then turned on her own kind. But either way she was bad. I mean, she was real bad."

"And you think there's a possibility she might be involved with what's going down around here?" Lyons asked.

Blancanales turned from the gunwale and looked at Vong again.

"I hope not," the detective finally managed to say.

# 14

The one they called Phom-do watched from the shadows at the end of the warehouse. Although apparently relaxed, half seated on a packing crate, the fingers of her left hand continued to tap against her thigh. There was also a degree of intensity to her eyes, which were fixed on the slender girl who dangled from the rafters:

"What's her name?" Phom-do asked in Vietnamese.

Trang stepped out of the shadows of the doorway and moved to Phom-do's side.

"Lisa," he replied.

"Lisa what?" Phom-do asked.

Trang shook his head. "Does it matter?"

It was just after midnight, a full nineteen hours since Trang had received a telephone call informing him of what had happened to his runners in the bay, a full thirteen hours since he had ordered an investigation. Three members of Phom-do's team and the boy who had pointed his finger at Lisa Hoa were also present.

"Do you want one of my people to soften her up first?" Trang asked.

Phom-do shook her head and smiled. "I don't think that will be necessary," she said, again in Vietnamese.

She rose from the packing crate and slowly glided forward, her white silk trousers whispering with every step. "So, my little rabbit," the woman said, "you've been naughty, yes?"

Lisa Hoa shivered, struggling slightly against the nylon cords that bound her wrists above her head. She couldn't have been more vulnerable: her body was stretched out like a dangling fish on a hook, her bare feet just barely touched the cold concrete, and her back was drenched in perspiration. Her left cheek had started to swell, a result of the backhand blow she had received when the Ghosts had dragged her off the corner of Third Street and Ocean two hours earlier.

"Why don't we take it from the beginning?" Phom-do suggested softly.

Lisa shivered again, pressing her face against her upraised arm, her eyes fixed on a flickering candle wedged among the packing crates.

"From what I've been told, you originally met the roundeyes when they caught you in the Buddhist temple, correct?"

Lisa shut her eyes with another spasmodic shiver, but finally managed to nod.

"You'd been out for a little fun and games with your boyfriends, and those men managed to catch you running like a rabbit in the temple. Yes, or no?"

Lisa nodded again, then finally whispered the answer, "Yes."

"And then what happened? They talked to you? They told you that if you helped them catch Vietnamese drug smugglers, they would reward you beyond your wildest dreams? Is that what they told you?"

Lisa shook her head, but still didn't open her eyes. "No."

"Then what?"

"Nothing."

"Nothing, my dear? Nothing?"

"They just let me go. One of them was going to hurt me, so the other one just let me go."

Phom-do smiled, then slowly extended a finger and brushed Lisa's hair from her eyes. "I'll ask you one more time, my dear. What happened that night when those men caught you in the temple?"

But again Lisa just shook her head.

The general approached, carrying something that Lisa couldn't see, an edged weapon or tool that faintly gleamed in the moonlight from above.

"Why do you suppose they still continue to resist me?" the woman asked Trang in Vietnamese. "After all these years, you'd think they'd learn. But they don't, do they?"

"No," Trang sighed. "They never learn."

He handed the woman the razor, and she gently slit the seams of Lisa's clothing. She seemed intensely concerned with the precision and fluidity of every stroke. She was very careful not to let the blade touch the young woman's skin.

"Like the petal of a dying rose," Phom-do whispered as she slowly picked away the strips of cotton.

Although Lisa's eyes remained closed, she knew they were studying her intensely, knew that every eye in the room was fixed on her naked body. Then, without warning, the woman ran a finger along Lisa's ribs.

"She may be small," Phom-do said, "but she's strong. She'll withstand a great deal of pain before she breaks. I'm ready," the Woman in White said softly to Trang.

Trang nodded, whispered something to one of the thin boys in the shadows and then handed Phom-do a long bamboo rod, two inches wide and an inch and a half thick.

Taking the rod in her right hand, Phom-do began to lightly test it against her open right palm, then against Lisa's naked thigh. Next the Woman in White spread her stance and drew back her arm. Then she brought the rod whistling into the small of Lisa's back. The young woman arched in pain and sucked in her breath, but she remained silent.

Phom-do smiled. "That's one."

She delivered the second and third cut to the top of the thighs, leaving long, intersecting welts. Lisa jerked against her bonds, throwing back her head and softly moaning behind clenched teeth. Then, as the rod whistled down and slashed her buttocks, she finally collapsed with a shriek.

"Hurts, doesn't it?" Phom-do whispered. Then, actually pressing her lips to Lisa's ear, she added, "But

I'll let you in on a little secret, my darling. This is only a prelude, a little appetizer before the main course.''

The woman withdrew again, contemplatively swishing the rod back and forth while she examined the earlier welts. Then, without warning, she laid down eight more cuts between the small of the back and the top of Lisa's thighs. The attack left Lisa bathed in perspiration and nearly hysterical.

Phom-do smiled. "There. I think that should do it." She turned to Trang, although her eyes didn't entirely leave the trembling girl. "Bring me the battery."

There were whispers next, someone saying something about water and wire, and then the sounds of footsteps behind a squealing dolly.

"Tell me something," Phom-do rasped. "Have you ever stuck your finger into an electrical outlet? Ever had a little accident while changing a light bulb?"

Lisa couldn't keep herself from shivering. She finally whispered, "Please."

"Please, my dear?" Phom-do gently tugged on Lisa's lower lip. "Please, what?"

"I've told you everything I know."

"So you claim, but we'll soon see if that's the truth." Phom-do looked down and examined the tiny alligator clamps that were attached to the battery cables. There was also a roll of electrical tape. "You'll find that this will hurt," Phom-do said, smiling. "A slight pinch." Then, briefly examining the connection, she attached the first clamp to the nipple of Lisa's left breast.

The young woman sucked in her breath at the stabbing pain, then found herself pleading again as the woman attached the second clamp to the right nipple. She was also conscious of the observers: the general and the boys. Then, catching another whisper from over her shoulder at what sounded like a switch, she was finally conscious of nothing except the exploding pain.

It left her gasping for air and shaking her head from side to side with involuntary spasms. It left the stench of burned flesh in her nostrils and the taste of old pennies in her mouth. It also gave her a warped sense of time, as if her childhood had only been yesterday, although the pain was at least a thousand years ago.

"Now I think we're getting somewhere," Phom-do said. "Again," she ordered.

A second explosion of electricity coursed through Lisa's body, leaving her limp and nauseated while the echo of her own screams rang in her ears. Then came a third jolt, then a fourth and a fifth...until finally only blackness.

A hand grasped her hair and yanked back her head. Burning lips brushed her ear again, while a scorching finger traced the curve of her lips. Although her eyes were still closed, she couldn't seem to block out the burning light. The air was also too hot.

"Now let's have a little talk," Phom-do said.

Lisa found herself crying in gratitude, desperately wanting to please the woman now. "Yes," she managed. "Talk."

"What did you tell the roundeyes about the general's business?"

"I . . . I told . . . I told them . . ."

"Go on, my dear. What did you tell them?"

"About boats."

"What about boats?"

"Boats bring dope."

"So you told them about the shipment. Is that it?"

Lisa nodded, then found that she couldn't stop nodding. "Yes. Told them about shipment."

"Why?"

"Because."

"Because?"

"Dope . . . not . . . good. Dope not good for Vietnamese people."

The woman smiled again. "Well, that was certainly naughty of you, wasn't it, my dear?"

Although Lisa nodded again in a frantic effort to show how sorry she was, the woman stepped back and whispered, "Again."

This time the jolt hit her like a club, a spiked club across her breasts that left her spinning in white light while her lungs seemed to fill with blood and her bones turned to glass. When it finally ended, she found herself shamelessly sobbing like a child in the woman's arms.

"There, there," Phom-do cooed. "I know it hurts. I know it hurts terribly, but in the end I think you'll thank us for it. Yes, thank us because it'll make you a much better person." Then, casually stepping back with a shrug, she ordered, "More."

Lisa heard a sound like wind in her ears, and she supposed that it must have been her own raw scream. And there was a taste of crushed pencils in her mouth, most likely blood. She was vaguely aware of the general's voice, echoing from what seemed like ten thousand miles away. "Don't you think that's enough? She's told us everything she knows."

"What difference does it make?" the woman responded. It made no difference at all. Although they must have jolted her at least another dozen times, Lisa was finally conscious of nothing except an undulating blackness and numbing cold.

# 15

It was another gray morning, with cool winds from the bay and low clouds to the north. In addition to Blancanales, Lyons and Schwarz, five or six cops were in the warehouse. A crowd had gathered outside, but the police kept them back from the building.

"Isn't anyone going to cut her down?" Blancanales asked softly.

Lisa Hoa dangled from her blackened wrists. The air stank of perspiration and vomit. Bits of copper wire lay on the concrete.

"Isn't anyone going to cut her down?" he asked again.

But the only response was a soft hand on his shoulder while Lyons whispered, "It won't be much longer, man."

A photographer appeared and began taking photos of the scene; the body seemed to shift positions under the flashing strobe. Someone said something about the bits of charred wire, and a small debate ensued about whether or not samples of the vomit should be collected. Then, at last, Dennis Loft, the coroner, told Vong he could have the body cut down.

"Any idea what finally killed her?" Blancanales asked, stepping to the coroner's side.

Loft shook his head, his eyes still fixed on Lisa's empty gaze. "Heart," he finally replied.

"And how long would you estimate . . . ?"

The coroner shrugged, then took a deep breath and exhaled through his teeth. "An hour, maybe two."

"You want me to check the door for prints?" a thin, hawk-faced man asked Vong, interrupting the coroner's brief report to the group.

Before Vong could respond, however, Blancanales interjected. "Why the hell do we need prints? You know who did this as well as I do."

"Take it easy, Pol," Lyons cautioned. "Just take it easy and let these boys do their job. We're not going to accomplish anything without real proof."

Blancanales glanced at the dead girl again, at her blackened wrists and blistered nipples. But before he could say anything, Schwarz took him by the arm and led him to a corner.

"The Ironman's right," he told Pol quietly. "We can't just go busting into Gook Town and start asking questions about the Woman in White. Not at least until we get a little more information about what's going on around here."

Blancanales glanced back over his shoulder at the girl. Although half encased in a body bag, her horrified eyes seemed to be gazing at him . . . accusing, pleading.

Pol frowned. "Yeah, and where are we going to get that information?"

"From the inside," Vong said.

THE INSIDE TURNED OUT to be a sprawling, white-washed colonial estate in the Laguna Hills, high above the Pacific. There were horses grazing in fenced pastures, the narcotic scent of eucalyptus, and bougain-villeas aflame with purple buds. A discerning eye, however, would have noticed things that set the house apart from the others: surveillance cameras cleverly concealed in the leaves, trip wires strung along the wrought-iron fence and razor wire along the surrounding walls. The owner of the house, William Lyle Wells, had spent his life in the CIA.

Wells, a slender man, was an attorney by trade and originally a Harvard man. He was known to be a formidable historian of the Middle Ages, and was also something of a linguist. Although chiefly remembered for his twenty-one years in Southeast Asia, he had served in many places. Chile, Iran, Cuba, Chad—at one time or another Wells had seen them all. Indeed, he had even spent time in El Salvador, which was where he had originally met Carl Lyons.

"But I'm officially retired now," he told Able Team.

It was just after two o'clock in the afternoon. Although it had been more than six years, Wells recalled every aspect of his initial meeting with Lyons—the names of cocaine lords that Lyons had been hunting, the name of the pilot who had flown him out after the kill, the fact that Lyons had been carrying a 9 mm slug in his left shoulder, and that Wells had promised Lyons a glass of fifty-year-old Scotch if they ever met again.

"The other thing you gentlemen have to know," Wells continued, "is that I'm not only retired, I'm off the team. I don't advise, I don't consult and my close friends are all dead." He moved toward a varnished cabinet. "But I do happen to have that Scotch I promised . . . for whatever it's worth to you, Carl."

Lyons smiled and moved to the opposite corner of the room in order to examined a Walther PPK that had been framed and mounted on the wall. Beside it were two tiny nudes from Prince Bandar of Saudi Arabia's Rembrandt collection, a vial of cyanide from Jonestown and two petrified cigars from Castro's private stock.

"Well, to be quite honest with you," Lyons said, "it's not your connections that interest us. It's your memory."

Blancanales withdrew three photographs of Lisa Hoa's body and dropped them onto the coffee table.

Wells spent a long time studying the photographs. "I was afraid something like this was going to happen," he said finally.

"Her name was Lisa Hoa," Lyons said.

"A local girl?" Wells asked.

Lyons nodded. "Ran with the Black Ghosts but never counted herself as one of the inner circle. She also didn't much care for Sonny Trang."

"Who does?"

"Well, that's the million-dollar question, isn't it?"

Wells picked up the photographs again. He was particularly intrigued by the close-up of the girl's face, the agonized eyes and blood-clotted nostrils. "Any idea what actually killed her?"

"Electricity," Blancanales replied. "A lot of it applied over a long period of time."

"And you don't think the local talent is capable of such a thing?"

Lyons shrugged. "Do you?"

Wells took one last look at the eyes, then tossed the photographs back onto the table and returned to the cabinet to pour drinks. "We're talking about rumors, gentlemen. Old legends and rumors."

"And what do those rumors say?" Blancanales asked.

Wells cocked an eyebrow. "They say that maybe, just maybe, Sonny Trang has cut a deal with Hanoi."

"To reactivate the Golden Triangle connection?" Lyons asked.

Wells nodded. "Yes."

"But you don't think that's likely?" Blancanales asked.

Wells shook his head again. "On the contrary. I just don't think Sonny Trang's the only player, which means that you gentlemen are going to have one hell of a difficult time trying to crack it."

Wells moved to a curio cabinet and picked up what appeared to be some sort of musical instrument. On closer inspection, however, Lyons realized that it was a Burmese opium pipe—hand-tooled and inlaid with ivory.

"You can't separate the politics of Southeast Asia," he said, "from the politics of opium. The Chinese learned that the hard way in 1560. The French learned it the same way in 1954. And we learned just as hard in 1966. You want to be king of the Asian jungles, then you'd better pay your respects to the Great God of Opium."

He pressed the pipe against his lips with a wistful smile, then put it aside and whispered, "Opium, the Black Mother."

Geographically, Wells told them, the Golden Triangle was actually a hundred and fifty thousand square miles of forest highland between Laos, Burma and the northern reaches of Thailand. For the most part, the poppies were planted among the mountain peaks where the light was bright but the air was still cool. Just before the harvest, the view was actually quite spectacular with hundreds of acres in yellow bloom.

"Of course, the poppy isn't new to that region," Wells continued. "The tribesmen have been planting and harvesting it for at least a hundred years, or since the British East India Company decided to market the drug in China. But it was only with the start of the secret wars that the Triangle became so powerful."

As for the specific details, Wells said that it really all began when Western intelligence services decided to employ exiled Kuomintang armies to patrol the Chinese border lands. "Essentially we're talking about a pirate force," Wells continued. "A lost army from a lost cause that fled the mainland and settled in those mountains. Although they continued to talk about mounting an invasion and kicking out the Chicoms, they were actually quite content to sit there and let the local tribesmen milk those lovely poppies. The only problem, however, was that they lacked the distribution facilities, which meant they lacked the aircraft needed to fly the opium to market. Initially it was primarily a French play. After all, the French needed money to conduct their war in Vietnam, and if nothing else, opium can be an extremely lucrative commodity. But it wasn't until the Agency entered the game that the business really began to soar.''

The plan had been a simple one, Wells said, a relatively straightforward trade. The CIA wanted an indigenous buffer between the Communist Chinese to the north and the somewhat less hostile governments to the south. The Kuomintang contingents wanted military support to remain in place and needed the aircraft to transport their opium to market. It was truly a case of one hand washing the other. Opium for arms and arms for anticommunism. ''The only hitch,'' Wells sighed, ''was that the dope started spreading in embarrassing directions, and soon the U.S. Marine Corps had one hell of a heroin problem.''

''Not to mention what was happening in the streets of New York and Chicago,'' Schwarz added quietly.

''Exactly,'' Wells said.

''So what happened to the Triangle after we pulled out of Saigon?'' Lyons asked.

Wells took another thoughtful sip of Scotch, then moved to the far wall where a yellowed map of Southeast Asia hung behind a dusty sheet of glass.

"There were actually several theories," he said at last. "Some claim the Thais took it over. Others say it's mostly the Burmese. Then, of course, there are those who say it really doesn't matter as long as the stuff still gets to market."

"What does William Lyle Wells say?" Blancanales asked.

Wells shrugged, then shook his head. "He doesn't say anything on the record."

"All right, then, off the record."

Another shrug, then another thoughtful sip of Scotch. "Let me put it like this. Although Hanoi may frown upon heroin use within its own borders, I really can't imagine there'd be much objection to exporting the stuff to America, particularly if they were able to set up an effective distribution network."

"And Sonny Trang?" Lyons asked.

"Sonny Trang is an unscrupulous pig who would sell his own daughter if the price was right. But ultimately he's not the one you need to worry about. The one you need to worry about is the person behind him, the person who's really calling the shots."

Wells finished his Scotch, moved to the window and gently drew back the shade. Although the hills were still bathed in sunlight, rain clouds were gathering in the west.

"Following the U.S. withdrawal from the south and the Vietnamese invasion of Cambodia, Hanoi began to draw up plans to replant the poppies," he continued. "Now, my guess is that it was as much a financial decision as a political one. After all, we're talking about a multibillion dollar industry, and Hanoi isn't in a position to ignore those kinds of profits, particularly when there are distribution links just waiting for the product."

"What about the politics?" Schwarz asked.

"Oh, the politics mean nothing in this context. All that matters are the profits. If a guy like Sonny Trang, a great hero of the anti-Communist cause, needs smack to supply his dealers, then he's going to get it anywhere he can. And if Hanoi needs reliable distributors, then they're going to play by the same rules. Although things do tend to get complicated when one factors in the people who supply the air cover."

"Air cover?" Lyons asked.

"Well, surely you don't think an arrangement of this sort could continue without at least some tacit support from Agency personnel. Besides, I should think that dealing heroin is almost as addictive as injecting it."

"Any idea exactly who's involved?" Lyons asked.

Wells shrugged. "Well, obviously we're talking about people who were involved with the trade during the war."

"But we're not talking about something that's necessarily sanctioned from the top?" Blancanales asked.

"No, I think we're talking about a renegade contingent, people who have simply come to the conclusion that the financial gains justify the risks, particularly in light of the fact that the dope will flow regardless of who profits.''

"Fine, but what's the real motive?" Lyons asked.

Wells shrugged again, this time with a wry smile. "What do you think the motive is? The motive is El Salvador and Chad. It's anywhere they want to mount a covert operation but can't get the funds through Congress."

"So then basically you're saying that the officers within the CIA have sanctioned a heroin deal with Vietnamese Communists in order to fight communism in Africa and Central America," Lyons said. "Is that it?"

"In a nutshell, yes."

"And Sonny Trang is just their front man."

"Correct. But before you start busting heads in Langley, I suggest you turn your attention back to the source of the problem." Wells picked up the photographs again, and tapping his finger against the brutal image of Lisa Hoa's body, he asked, "Because this is where your talents will come in handy, gentlemen. Right here."

# 16

It was four o'clock in the afternoon when Lyons and company descended from the Laguna Hills. They followed a circuitous route past Huntington Harbor and the Seal Beach swamps. Then, turning east through the flatlands, they once again found themselves in Gook Town, where a red dusk cast its garish glow along the waterfront.

They entered Gook Town from the east through nameless back streets flanked by dry cleaners and video shops. Here and there newspaper kites hovered above the low skyline, while children darted in and out of the parking lots. Closer to Little Saigon Plaza, teenagers in oversize clothing and wraparound sunglasses slouched at tables in the Tranh Café.

Finally Lyons pulled up in front of a nondescript duplex sitting amid dying palms and exhaust-choked shrubbery. Two half-naked Amerasian children were playing with rubber soldiers in the dirt, lining them up with some care and then mowing them down with a squirt gun. There were also dogs barking from somewhere beyond the chain-link fence and strains of a radio tuned to the All-Asia station.

"You sure this is the place?" Gadgets asked.

Lyons pulled out a crumpled slip of paper and examined Sammy Vong's scrawl. "Yeah, this is the place."

There were two South Vietnamese flags suspended from either end of the building, while the U.S. Marine Corp colors hung from a second-floor window.

"Looks like he's kind of gone native," Blancanales said.

"Exactly," Lyons breathed.

Another Vietnamese child appeared in the window, this one holding a plastic M-16.

"You want me to wait here?" Schwarz asked.

Lyons shook his head, then popped open the glove compartment. Inside was a .45 auto and two spare magazines. "No. I want you to watch my back."

"What about me?" Blancanales asked.

Lyons glanced out across the dusty yard at the shabby steps and cracked green doors. He turned back to Blancanales, briefly meeting the man's smoldering gaze. "How long did you say you were at Khe Sanh?" he finally asked.

Blancanales shrugged. "Long enough."

"Yeah, well, in that case maybe you'd better come along with me."

They moved out slowly, casually, armed with only their .45s beneath their jackets. Once past the green doors, the odors along the foul corridor brought back many memories: fried fish and allspice, camphor and curry. The sounds were also reminiscent of the late sixties: sobbing children, muggy rock and the hypnotic drone of a Buddhist prayer on the radio.

They stopped at the last door at the end of the corridor, a half-glazed beige affair with missing numerals. Before knocking, Lyons flicked off the safety of his .45 but still kept it hidden.

A woman responded to his knock, her pale but beautiful Vietnamese face peering through the half-opened door.

"I'm looking for Billy Swann," Lyons said.

The woman seemed to shiver slightly, and her eyes darted to something just out of sight. "No Billy Swann here," she replied.

Lyons peered past the woman to the interior of the apartment. He could see a cheap lamp shade with a pattern of gray diamonds, a frosted mirror and an anonymous landscape of a rocky coast. There were also more rubber soldiers on the carpet and a couple of tiny plastic tanks. "Look, we just want to talk to him, okay? We're not cops and we're not FBI. We're friends."

"Yeah? Well, I don't have any damn friends," a man's voice boomed out.

Lyons slid away from the door and pressed himself against the wall. "Billy, that you?"

"Who wants to know?" came the question from deep within the shadowy room.

"My name is Lyons. Guy with me is named Blancanales. We're friends of Sammy Vong's."

There was a moment of silence, then the two Able Team warriors heard when might have been a dropping safety on a Browning automatic.

"We got your name from the VA. We just want to talk."

"About what?"

"Look, if you'd just let us in for a moment—"

"About what?"

Lyons looked at Blancanales, and Pol responded with a grim nod. "About the Woman in White," Lyons said at last.

After a deadly silence, the door partially opened to reveal a stocky man with an uneven thatch of fair hair and gray-blue eyes. His features were hard and bony, but also vaguely boyish. Two thin scars ran along his jawline, and a third along his left forearm.

Lyons and Blancanales entered the room, and immediately both men saw a man slouched against the far wall. He wore jeans and a torn gray T-shirt with Broken Heart stenciled across the chest. The Browning automatic was jammed into his waistband.

"Let's just get one thing straight," he said. "This is my house. This is where I live with my wife and kids. So if you guys get weird, I won't hesitate to do some damage."

"Like I said," Lyons replied, "we just want to talk to you."

The slender Vietnamese woman who had answered the door disappeared through a curtain of beads. When she returned, she was carrying three cans of beer on a copper tray. There were no glasses.

"So why don't you just run it by me from the top?" Swann suggested.

"All right," Lyons said, nodding as he popped the beer and took a sip. "Basically we're interested in talking to guys who might be able to tell us something about a certain Colonel Phom-do."

Swann also popped a can. "Yeah, well, what makes you think I've got anything to say about that bitch?"

"We checked your VA records," Blancanales said. "We also wired your CO and got hold of your citations."

"Yeah, well, fuck the citations. And fuck the Veterans Administration. I still don't have anything to say about Phom-do."

"Is that so?" Lyons breathed.

"Yeah, that's so."

"Well, what if I told you that she's back? Right here in Gook Town."

Swann met Lyons's gaze for a moment, turned to the woman and said something in Vietnamese. When the woman had vanished again, he set the Browning aside and told his guests to sit.

Then, for a long time, he was silent—the only sounds were the television voices from the corridor and the faintly hypnotic prayers.

"Look, I spent a long time trying to forget, okay?" Swann finally sighed. "I mean, I spent years trying to forget, so if you guys are messing with my head . . ."

But at this point Lyons withdrew the photographs of the girl's tortured body and tossed them into Swann's lap. Although the man said nothing at first, his face was studded with perspiration and his mouth was twisted into an awful grimace.

"Her name was Lisa Hoa," Blancanales said, "and she was acting as an informant. We're not really sure how they tumbled on to her, but it's pretty clear how she died."

"All right," he finally breathed. "What the hell do you want to know?"

"We just want you to tell us what you know about her," Lyons said.

"Okay," Swann sighed, "but not here. Not with my wife and kids around."

The three men withdrew to the kitchen, then down a flight of wooden steps to another shabby garden littered with more toys. Beyond the garden lay a converted garage.

"This is my place, okay?" Swann said as he fumbled with the lock and pushed open the door. "No one comes here without my permission."

Inside it was very dark, so that initially Lyons and Blancanales only saw shapes and shadows. Then, by degrees, as Swann inched the blinds inside, the Able Team warriors realized they were surrounded by photographs of charred bodies and smoking ruins, a bullet-riddled helmet and the remnants of a boot, a dozen dangling dog tags, a tattered flak jacket and what looked like a necklace of petrified ears. There was also a vaguely sweet stench to the place.

"Sometimes I just come here to think," Swann said. "Know what I mean?"

"Yeah," Blancanales said. "I know what you mean."

There was a battered rocking chair and an old sofa that vaguely smelled of cats. Swann slid down to the floor, knees drawn up to his chest, right hand still clutching his can of beer, eyes fixed on a yellow map of Vietnam that had been tacked to the far wall.

"First thing you've got to know," Swann said after a long silence, "is that this isn't just another war story. You understand? This isn't just one of those war stories vets are always telling."

"Sure," Blancanales said softly. "We understand."

"Second thing you've got to know is that I don't want to hear it repeated. I don't want to walk into some bar and hear some dumb grunt talking about what the White Bitch did to Billy Swann. Agreed?"

"Agreed," Lyons said.

"Okay, then, this is how it went down."

He let his head fall back against the wall, shut his eyes and began. He began with the date and the place—June 1967, a spooky little valley just inside the Cambodia border. Command called it Sector Twelve, Swann explained, but the grunts just called it the Rat Trap. All in all, there were supposed to have been at least two companies of NVA regulars dispersed beneath the canopy. "But all we ever saw were the footprints. Footprints and bodies."

Then, one night toward the end of the second month, Swann found himself outside the wire on a little recon patrol. Although there had been a little action to the south earlier that evening, the landing zone perimeter had been quiet for more than a week. "So we all thought it was going to be a walk in the park," he added. "We all thought it was going to be a damn picnic . . . until they started opening up with a couple of mortars."

Swann said that he never really saw what hit him. One moment he was screaming for a medic, because a kid named Cherry had taken a wad of shrapnel in the groin. The next moment he was sailing into the elephant grass with a mouthful of blood. When he finally woke again, he found himself in a bamboo cage suspended from a mango tree.

"They had four of us," Swann said. "Two brothers called Skeeter and Tubbs, and this skinny kid everyone called Climax. Later I found out they had also taken the squad leader, but he kicked it before anything really happened."

In all, they waited in the cages for about six or seven hours, Swann said. Then, finally, this ugly little colonel appeared. He took one look at the prisoners, then ordered everyone to move out. "But by this time they had us blindfolded," Swann said, "so that we wouldn't know where we were going."

There had always been rumors that Charlie had a major facility just across the Cambodian border, Swann said. Some thought it was in the Parrot's Beak, buried in all that steaming jungle. Others thought it was in the high country, hidden among the northern trees. But no one, not even the high command, could have imagined what the place was really like—deep under the ground.

"From ground level," Swann began, "all you saw were these weird-looking mounds, like huge anthills or something. Then we started descending, moving down a slimy, black passage. There was also a smell . . . like ten-year-old death. They took us to a kind of cell, a dark little cell off one of the passages. I don't know how far down we were. It could have been thirty feet or thirty miles."

In retrospect, Swann supposed that he and his buddies must have waited in the cell for at least another fifteen or twenty hours. Although at the time, he said, it felt like weeks. There were no sounds except the distant throb of generators and the squeal of unseen rats. And there was no food, no water, no lights.

"We were sleeping when they finally came for us," Swann said. "All of a sudden the door slid back and these two dinks walked in. Then, after checking us out for a minute or two, they finally grabbed Climax and dragged him away. Finally, after maybe thirty minutes or an hour, we began to hear screams—long, wailing screams like something from a real bad dream."

Another six or seven hours passed. For a while Swann tried to keep morale up by working out an escape plan, calculating the distance between the far wall and the door and then working out the details for a jump on the guards. In the end, however, there really wasn't anything to do but sit and wait in the darkness.

"I must have been dozing when they finally came for me," Swann said, "curled up in a little ball and dreaming about my girl back home. Then, the next thing I knew, the guards were back...just standing in the doorway and looking at me. As they dragged me away, I remember hearing Tubbs telling me to hang in there, but he didn't have a clue what was waiting out there, not a damn clue."

There had always been stories of elaborate tunnels, Swann told them, virtual cities beneath the soft jungle soil where hundreds of VC lived in undetected safety. But it wasn't until he'd been dragged from the cell and into the main passage that he even began to imagine the sheer magnitude of the place.

"It was kind of like a giant beehive," he said. "There was this huge chamber in the center and hundreds of smaller chambers radiating out in all directions. The ceiling was at least twenty feet high, and the walls were paneled with teak. But the most impressive thing about the place was the circular White Room at the end of the passage.

"At first I thought I was dreaming again," Swann continued. "All of a sudden there I was in this really bizarre white room. There were thick rugs on the floor, gold mirrors on the walls and beautiful alabaster birds cut into the ceiling. There were also incredibly lush ferns in porcelain bowls. I thought there could only be one explanation: that I'd died and gone to heaven. But it wasn't heaven. It was hell."

A complex arrangement of pulleys and chains were attached to the far wall, Swann told them. There were also chains bolted to the floorboards and what looked like some sort of restraining device cemented to the central column. Swann, however, was hung from a beam, strung up by the wrists.

He waited an hour, two hours—it was difficult to tell. Occasionally he heard soft voices that seemed to echo from deep within the walls or from below the floorboards. At other times it was very quiet, with only the sound of throbbing generators. "At one point I think I even managed to sleep," Swann added. "I like to think I was actually sleeping when that bitch finally entered the room."

"Maybe you'd like to take a break now," Lyons suggested softly. "Maybe have another beer or go for a walk."

Swann, however, shook his head and lit a cigarette before slowly starting to speak again. He said that at first he'd hardly known what to make of the woman. "I mean, here was this very cool bitch, right? This woman all dressed in white with long black hair down her back. And she just looked at me. She just glided into the room, and looked at me. Then, after maybe five or ten minutes, she took out a knife, like one of those butterfly knives you can pick up in the Philippines. But she didn't cut me with it. She just used it to strip off my uniform.

"Then she just stepped back and looked," Swann whispered. "She just kept circling around me like a hungry shark and then she finally brought in the electrodes.

"There's really no way to describe the pain. She probably began with just a small charge, enough to tickle my toes. Then she increased it and pinned the electrodes to my earlobes. Finally she delivered an incredible jolt to my balls. In between the bouts of pain she seemed to take a lot of pleasure in running her fingers up and down my body while whispering softly into my ear. There was also something very weird about her eyes, about the way she looked at me whenever she turned on the juice."

Swann had never really been able to remember how it ended. At one point they must have thought he was either dying or insane, so they simply dragged him back to the cell. Then, for a long time, two or three days at least, he lived in a kind of gray twilight zone. He was conscious of the little things—of the rats along the rafters, of the sweet stench of the walls, of the voices around him—but he really had no idea where he was. Then, one evening about four or five days after his arrival, he found himself on the back of a flatbed truck bound for Haiphong. Eight days later he arrived at the Happy Ho Prison Camp where they kept him locked in a stinking cell for another four years, seven months and sixteen days.

It was early evening when Swann finished his story. Although his voice had remained calm throughout, his T-shirt was drenched with perspiration and his left hand was still locked around the can of beer.

"You ever see her again?" Lyons asked quietly.

Swann shook his head, shifting his eyes to the narrow band of moonlight that filtered through the dusty blinds. "No, I never actually saw her again, but I've heard about her from other guys who'd fallen into her clutches."

"What about lately?" Blancanales asked.

Swann shrugged, his eyes still fixed on the moonlight. "There's always rumors, you know. There's always some guy who claims to have seen her in Hong Kong or Paris or someplace like that. But after a while you just stop thinking about it. You just tell yourself the bitch is long gone and stop thinking about her."

"And what if she isn't long gone?" Blancanales asked. "What if she's right here in Gook Town, along with a couple of NVA squads and her nasty little battery pack. What then, Billy?"

Swann slowly shifted his eyes from the window, past the dangling dog tags, until he finally met Blancanales's gaze. "Then I'd appreciate it if you'd give me a call. I mean, if you're really serious about her being here and all, then I'd appreciate if it you'd give me a call when it's time to move out."

# 17

Sammy Vong tore open a pack of gum and popped a stick into his mouth. He was the only guy on the Force who still chewed Juicy Fruit; everyone else had switched to one of the sugarless brands. But Sammy liked the real thing, the stuff he'd grown up with in the streets of Saigon.

It was half past eight in the evening. The fog had moved in from the bay an hour ago, quickly spreading through the back streets of Gook Town. There was no moon, and kids had shot out most of the street-lamps with pellet guns. For a long time, twenty or thirty minutes, Vong had remained absolutely still be-hind the wheels of his car. Then, finally noting the sweep of headlights from the end of the alley, he stepped out onto the curb. His heels echoed like tiny gunshots as he moved across the pavement. Drawing closer, he watched two figures emerge from the shad-ows and into the headlights of a Ford Bronco—Mr. Smith and Mr. Jones.

"Hello, Sammy," Jones said. "How the hell are you?"

Vong stopped, casually jammed his hands into his pockets and nodded. As always the the two CIA officers were dressed almost identically: checked sport coats, tan slacks and white loafers. And, as far as Vong could tell, they were both armed.

"Didn't think you'd come," Jones said. "We thought you might be too scared."

Vong shifted his gaze from the squat outline of Smith to the angular outline of Jones. Then, glancing up at the blank tenement windows and the piles of garbage heaped on a fire escape, he slowly fixed his eyes on Jones again. "What makes you think I'd be scared?"

Jones smiled. "No reason...except that maybe you thought we'd cut you into little pieces and smear you all over the city."

Vong glanced back over his shoulder, his eyes following the long spears of light from the Ford's headlights into the swirling mist. Then, shivering slightly with the breeze, he turned up the collar of his raincoat and faced the men again. "Sonny Trang's a losing bet. We got twenty-five keys off a cigarette registered in his name. We've got a witness who'll testify to the fact that his boats have been picking up junk off the Oregon coast. We also have a witness who'll testify to the fact that he's been hanging out with some very bad company—no pun intended."

Jones glanced at Smith and then off into the fog.

"Tell me something, Sammy," Smith finally said, "who do you think you're dealing with here? Do you think we're just another couple of pencil-pushing flatfeet?''

"No," Vong replied. "I think you're a couple of creeps who've gone so far out you think you're in. I also think it's only a matter of time before you fall, and I'm definitely going to enjoy watching that happen. Now, does that answer your question?''

Smith withdrew a Browning automatic from beneath his sport coat and leveled it at Vong's skull. "Yeah, that definitely answers my question." Then, pressing the muzzle of the weapon to Vong's throat and easing off the safety, he continued, "Now, how about we go meet the Woman in White?''

But before Vong could answer, a single shot cracked out from above, leaving Smith screaming on his knees as the blood pumped from his shattered wrist and the Browning clattered to the concrete.

Jones responded with a furious cry and also withdrew a 9 mm Browning. But before he could even cock the gun, three more shots resounded from the fire escape. The impact of the high-velocity rounds lifted him into the air, held him suspended for a moment and finally tossed him back onto the pavement. Then there were no sounds at all, except for Smith's agonized groans and the approaching footsteps of Able Team.

Lyons appears first, stepping out of a dark doorway, a .45 dangling in his right hand. Schwarz emerged from an opposite doorway, carrying a MAC-10 and a Starlight scope. Blancanales was the last to appear, slipping down from the fire escape with a modified M-16. By the time they reached the glow of headlights, Smith had managed to strap his belt around his forearm. Jones lay sprawled on the pavement, his sightless eyes fixed on the swirling mist.

"Isn't somebody going to call an ambulance?" Smith groaned.

Lyons glanced at Gadgets and nodded. He then moved to Jones and examined the man's wounds. There were two widening stains on the left hip, another in the chest.

"Is he dead?" Smith asked, drawing the belt a little tighter on his forearm and wincing with the pain.

Lyons nodded. "Yeah, he's dead."

Smith shook his head and swore under his breath.

Blancanales appeared with a first-aid kit, and took one look at Jones, then put the kit down and backed off into the mist. Meanwhile Vong had collected the handguns from the pavement and deposited them in plastic evidence bags.

"You know, if you'd waited a little longer," Vong said, "they would have probably led us right to Phomdo's doorstep."

Lyons shrugged and drew back the bolt on his .45 auto. "If we'd waited any longer, Sammy," he said, "you'd be dead. Besides, I kind of got a feeling that Mr. Smith here is going to tell us all about Phom-do, anyway. Now, why don't you go take a walk?"

Vong looked at him with an oddly dazed expression in his eyes. "What are you talking about?"

Lyons shrugged again. "I just think you might like to take a walk, that's all."

Vong shifted his gaze from Lyons to Smith, then slowly shook his head. "Look, Lyons, you want to play rough with a doper, that's one thing. But there's no way can I let you do it to a federal employee. I mean, we're talking about an agent of the U.S. government here. Do you understand what I'm saying? The guy may be dirty as sin, but he still works for Uncle Sam."

Lyons, however, just looked at Vong. "Take a walk, Sammy."

"Lyons, I'm serious. I can't let you do it!"

But by this time Blancanales had reappeared to lead the cop away gently.

Lyons waited until Vong and Blancanales had gone. Then flicking the safety off his .45, he knelt beside Smith and pressed the muzzle against the CIA man's rib cage. "Way I figure it," he said, "we've got about fifteen minutes before the medics arrive. Now they can either take you to the hospital with a fractured wrist or they can cart you off to the morgue in a body bag. It's up to you."

Smith glared at Lyons, his lips curling back from his teeth. "Go screw yourself," he spit.

Lyons smiled. "Oh, I get it. You think I'm bluffing. You think just because we both work for Uncle Sam that we're on the same side. Well, I've got news for you, pal. We're not even close to being on the same side."

Lyons slid the muzzle of the .45 just past Smith's leg and squeezed the trigger. Smith was still looking at him when the weapon discharged. The bullet missed the flesh by less than an inch, although the blast blackened the polyester and left an ugly powder burn along the skin.

"Shit!" Smith screamed, rolling onto his side and clamping a hand over the wound. "Are you out of your mind or what?"

Lyons pressed the muzzle against Smith's hip. "Next time it won't be just a powder burn," he said. "Now, how about you start talking to me?"

Smith shut his eyes and took a deep breath. "All right," he finally sighed. "What do you want to know?"

"What's the arrangement with Sonny Trang?"

Smith gritted his teeth, then shut his eyes again. "Sonny's the distributor."

"And Phom-do?"

"Oversees the delivery."

"From Nam?"

He took another deep breath and exhaled it through clenched teeth. "Yeah, from Nam."

"So what's your role? How do you figure in?"

Smith winced. "You still don't get it, do you? You still don't have a clue about what makes the world go round." He extended his good hand and eased the muzzle away from his leg. "Okay, I'll tell you how the big boys play."

There were echoes of sirens in the distance now and whispered voices from curious citizens watching from the windows. But suddenly Smith didn't seem to be conscious of anything except setting the story straight.

"It's like this," he said. "You and your friends probably think you're pretty cool, don't you? I mean, some guy grabs a couple of co-eds and, man, you boys are right on him, jumping into rented vans and pasting America's enemies with unregistered automatics. Nothing finer, right? Well, I've got some bad news for you, son. You boys have no idea what's going on in the world. I repeat, no idea."

He leaned against the fender of the Bronco and shut his eyes with a cocky grin. Although his wrist was still oozing blood, he no longer seemed to care.

"You probably think I'm a real creep, don't you?" he breathed. "After all, I've been cutting smack deals with the Vietnamese Commies, and what could be worse than that, huh? Well, I'll tell you what could be worse. What could be worse is to let this great nation slide a little lower into the mud."

He sighed, then ran his eyes along the rooftops. "See, it's like this. Every day this nation is losing a little more ground. Every day the Third World barbarians are moving a little closer to our doorstep. And Congress doesn't give a shit. All those fools care about is staying in office. And the Senate doesn't give a shit because they're too busy looking good. So where do we get the money to fight the secret war? Where do we get the money to buy ourselves another year or two of prosperity? Well, I'll tell you where we get it—we get it anywhere we can."

The ambulance had rounded the last corner, and Schwarz had reappeared, speaking quietly into a portable phone. Smith, however, was oblivious to all of it.

"Okay, so dealing Asian smack is a nasty move," he said. "So I'm the scum of the earth for playing import-export with the White Bitch. But let me tell you something, hotshot. When the Reds start cutting off our oil supply and people start freezing to death in New York City, they're not going to worry about a few thousand junkies in California. All they're going to care about is staying warm. They're not going to worry about the ethics of the matter. They're just going to say, 'Hey, we're cold and hungry. Now fix it!' And, man, you better believe they'll mean *now*!"

He was still talking when they carried him away, mumbling something about the contra supply line and the Soviet menace in Mexico. By this time, however, Lyons was too cold and hungry to listen.

IT WAS NEARLY MIDNIGHT before the last cop departed and two bulldogs from Internal Affairs had finished grilling Sammy Vong. The fog had turned to a chilling drizzle. After driving aimlessly for nearly thirty minutes, Lyons and company finally found refuge in an all-night coffee shop called Pho Dinh's. It was a dreary place, filled with cracked formica and photographs of Asian pop stars whom no one had ever heard of. The clientele mainly consisted of thin teenagers with gel-slicked hair and wary eyes. Vong claimed that at least a dozen of them were probably members of the Black Ghosts, but neither Lyons, Schwarz or Blancanales cared.

"I know this judge," Vong said when they slid into the vinyl booth. "Not exactly the most cooperative guy ever to take the bench, but I think he'll probably give us a warrant."

"You mean to search Sonny Trang's place?" Lyons asked.

Vong nodded. "And not just the house. I think that, based on what we've got so far, we can probably get a warrant for his warehouses and building sites."

"And what do you think that's going to yield?" Schwarz asked with a frown. "Another twenty keys of Asian horse? Get serious. The moment Trang receives word that we broke his Agency contact, he's going to clean out his storage room pronto. Besides, Trang isn't the one I want. I want the White Bitch."

Blancanales nodded. "Gadgets is right. At this point the general's peripheral. We need to go to the source. We need to hit the Bitch."

"And how do you suggest we do that?" Vong asked.

Blancanales shrugged. "Same way we did it in Vietnam."

A waitress appeared with a pot of coffee. She was a tired but pretty Vietnamese woman with shrapnel scars on her arms and legs. There was also something wrong with her left hand, possibly the effects of a twenty-year-old napalm burn.

"You know, this isn't something you boys can just walk into," Vong said. "I mean, we could be talking about fifty or sixty NVA regulars. We could be talking about an extremely seasoned force."

Blancanales took a sip of coffee. "So?"

"So don't you think you'd better start considering getting some help? Maybe you should call Washington and tell them to send out a few Marines."

"Too much red tape," Lyons countered. "Besides, I kind of think we already have some Marines."

Vong cocked his head with a quizzical frown. "What are you talking about?"

Lyons smiled. "I'm talking about Billy Swann. I'm talking about all those poor bastards who were never given a chance to even the score."

# 18

"We leave tonight," Phom-do said in Vietnamese.

"How do you expect me to leave?" Trang asked.

Phom-do shrugged. "Think of it as the fall of Saigon, General."

Two slender Vietnamese men descended from the darkened staircase. In addition to the attaché cases, they also carried weapons: AK-47s slung across their shoulders, TT-33 Tokarevs jammed into the waistbands of their black trousers. There were further sounds of men in the courtyard, at least a dozen of them loading Trang's valuables into vans. In response to all this activity, however, Trang had hardly even moved his hand. His chair faced the blue-gray view of the bay. "May I at least be told where we're going?"

Phom-do shrugged again, her attention suddenly falling on a tenth-century Buddha that the general had obviously stolen from her homeland. There was also an exquisite collection of bronze deities pillaged from the ruins at Angkor in Cambodia.

"Where are we going?" Trang asked again.

"North," the woman replied. "We're going north to our main base of operations."

"And you actually believe we'll be safe there?"

The woman shook her head with a small sigh. "Not entirely, no."

"Then what's the point?" Trang questioned.

"The point, General, is that we'll be on our own ground."

Another thin Vietnamese youth entered from the study adjacent to the living room. Among the treasures in his arms was an ivory elephant from Phnom Penh and several hundred thousand dollars in negotiable bonds.

"Well, I'm not going," the general said suddenly. "Do you hear me? I'm not going to let you drag me from my home in the dead of night."

The woman turned to faced him, her long hair obscuring half of her face, her bony fingers still caressing one of the temple deities. "Let me explain something to you, General. Less than four hours ago your Mr. Jones was shot dead in the street and your Mr. Smith was arrested. Now, although the round-eyes have no real talent for interrogation, it will only be a matter of time before they begin to advance on us. And we're not in a position yet to fight them. Not here."

Trang rubbed his forehead, then stared at the perspiration in his palm. "Well, it's not my fight."

Phom-do sneered. "Really, General? Then what will you do? Wait in your lavish estate until they arrest you?"

Trang shook his head. "I don't know. Maybe I'll go to Mexico."

The woman put down the bronze statue and stepped a little closer to Trang's chair. "Mexico, General?"

"All right, Brazil. I'll go to Brazil."

"No, General. I don't think so. I think I'd rather have you at my base camp where I can keep my eye on you."

There were sounds of a struggle from the top of the stairs. Finally another black-clad Vietnamese youth appeared, leading Kim Kiet by the arm. Although obviously frightened and confused, her voice remained composed. "Sonny? Sonny, what's happening?"

Trang extended a hand and beckoned her forward. "Don't worry, baby," he soothed, smiling. "Everything's going to be okay."

"But what's going on? Why are they taking all your furniture?"

He placed his hands on her narrow waist, then gently eased her down to his lap. There were times, particularly when she was still half asleep, when he almost thought of her as his daughter, a long-lost daughter from the war.

"Your general has to go away for a little while," he told her softly.

"And what about me?" she asked.

He brushed her hair from her eyes, then a tear from her cheek. "Well, maybe you'd like to take a little holiday in Mexico?"

But before she could answer, Phom-do's voice cut through the silence like a cold knife. "The girl comes with us."

THREE HOURS LATER Kim Kiet sat beside the general in the Trang Enterprises Lear jet. Phom-do sat at the opposite end of the cabin, her lips pursed, her eyes fixed on the gray strip of pavement. There were also four silent Vietnamese men in the jet, but Kim didn't know their names. As the aircraft taxied into the rising sun between the dung-colored hills, she thought she caught a glimpse of at least another dozen young Vietnamese men, watching from an isolated terminal at the south end of the field. Despite the fact that she had only been given fifteen minutes to pack her things, she had still managed to bring her diary. It was wrapped in tissue and concealed at the bottom of her cosmetic case, waiting for a last, critical entry that would hopefully drag them all down.

Although there had been no specific mention of a destination, she felt fairly certain they would finally land in some lush but remote corner of Oregon that resembled the Asian jungles. She had heard Trang talk of such a place. She was also fairly certain that a lot of people were going to die, as the ghosts of far-off Asian jungles rose up for a last confrontation.

She felt the general's knuckles brush across her cheek, his hand close on her hand. "You're cold," he whispered. "You're as cold as ice."

She forced a smile, then shook her head. "I'm all right."

"Well, soon enough we'll be safe and warm in the beautiful woods."

She let her head fall against the window and gazed down at the cracked wastes stretching to a brown horizon. Although she supposed she should have been concerned, she actually felt quite calm. In fact, watching the ribbons of highways growing thinner, the cars becoming indistinguishable dots in the nothingness, she realized that she actually felt more than just calm. She felt pleased, pleased that Phom-do and Sonny Trang were finally on the run. And, as she shut her eyes, luxuriating in the warm dawn light through the Plexiglas, she even found herself slipping into her favorite dream—a dream in which she saw hundreds of tortured victims closing in on the White Bitch...a dream in which she even saw Jackie Minh.

## 19

Jackie Minh shivered in the cold. Although more than three weeks had passed since he had dragged himself out of the harbor and found refuge in a basement hovel beneath the Thanh Tong Seafood Company, hardly an hour passed when he didn't think about Kim. Minh had thought about her during the excruciating days when he had hovered between life and death. He had thought about her through all the lonely nights when he had lain in the blackness with only the mice for company. He had even thought about Kim in the predawn hours when planning his revenge on Sonny Trang and the Woman in White.

Apart from the mice and the tiny brown moths, the only one who knew that Jackie Minh was still alive was the Kite Man. Usually the Kite Man came in the morning, tapping three times on the steel door and then whispering his proper name through the keyhole: *It is me, Nguyen Hy*. More often than not he was accompanied by at least one cat, usually a mangy tabby called Tick Tack Toe. The cat, however, didn't bother the mice. In the beginning the Kite Man's concern had simply been to keep the young man from dying. To this end, he had administered numerous strange concoctions: rose petals, cobwebs and garlic, ginseng and eucalyptus leaves. At one point the old man had even mixed equal portions of honey and rice wine with the powdered bones of a black crow, and then forced his patient to drink it. Minh's strength gradually returned, and finally the old man had brought him a dog-eared copy of the *I Ching* as a remedy for a troubled mind.

It was about half past seven in the morning when the Kite Man knocked at Jackie Minh's door. As always, he carried an old oilskin bag across his shoulder. "So, *mon ami*, you are better today?"

Minh shrugged but said nothing. Although more than an hour had passed since he had risen from his bed, he hadn't dressed or washed. He sat with his knees drawn up to his chest, his eyes fixed on the tiny wedge of dusty light that filtered through a chink in the wall.

"I've brought you a very special soup," the Kite Man said as he put his satchel down. "One sip of this golden liquid and you'll feel ready to take on the whole world."

Minh just shrugged. "It's not the whole world I want to take on," he said. "Only one small part of it."

The Kite Man squatted at the edge of the mat, picked up the worn copy of the *I Ching* and turned to a page at random. He ran a crooked finger across each yellowed line and read softly, " 'The best charioteers do not rush ahead. The best fighters do not make displays of wrath. The greatest conqueror wins without joining issue.'"

Again, however, the boy just shrugged, his eyes still fixed on the dusty square of light above. "Just tell me this," he finally said. "Will you help me find out where Sonny Trang is?"

The old man smiled and flipped to another page.

"Look, I can't wait any longer!" Minh cried. "Do you understand?"

The old man nodded and put the book aside. "The general and the White Bitch left this morning on an aircraft bound for what was called the Great Northwest. Kim Kiet is with them, but otherwise she is well."

Minh shut his eyes for a moment. "You're sure about this?"

"Yes," the Kite Man breathed. "I'm sure."

"Then I must go and find them."

The old man shook his head and again picked up the book. "'The only effective action is no action. The only effective revenge is an embrace.'" He put down the book again, and then said, "Besides, there are dozens of them, *mon ami*, and you wouldn't stand a chance alone."

Minh rose from the cot and began pacing the room. "Well, I have to do something!" he finally exclaimed. "I can't just sit here and rot!"

The old man waited until Minh resumed sitting on the cot. Then, leaning forward in the faint light, he began to speak very slowly and softly. "You're too young to remember the war clearly, *mon ami*, but believe me when I say you're not the only one who's suffered at the hands of Phom-do."

Minh looked at him—for the first time he actually looked into his eyes. "What are you talking about, old man?"

"Even as we speak the word is softly spreading among those who suffered, among those who never had a chance to even the score. And even as we speak they're whispering among themselves."

Minh felt a slight twinge in the pit of his stomach. "How can I find them, join them? You must tell me!"

The Kite Man frowned and pressed his fist against his forehead. "We're no longer discussing poetry, *mon ami*. We're no longer discussing war. Do you understand? We're discussing what will be the last battle of a terrible war. It's a battle for which these men have been waiting a long, long time. And when it comes, they'll give the last full measure of themselves without caring whether they live or die."

"Just tell me who they are, old man. Just tell me who they are so that I can find them and fight by their side."

Although the Kite Man hesitated for at least another three or four minutes, he finally whispered the name he had heard whispered so many times before: *Able Team*.

FOR A LONG TIME after the old man left, Jackie Minh remained seated on his cot. Although his right hand was still slightly swollen and the electrical burns hadn't completely healed, he generally felt fit enough to fight, fit enough to kill. He clenched his right hand into a fist, then extended the fingers to form the tiger's claw. He tucked the thumb beneath his palm, to form the ridge hand. He cocked the hand down and closed the fingers with his thumb to form the crane. Yes, he was definitely fit enough to kill.

Minh slid back onto the cot and shut his eyes. He heard mice scurrying on the pipes above and the distant echo of foghorns and the clang of a ship's bell. And then, deep within himself, he heard the rattle of machine gun fire that had terrified him so much as a child.

# 20

Blancanales ran a finger along a map of the Oregon coast, then glanced at a partial list of Sonny Trang's holdings. He took another sip of coffee, shut his eyes and briefly caught a vision of a dark, damp forest.

"I suppose you realize that you look like hell," Schwarz said from the far corner of their hotel room.

Blancanales glanced at his reflection in the mirror, at the eyes mottled with red, at the two-day growth and the cracked lips. "I'm not wrong, Gadgets," he said, ignoring his friend's comment. "They're up there in the Oregon woods, waiting for us."

Schwarz also ran a finger along the Oregon coast. "You know, that's pretty wide-open country up there. What makes you think we're ever going to find them?"

Blancanales picked up the list of Trang's holdings and jabbed a finger at the last entry. "See that. Northwest Developments."

Schwarz shrugged. "So?"

"So look at the map. We're talking about an area twenty miles southwest of Eugene. A piece of land that's virtually out in the middle of nowhere. Now you tell me what Trang's doing with the land."

Schwarz shrugged. "How should I know? Maybe he's building a house."

"On two hundred acres?"

"Okay, so maybe he's building a resort."

"No roads."

"All right," Schwarz finally sighed. "I give up. What's he doing out there?"

Blancanales jabbed a finger at the map. "He's built himself a base camp and he's bringing in dope."

"And you think that's where he and the White Bitch have gone? Is that what you're trying to tell me?"

"I don't think it," Blancanales said. "I know it."

Schwarz rose from the table, moved to the sliding glass doors and pressed his palms against the glass. For a moment a lot of odd thoughts went through his head—memories of action in the Delta, of a rocket attack in Saigon and the tunnels in the Highlands. "Well, even if you're right, how the hell do you expect the three of us to flush them out of there?" he finally asked.

"Well, for one thing," Blancanales replied, "it's not just going to be the three of us."

IT WAS HALF PAST TWELVE in the afternoon when Lyons returned with more maps of the Oregon coast. Although they had changed hotel rooms twice since the mission had begun, he still refused to speak until he had shut the windows and turned the television on.

Then, for a moment, all eyes turned to the television station's midmorning classic, *Casablanca*.

"I'm not going to lie to you guys," Lyons began. "I'm not going to tell you this is just business as usual, because it's not. We've got authorization from Stony Man, but that's as far as it goes. Washington doesn't want to know about this one. Do you guys understand what I'm saying?"

Schwarz and Blancanales couldn't help glancing at the screen where Peter Lorre was pleading with Bogart for refuge from the Germans.

"So what's the bottom line?" Schwarz finally asked.

Lyons riffled through a stack of papers in his briefcase, then finally withdrew a State Department cable. Although the point of origin and signature had been deleted, the meaning was clear enough. "This is the bottom line."

Schwarz picked up the cable, scanned it quickly and passed it to Blancanales. "So basically we're talking about a hostile invasion of this nation's coastline, and Washington is calling it an immigration problem. Is that it?"

Lyons nodded. "It's a political call. The White House doesn't want to make a fuss because they don't want any bad press. And the DEA won't move without a nod from the White House."

"What about Special Ops or one of the antiterrorist teams?" Blancanales asked.

"Same problem. Washington has no problem fighting Arabs, but no one wants to believe we're still at war with Hanoi."

"So where does that leave us?" Schwarz asked.

Lyons glanced at the screen and watched a pensive Bogart reach for another glass of whiskey. "It leaves us on our own. It leaves us facing forty to fifty communist sappers from the Vietnamese army."

"What about tactical support?" Schwarz asked, watching Ingrid Bergman snake her way between potted palms.

"What about it?" Lyons growled. "You want a chopper? Forget it. You want satellite links? Keep dreaming. You want a few unregistered M-16s? They can probably help us out.'

"And personnel?"

Lyons glanced at Blancanales, then back at a brooding vision of Bogart in a wrinkled tuxedo. "Personnel," he finally said. "We should probably talk about personnel."

Lyons produced fifteen manila envelopes, each embossed with a stamp from the Veterans Administration. Some contained photographs, dull shots of empty-eyed men in combat garb. Others just contained copies of service records and discharge reports.

Schwarz opened two or three enveloped at random, scanned the contents, then tossed the papers onto the table. "You're kidding, right? I mean, this is a joke, right?"

Lyons glanced at Blancanales, but Pol only shrugged.

"Most of these guys haven't touched a weapon in fifteen years," Schwarz added. He leafed through the contents of yet another envelope. "And what about this guy? Looks to me like this one can barely walk."

"They're part of an informal veterans' network," Lyons said at last. "A kind of mutual support group of guys who spent time in one of the Hanoi POW camps. They meet once a year in Hawaii and stay in regular communication with letters and telephone calls."

Schwarz shook his head and frowned. "Well, that's great. We're about to meet fifty seasoned Vietnamese sappers and you want to enlist a dozen wasted grunts from the Vietnam Memorial Barbecue Club. Take 'em up in the woods, give 'em a few M-16s, let 'em pop off a few rounds and then we'll crack open a case of beer and talk about the action. Yeah, well, that's just great."

"Look at it this way," Blancanales said. "These guys may be a little out of shape, but they're all we've got right now. Besides, what they lack in physical skill will be more than compensated for in determination."

Schwarz shifted his gaze from the TV to Blancanales. "What are you talking about?"

"I'm talking about the fact that these guys all have one thing in common: each and every one of them has a personal score to settle with Phom-do."

"Okay, I'm listening," Schwarz finally said.

A third map of the Oregon coast was spread out on the coffee table, as well as two aerial photographs of what looked like a deep-cover construction site. Finally there was also a handwritten list of weapons that Lyons had ordered from the Stony Man compound.

"Basically we're talking a search-and-destroy mission," Lyons said. "Phom-do's probably going to be expecting a chopper assault. But we're not going in with choppers. We're going in on foot."

Schwarz ran a finger along the map, quickly calculating distances. "That looks like one hell of a walk. Are you sure those vets are up to it?"

Lyons looked at Blancanales, and Pol shrugged again.

"Put yourself in their position," Blancanales said. "You've spent the past ten years of your life waking up in the middle of the night with visions of what the White Bitch did to you. You've stayed in touch with twenty or thirty other guys around the country who've had similar nightmares over the years, but up until now all you could offer was a reassuring word. Then it happens. You get a call from one of your buddies: the Bitch is back. Now, are you going to let anything stand in the way of a chance to even the score? I don't think so."

Schwarz glanced at the map again, then picked up another envelope. "So we tramp in, catch them with their pants down and then blow them back to Hanoi. Is that roughly the plan?"

Lyons nodded. "Roughly, yeah."

"But if anything goes wrong, we're completely on our own. No backup, no air support, not even medical?"

"That's right," Lyons said.

Schwarz rose to his feet and grinned sardonically. "And I thought Khe Sanh was fun."

PHOM-DO HAD BEGUN to plan her defense. She had first sketched out a rudimentary diagram of her fire base on the back of an envelope. Then, recalling how the NVA had defended the Central Highlands in 1969, she had sketched the machine gun emplacements. Although not entirely certain of her technical superiority, she felt fairly confident that her men could withstand anything the enemy might throw at them. She was also confident, as she looked down through a break in the clouds, that the terrain would work to her advantage.

One of her lieutenants appeared to tell her that the aircraft would be landing in fifteen minutes.

"Very good," she replied.

She shifted her gaze to the general, who was apparently dozing beside the sleeping girl. It was odd, she thought, that of all her former enemies in the South, she would find herself allied with General Sonny Trang. Not that the general had ever been much of an enemy. Rather he had been more like a sucker fish that attaches itself to a shark. He let others do the killing, and then moved in to gorge himself on the scraps.

She turned her attention to the sleeping girl, fixing her gaze on the curve of the girl's shoulder and the outline of her thigh beneath her skirt. Since the very first moment she had set eyes on Kim Kiet, she hadn't been able to get the girl out of her mind. She couldn't seem to keep herself from dreaming about the girl . . . perhaps writhing under the electrodes, her delicate wrists straining against a nylon cord, her eyes pleading through tears.

The lieutenant's voice again broke her reverie. He was kneeling between the seats, his face pressed against the Plexiglas. "It almost looks like home, doesn't it?" he said.

She let her gaze fall back to the window, to the vast green-black forest below mountains of churning rain clouds. "Yes," she whispered. "It's just like home."

# 21

One afternoon in the summer of 1967 Blancanales had
been called in to advise the Fourth Division LURPs on
a search-and-destroy into Ia Drang. The commanding officer was one of those tough young men from
West Point, the sort of kid who was always talking
about "attack posture" and using the word *outstand-
ing* to describe the performance of his men. At issue
was what the CO called a "selective foray" into "dis-
puted" ground, which meant he wanted to send about
fifty Marines into a meat grinder. When Blancanales
tried to explain the futility of such a mission, the CO
turned to him with an unexpected fury.

"Look at it this way. We can either fight them in the
jungles out there or we can fight them in the States.
Now what's your choice?"

"Well," Blancanales replied, "maybe we can beat
them in the States, sir."

It was a phrase that had come back to haunt the
Able Team warrior.

It was very early and very cold when Blancanales
and his compatriots left their rooms and moved out
into the parking lot. After loading the van with their

personal gear, they drove due north along California
State 14. Although the sky was clear, the air was still
cold with high desert winds whipping through the
pass. When they reached the airstrip and he caught his
first glimpse of the ragged volunteers, the phrase came
back to him. *Maybe we can beat them in the States.*

The airstrip was an ancient ribbon of pavement set
among the lower Mojave Hills. Thirty, possibly forty
years ago, Blancanales supposed the place had been
the launch site for numerous covert missions: supply
runs into Central America, support runs into the
Asian rim. Today, however, it was just a cracked runway amid the tumbleweed, a crumbling tower beside
a junked fuselage and a row of rusting Quonset huts
where the volunteers had assembled.

From a distance and through the rising clouds of
dust, the men actually looked pretty formidable: a
ragged line of about thirty lean figures in camouflage
jackets and boots. As Lyons pulled the van a little
closer, however, all the flaws became evident: the
frightened eyes, the slouched shoulders, the bellies
hanging over their belts.

The first to emerge from the rank was Billy Swann.
In his jacket and field trousers he looked marginally
tougher than he had in his apartment. But the moment he removed his sunglasses it became obvious that
he was in way over his head.

"All present and accounted for," he said as Lyons
and Blancanales stepped from the van. "As a matter
of fact, we've even got a few more than we figured
on."

Blancanales scanned the faces that peered out at him from the shadows of the hut. There were at least four that he recognized from photographs: a slender ex-private named Hopper, two marginally disabled black men named Anderson and Flood, and a graying ex-gunnery sergeant named Moulton. As for the others, the best anyone could say about them was that they looked determined, hopelessly past their prime and pitifully out of shape, but determined to end their lives of quiet desperation in one way or another.

"A few of the guys brought their own weapons," Swann said, "but basically we're going to need a little help on that score."

Lyons nodded, then turned to Schwarz. "What's the word on equipment?"

Gadgets glanced at his wristwatch, then at the empty sky. "Due here any minute."

"And the transport?"

"Any minute."

Although the sky remained empty, there were suddenly sounds of an approaching vehicle—a beat-up gray sedan plowing through the billowing dust. A few moments later all eyes watched Sammy Vong step from a dented Plymouth. He had a flight bag over his shoulder and a green umbrella under his arm.

"What's going on?" Lyons asked as Vong approached.

Vong let the flight bag slide from his shoulder into the dirt. "What's it look like?"

Lyons shook his head, not quite able to suppress a grin. "I don't know, Sammy. Why don't you tell me?"

Vong shifted his gaze past Lyons to the sad crowd of elderly soldiers. "Well, it's like this," he finally said. "Oregon may be out of my jurisdiction, but this is still my case."

Blancanales stepped forward and placed a hand on Vong's slender shoulder. "You don't have to do this, Sammy. It's not your fight."

But Vong just shook his head. "Yes, it is."

THEY WERE STILL STANDING on the runway when the C-47 appeared, banking in low from the east and then skimming above the sage-covered flatlands. As the ancient twin-engined aircraft drew closer, Blancanales was able to make out the words Freedom Transport stenciled across the gray fuselage. All other markings, however, had been obliterated.

"Well, I guess this is it," Swann said as the aircraft taxied to a halt in front of the Quonset huts.

"Yeah," Lyons sighed. "This is it."

"You want me to get the men aboard?"

Lyons glanced at his wristwatch, then shook his head. "Not yet. First I want to talk to them."

Swann tugged at his ear, then shifted his eyes to the waiting ranks beneath the corrugated awning. "Nothing you can say will make any difference. These boys are committed, and that's final."

"Maybe so," Lyons breathed, "but I still want to talk to them."

"All right," Swann sighed, "suit yourself." Then, extending an arm above his head and cupping his hand to his mouth, he shouted for his men to gather.

Once the men had lined up in front of Lyons, the Able Team warrior talked about the dangers ahead. He knew, however, that danger was meaningless to these men. He talked about the fact that they were essentially an illegal force, but he knew the law was also meaningless. Lyons told them that in all likelihood at least a third of them would die, but that wasn't a deterrent, either. In closing he said that if anyone wanted out, he wouldn't think any less of them... naturally there were no takers.

IT WAS DAWN when they were finally ready to depart. Although the pilot, a lean kid who called himself Hamster, complained about the weight, Lyons told him that nothing could be left behind.

"Well, I guess this is it," Vong said. He was standing beside the members of Able Team.

"You know, you can still change your mind about this, Sammy," Lyons said. "You can turn around and no one will think any less of you."

Vong shook his head. "I may be an American citizen now, but I'm still Vietnamese... and this is still a Vietnamese war." Then, tapping out another cigarette and flipping it into the corner of his mouth, he picked up his bag and started forward with the others.

When the pilot finally started the engines, there were one or two feeble cheers from within. Then, as Lyons tossed in the last of the luggage, he heard another faint cry from the end of the airstrip. "Who the hell's that?'' he asked, shouting above the roar of the twin engines.

Schwarz and Blancanales leaned out of the fuselage, shielding their eyes from the glare of the rising sun. In the distance a tiny figure could be seen sprinting across the tarmac.

"I think," Vong said after a long pause, "that it's probably Jackie Minh."

Lyons turned with a wide-eyed stare. "What are you talking about?"

"Minh," Vong repeated. "I think it's Jackie Minh."

"Minh?" Schwarz exclaimed. "I thought you said he was dead."

"Well, I was wrong."

"Fine, but what the hell's he doing here?" Lyons asked.

Vong smiled. "What do you think?"

# 22

They landed at the deserted airstrip in a cold rain that fell in wavering sheets and smelled of the deep forest beyond Eugene. It was eleven o'clock in the morning, but it could easily have been mistaken for the early evening.

"For the next fifteen hours you men are going to be on your own," Lyons told the veterans when the plane finally taxied to a stop. "I suggest you team up in twos and threes, find yourself a hotel room and get some sleep."

"When and where do we meet up again?" a rangy ex-platoon leader named Tigue asked.

"That information will be found on an instruction sheet that Gadgets will now pass out."

"What happens if we run into trouble?" a balding ex-chopper pilot named Butane Dempsey questioned.

"Yeah," said someone else. "What happens if we run into a curious cop or somebody like that?"

"See that you don't," Lyons replied.

THE NEXT THIRTEEN HOURS were consumed with preparatory work. Lyons placed three telephone calls to Stony Man Farm in order to coordinate the deni-ability factor. He met briefly with a general from the local National Guard who told him the Guard would cover for them, but only if there were no civilian cas-ualties. It was also during these hours that Lyons ar-ranged for a shipment of what he called "the new-generation weapons."

It was nearly two o'clock in the morning when the preparatory steps had been completed. As a base of operations, Vong had secured a dull room in a Sleepy Time Travel Lodge that lay just past the north end of the University of Oregon campus. Although earlier there had been sporadic shouts of students from a neighboring fraternity house, by midnight things had grown quiet. Only Blancanales, however, had ac-tually been able to sleep for a couple of hours.

"I used to know a guy who played for the Ducks," Blancanales said softly. He stood at the window, fac-ing a dark view of dripping pines and oaks along the edge of the Eugene campus.

"The Ducks?" Schwarz asked.

Blancanales nodded. "University of Oregon Ducks. Used to have a pretty good team back in the sixties. Guy I knew played tight end, or maybe it was middle linebacker."

Schwarz met Blancanales's eyes. "So?"

Blancanales shrugged. "So, nothing. He was just another guy who happened to eat it in Nam."

There were sounds of a truck pulling into the park-ing lot, then the slam of a door. A moment later Vong appeared in the doorway with bags of cheeseburgers, fries and Cokes. Lyons followed Vong, wearing a pair of field trousers and a camouflaged poncho.

The detective put the food on the table, but no one touched it.

"You guys might regret it later if you don't eat something now," Lyons said.

In response, Schwarz and Blancanales reached for the greasy bags. After two of three bits of their burgers, however, neither man seemed able to continue.

"Any idea how the others are doing?" Blancanales asked after a long silence.

Lyons shrugged. "Nervous."

"What about Stony Man?" Blancanales asked. "What's the word from back there?"

Lyons shrugged again. "Unofficially they wish us the best of luck. Officially they don't know us."

"So where does that leave us if things go wrong?" Vong asked.

Lyons shook his head with a grim smile. "Where do you think it leaves us?"

IT WAS TWO O'CLOCK in the morning when Lyons and company rendezvoused with the volunteers. Although the rain had finally stopped, it was still quite cold and the sky remained capped with clouds. They met in a deserted parking lot on the far west edge of the city, some arriving in rented cars, some in taxis, others on foot. After lingering in the damp mist for about ten or fifteen minutes, Lyons ordered everyone into the back of the rented truck. Although there were one or two halfhearted cheers when Lyons started the engine and eased the truck onto the road, it soon grew quiet again.

"Nasty-looking country, isn't it," Schwarz said. He was seated between Lyons and Blancanales, his eyes fixed on the road ahead, on the black humps of mountains and on the dark shapes of pine trees.

"No worse than the Delta," Blancanales replied. "No worse than anywhere in Nam."

Schwarz thought about that for a while, then finally nodded. "You've probably got a point there." But his eyes were still fixed on the shifting black shapes beyond the glare of headlights.

It was half past three when Lyons finally pulled the truck off the highway and coasted to a stop among the massive pines. En route from the city he had mentally rehearsed the speech he planned to deliver before moving out. When he climbed out of the cab and faced the ragged circle of men, however, he changed his mind. "Okay, let's get those weapons unpacked," was all he said.

A hush descended when the M-16s were distributed. Some, upon receiving their weapons, simply held them at arm's length and stared. Others immediately began to refamiliarize themselves with the feel of the stock against their shoulders, the weight of the barrel in their hands. Swann actually began to talk to his weapon, whispering a long-forgotten endearment and giving it a name.

Next came the grenades, the handguns and the light antitank weapons. But it wasn't until Lyons unpacked the last crate, however, that either Schwarz or Blancanales showed any similar emotion.

"What the hell's that?" Vong asked as Lyons withdrew a truncated fire hose attached to a massive backpack.

"This," Lyons said, "is our edge."

"Great, but what is it?" Vong persisted.

Schwarz knelt to examine the weapon, inspecting what appeared to be its firing mechanism. "It's a minigun. It's a goddamn hand-held minigun."

Lyons nodded. "That's right. A minigun. Otherwise known as a 7.62 electric Gatling gun."

"Yeah, but what's it do?" Vong asked.

Blancanales allowed himself a slow, knowing smile. "It fires six hundred rounds per minute," he said. "That's what it does."

Vong whistled incredulously. "Six hundred rounds per minute?"

"Correct," Lyons replied.

"Then what the hell are we waiting for?" Vong asked. "Let's go get them."

By the time they actually started moving, however, the smiles had entirely faded. They moved out at a moderate pace, first along the fire trail, then along a deer path. They moved in single file like some segmented predator slithering between the ghostly pines. Now and again echoes of snapping twigs and branches broke the predawn stillness, but for the most part they were as quiet as they had ever been in Vietnam.

# 23

Phom-do stood on a rise and surveyed the landscape. She swept her gaze along the far pines to a shallow meadow filled with skunk cabbage, piles of leaves and dogwood. Then, slightly shifting toward the north, she let her eyes fall on the concealed entrance to the tunnels.

She was particularly proud of the tunnels. She felt that they represented the ultimate blend of Western technology and Eastern design. From a distance or from the air one saw nothing more than freshly turned furrows in a tiny clearing. But below the earth's surface existed a whole new world. Although originally constructed as a distribution base and laboratory for the heroin operation, she had also realized that it would be a wonderful place to fight a battle.

A young lieutenant emerged from a tangle of dogwood where he had been supervising the deployment of claymores and .51-caliber heavy machine guns. Although only fifteen years old when the Americans had withdrawn from Saigon, his memories were still vivid.

"All the weapons have been properly placed, Comrade Colonel," the boy said in Vietnamese.

Phom-do nodded, but her eyes and thoughts remained elsewhere. "Tell me something, Comrade Huong, are you afraid to die?"

The young lieutenant looked at her. Although his eyes grew slightly wider, his expression was otherwise unchanged. "Not if the cause is right."

Phom-do smiled. Excellent, she thought. Leaving the boy still slightly dumbfounded, she moved into the forest. Beyond the pines lay a grove of black oaks carpeted with tassels of Solomon's seal and wild geranium. There were also coils of razor wire and more claymores strategically placed along the stream. Then, closer to another tangle of ivy and dogwood, was a secondary entrance to the tunnels.

In all, Phom-do's people had spent more than six months digging the tunnels below this stretch of forest. Although the ground had ultimately proven to be reasonably firm, there had initially been problems with seepage and flooding. Despite the fact that it was fairly remote country, there had also been a fair amount of local curiosity about what was being built.

But regardless of the expense and risk of exposure, it all seemed well worth the effort whenever she crossed the threshold and descended into the darkness. There were no less than a dozen separate passages, each radiating out from a central chamber like the tentacles of an octopus. Whenever Phom-do shut her eyes, however, she envisioned a spiderweb—a vast and complicated network from which nothing could escape.

"I suppose you realize it's only a matter of time before they find us," Trang said from the mouth of the passage below the entrance.

Phom-do turned, searching the man out in the darkness. She met his gaze across twenty feet of tunneled earth and shaved timber. "Hello, General," she said softly. "How are you feeling this morning?"

Trang ignored the question. "It's elemental," he said. "The property we stand on is registered in my name. The building permits are also in my name. Now, how long do you think it's going to take them to connect those facts with the rumors of smuggling along the Oregon coast?"

Phom-do smiled again, running a hand along the smooth surface of a support beam. "They've already figured it out."

"Then why are we just sitting here?"

Phom-do shrugged. "We're not *sitting*, General. We're *waiting*. We're waiting to teach these Americans one last lesson in revolutionary warfare."

Thirty yards beyond the entrance lay what Phom-do considered to be her first real line of defense—a sandbagged alcove fitted with two .51 heavy machine guns. There were also booby traps here: stainless-steel spikes embedded in the soft earth, claymores beneath the floorboards and concealed fire bays for riflemen. Farther along the tunnel Phom-do's engineers had put down C-4 charges, but apparently the general still wasn't impressed.

"Let me ask you something," he said as they continued along the dark tunnel. "Have you ever seen an American combat unit in action?"

Phom-do shrugged with a slight smirk. "Yes, General, indeed I have."

"Then you'll know what I'm talking about when I say we don't stand a chance. Even if they don't bring in the choppers, we'll never succeed in keeping them out of the tunnels."

Phom-do turned and smiled enigmatically. "And why should I want to keep them out of the tunnels, General? The tunnels are my killing ground. Besides, we won't be fighting an American combat unit here. It would prove much too disruptive politically if the present administration had to admit they'd been forced to defend their own soil against a Vietnamese invasion. No, at best they'll muster only an irregular force of foolish volunteers."

"And if those volunteers fail, then what?"

"Then I'm sure they'll send in others, but by that time our mission will have been accomplished and we'll be long gone."

Trang stopped, turned and slowly shifted until his eyes encountered the woman's gaze. "What do you mean, our mission will have been accomplished? I thought our mission was to set up our distribution network, to establish a thriving and lucrative business concern."

Phom-do smiled crookedly. "You really are naive, aren't you, General?"

"What are you talking about?"

"I'm talking about the fact that this has nothing to do with investments and profits, General. It has nothing to do with drugs or money. We're making a political statement here, a political and military statement that has been a long time coming. We're showing the Americans that not only can we defeat them on our ground, but we can also defeat them on their own ground, as well. We're showing them that they'll never be free of our shadow, of our memory and our will. Now why don't you return to that little kitten of yours and comfort her? I'm sure all this excitement has left her feeling a little insecure."

Although the general started down the passage, he couldn't seem to keep himself from turning and facing her one last time. "You really are insane, aren't you?" he whispered.

The Woman in White merely smiled.


KIM KIET WAS STILL dozing on the narrow cot when the general entered her chamber. Now and again she had been disturbed by the sounds of footsteps in the passage, but after a while she had finally managed to slip into a shallow dream about Jackie Minh.

"Are you awake?" the general whispered. "Kim, are you awake?"

She opened her eyes but couldn't bring herself to meet his gaze. "What time is it?"

He glanced at his gold watch, a symbol of better days. "It's just after nine."

"Morning?"

He nodded. "Yes, a beautiful morning."

"May I ask a question?" she said after a long silence.

"Of course."

"How much longer will we have to stay here?"

He smiled, then extended his hand to her forehead. "What's wrong, my dear? Are you really that frightened?"

She nodded, knitting her eyebrows together for a convincingly concerned frown. "Yes," she lied. "I'm frightened of what might happen to you, of what might happen to us."

"There's no reason in the world to be frightened. After all, there are more than fifty crack soldiers to defend us. Now, how can you be frightened on such a beautiful day with more than fifty of the world's finest soldiers to protect you?"

She let her head fall back on the pillow and shut her eyes again with an imperceptible smile. "They won't come for us during the day," she whispered. "They'll come at night."

# 24

It was dusk when Lyons and company reached the edge of Trang's property. Although there were no signs of human presence beyond a barbed wire fence, Blancanales still insisted that they retire to the deeper glades. A cool breeze off the sea blew through the western peaks. The forest floor was filled with small indications of life: box turtles beside a brook, squirrels among the pines, blue jays, crows and a circling hawk.

"What's your call, Pol?" Lyons asked.

The Able Team warrior was kneeling in the matted leaves, surrounded by veils of ferns and clustered dogwood. Behind them, in the deeper foliage, sat Sammy Vong, Billy Swann and the rest of their squad. Only Jackie Minh, intense and brooding, sat alone.

"We need a little physical recon," Blancanales said as he scanned the ground beyond the fence with his binoculars.

"You want me to hold your hand?" Schwarz asked.

Blancanales glanced over his shoulders, his gaze lingering on the anxious faces of those behind him: an ex-rifleman named Egan who had lost three fingers and his left ear to the White Bitch, an ex-gunner named Weed who still dreamed about the electrodes, and at least another dozen ex-grunts who owed her one.

"I think I should probably take Swann," Blancanales said at last. "I think it'll do a lot for their confidence if I take Billy Swann."

LONG SHADOWS WERE FALLING when Blancanales and Swann moved out from the pines. A pale moon had climbed above the eastern hills, and the breeze had risen.

"We're just going to take a look," Blancanales whispered. "You see something, just let it pass."

Swann nodded and flipped off the safety on his M-16. They were lying in tall grass just below a shadowy knoll. Ahead lay more than two hundred yards of relatively open ground. There was a stench of rotting leaves and stagnant water, and the air was alive with insects.

"What happens if they spot us?" Swann asked, nervously peering over the stalks of grass to the rusting barbed wire fence in the distance.

Blancanales looked at him and smiled. "You scared, Billy?"

Swann was also smiling now. "Sure, I'm scared."

"Well, that makes me feel better."

They moved out slowly in a half crouch. Beyond the barbed wire a bullet-riddled sign warned that trespassers would be prosecuted to the full extent of the law—a five-hundred-dollar fine, six months in jail or both. There were also notices against hunting, fishing and camping.

"Definitely takes you back, don't it?" Swann said as they continued stalking forward.

Blancanales scanned the meadow ahead, then lifted his gaze to the clustered pines beyond. "Yeah," he breathed. "That it does."

"Of course, at least this time we're doing it on our ground," Swann added.

"I wouldn't be too sure about that," Blancanales answered as he continued to scan the tree line.

The ground grew moist beyond the wire and the air was filled with choirs of crickets. Ground fog had begun to rise, oozing out from hollows and spilling into the meadow. As the light continued to fade, there were deeper sounds of frogs from the marsh and squirrels scurrying in the nightshade. Then, from deep within the oaks, there were also sounds of someone moving across the carpet of leaves. Blancanales motioned Swann down, and they lay very still among the sodden foliage.

"Now what?" Swann whispered.

"Now we wait," Blancanales replied.

There were sounds of what sounded like a water rat, dragging its belly through damp willows. There were also sounds of chattering squirrels and the whisper of a wasp.

And then, from deeper shadows between the pines and black oaks, they heard footsteps on brittle leaves and branches.

"Could be just a civilian," Swann whispered. "Local boy hunting cottontail with his old man's shotgun."

But by this time Blancanales had withdrawn his binoculars and had finally focused in on a slender figure in black with an AK-47 slung across his shoulder.

"Wait here," he said quietly. He put down the binoculars and withdrew a doubled-edged knife. "Just wait here and be quiet."

Blancanales started out slowly, inching forward on his elbows and knees. He held the knife in his right hand and kept the left hand empty and free. He crawled with slow, fluid movements. At twenty yards he paused to watch another water rat slide into the muddy reeds. Then he paused again to watch the slender figure up ahead light a cigarette.

The Able Team warrior took a slow breath. Although there were those who claimed the best hunters were able to focus their concentration like a laser, Blancanales had always believed in the opposite approach. He liked to think of his consciousness as elastic, as a limitless but silent intelligence blanketing the foliage. So for two or three minutes he continued to lie in the grass, listening to the twilight cries of the crows and the chirp of crickets. Eventually he grew conscious of the smaller sounds: the faint clicking of beetles, the beating wings of wood nymphs and months. Then, finally noting the crackle of a boot heel on leaves, he gradually started moving again.

Once past the first rank of oaks he was able to see his prey quite clearly—a hunched figure with one foot resting on a fallen log, an AK in the crook of the right arm. Although it had been said that Charlie had eyes in the back of his head, Blancanales had never believed it. All you had to do was choose the right time, he used to say. Choose the right time and then go for it.

He waited until he could smell the man before he finally rose to his feet. Then, slipping into another long shadow and shifting his weight to the balls of his feet, the Able Team warrior gradually started closing in. He moved with liquid steps, the right foot crossing over the left while his back remained perfectly straight. Although his eyes remained fixed on his prey, he was still also conscious of the little things: of the ground beneath his feet, of the breeze through the trees, of the weight of the knife in his hand.

And when he finally stepped in for the kill, he was also conscious of the hatred he felt in his gut.

He struck for the throat, with his left hand clamped around the soldier's mouth. He was surprised at how muscular the man was, at the ferocity of his struggle beneath the knife. He was also surprised at the heat of the blood and at how easily the blade cut through the tendons. The man died quickly with only the slightest whimper.

Blancanales wasn't, however, surprised at the time warp, at the growing realization that this wasn't simply *like* Vietnam... this *was* Vietnam.

He waited a full six minutes before returning to Swann, a full six minutes scanning the landscape below and watching dark shapes of soldiers among the far oaks. Then, dragging the body into the deeper bush, he started back across the field. When he finally reached the hollow where Swann lay, he took another two or three minutes to catch his breath.

"Contact?" Swann asked, noting the bloodstains.

"Yeah," Blancanales breathed. "Contact."

"How many?"

"Just one."

"So what do we do now?"

"I want you to go back to the others. Tell Carl he can move them out when he's ready."

## 25

Like many North Vietnamese commanders, Phom-do primarily relied on *The Art of War* for her tactical inspiration. A collection of essays generally attributed to a sixth-century Chinese general by the name of Sun Tzu, the work had long been a standard of Asian strategists. It was rumored to have been the inspiration for both the Long March and the victory at Dien Bien Phu and was currently the inspiration for Phom-do's defense of her outer perimeter.

Phom-do had determined that the defender must conceal himself and take advantage of the terrain—in this case the clusters of dark pines and the deep marsh.

It was close to midnight when she finished deploying her troops. Although the wind had died, the woodland fog had risen—an usually thick fog that vaguely disturbed her. She took comfort, however, in the fact that she had placed no less than fifteen of her top men along the outer perimeter and concealed another six-man fire team in the darker pines. In support of these men she had placed two 12.7 mm heavy machine guns and a .51-caliber machine gun on the rise. There were also mortars although her faith in them had been shaken since the incident at Sunset Cove.

"Any sign of them?" she asked a young squad leader named Dien.

The boy glanced over his shoulder, vaguely disturbed that he hadn't heard the woman approaching. "No, Comrade Colonel. No sign of them."

She slid into the trench beside him, nodding at the other soldiers guarding the flanks. Although she rarely got particularly close to her troops, she had always believed a few words here and there were necessary for morale.

"Tell me, Comrade," she said, "are you anxious for this fight?"

The boy nodded, tapping the barrel of his weapon. "Yes, I'm anxious."

"Anxious to hear them scream, to see their blood in the moonlight?"

"Yes."

She placed a hand on his shoulder, then whispered in his ear with a smile. "Of course you're lying, but I admire your spirit."

She moved a little farther down the line until she found a wiry lieutenant whom everyone called Dak. A veteran of four campaigns against the Americans, including the Tet offensive, he had been one of the first to volunteer for this mission.

"So how goes the night?" she asked, intentionally using the archaic phrasing.

The lietenant smiled, his face suddenly become a mass of tiny wrinkles. "Obscure," he replied. "Obscure with a fog that behaves like a ghost."

Phom-do picked up a Starlite scope, one of the few pieces of Western technology in her arsenal. She scanned the low ground, following the stream bed to a cluster of willows, then scanned the higher ground to the rise of the knoll.

"Tell me something," she said at last. "If you were the American commander, where would you begin your attack?"

The lieutenant hesitated, also scanning the far ground. "From the south," he finally replied. "I'd attack from the south, concealing my men in the fog."

"With machine gun fire?"

"And mortar."

"What about one man?" she asked. "What about a lone man in those trees to the north?"

"The lieutenant picked up the scope and scanned the stream bed. Although he thought he saw something, a fleeting glimpse of a hunched figure sliding into the fog-shrouded willows, he said, "Impossible. What kind of American would fight like that?"

But before she could reply, a thin soldier named Pham Sang suddenly collapsed not twenty yards away.

She saw it from the corner of her eye, saw it before she actually heard the shot. One moment Pham Sang was gazing out from the shadows of an oak, the next he was crashing into the surrounding leaves with a trailing spray of blood and bone. Then, although one part of her mind was still calm, another part had suddenly grown numb with a terrible possibility. Had she committed the gravest sin in Sun Tzu's book? Had she failed to know her enemy?

BLANCANALES EASED himself into the sodden willows and slowly took another breath. He lay very still while at least twenty or thirty rounds trimmed the foliage around him. In addition to the AKs he heard the deeper crack of a .51 and twin 12.7s. But he wasn't particularly concerned.

He lifted his M-16 and sighted down the scope until a second head and shoulders filled the eyepiece—a wiry figure with rabbit's teeth and a hard jaw. Ten or twelve more heavy slugs tore at the leaves above, while a frantic mortar team dropped a shell just up the rise. But, finally squeezing the trigger again in a concentrated moment of quiet fury, he watched another explosion of blood.

*Welcome back to Vietnam.*

"ANY IDEA WHAT'S GOING ON?" Schwarz whispered.

Lyons lowered the Starlite scope and shrugged. "Nothing much. Pol's just kicking a little ass."

"So then why are we still sitting here?"

Lyons shrugged. "Good question."

They lay among the damp leaves approximately two hundred yards east of the stream. Behind them, also utterly silent, lay Swann, Vong, Minh and the others. Although more than ten minutes had elapsed since Swann had returned, it was only now that there was any meaningful discussion.

"I can tell you how we would have played in the war," Schwarz said. "Send six or seven guys into those pines and then kick them in the ass while they're still trying to nail Pol."

Lyons shook his head. "Yeah, but I don't want to kick them in the ass. I want to stick them right in the gut. Pol's got them spooked. Now I want to make them bleed."

He signaled to Swann to bring up one of the anti-tank weapons. Lyons then motioned for an ex-rocket man name Hunter and picked up the scope again. "You boys think you can put one between the goal-posts?"

Hunter rose to his elbows and peered out at the black center of oaks and the flashes of the heavy Soviet 12.7s. There were also indications of fire from a ridge, but the range was still impossible. "I can give it a try," he finally said.

"All right then," Lyons breathed. "Let's move out."

PHOM-DO SANK into the shadows behind the clustered pines and tried to make sense of it all. On the one hand she still felt entirely in control; however, there was something that disturbed her about the nature of the American attack, something she couldn't quite grasp

A spray of heavy machine gun fire cracked from the blackness to her left. The mortar popped from the hollows to her right, and there were frantic cries from behind.

Yes, she thought. There was definitely something wrong.

She slipped a hand into her coat and ran a finger along the broken spine of Sun Tzu's book. Then she peered out from the pines again and watched another dozen tracers cut the fog-clotted air. It was obviously a matter of ferocity, she thought. For whatever reason, the Americans were fighting with an uncharacteristic ferocity, fighting like demons from hell. Very well, she told herself, then I'll simply have to match that ferocity with wisdom and flexibility.

But before she could even rise to her feet again, the night suddenly came alive with a blur of white light and the deafening explosion of a 66 mm rocket. There were screams from the far perimeter, and she caught a quick glimpse of a body hurtling fifteen feet into the air.

"They're fighting like ghosts," a soft voice said from the inky blackness behind her. "They're fighting like ghosts who have nothing left to lose."

She turned and found herself gazing into the cool eyes of Lieutenant Dak. Although his uniform was shredded at the shoulder and there were spots of blood on his trousers, he appeared to be unhurt. "How many casualties?" she asked.

The lieutenant shrugged. "Three, maybe four."

"Even so we must retaliate." Then, peering out from the pines again and noting a few far-off flashes from an M-16, she ordered her lieutenant to redirect his fire.

LYONS AND SWANN CROUCHED among the dogweed. Eight yards to their left lay Jackie Minh and seven others from the team of veterans. An ex-sergeant named Packer, however, had already fallen behind with a bullet in his foot.

"Something tells me that if we stay here much longer, we're going to start eating steel," Swann said.

Lyons lifted his head above the tangled foliage and peered out across the forest floor. Although the hollows were still shrouded, the fog seemed to be lifting from the higher ground. "How much piss can you squirt on that ridge?"

Swann glanced back at the anxious faces of his men, then took a peek above the vegetation. "We can give them another taste of the LAW, but those trees are going to cut the effectiveness."

"Well, let's try it, anyway," Lyons said. "Tell Hunter to squeeze off another rocket, and then let's see if we can't punch a whole through their forward line."

But before Swann could turn around and call out the rocket man's name, another dozen tracers sliced through the leaves around them. There were screams from the oaks behind, and a lanky ex-gunner named Hill staggered into the clearing. There were more screams as Hill collapsed to his knees with what must have been at least four slugs in his chest. Another spray of lead rained down from the ridge, and someone began crying out for a medic.

Lyons got on his knees, managed to squeeze off a few pointless rounds and then found himself kissing the earth. Three yards to his left a red haired ex-rifleman called Goofy was moaning with a sucking wound. As Lyons tried to drag the man behind an oak, six more 7.62 mm rounds cut through the dogwood and virtually severed Goofy's leg at the knee.

"We're taking some bad shit!" Swann yelled.

"Get me the grenade launcher!" Lyons shouted.

But when Swann rose again to call for the Armscor, he caught a glimpse of the meadow beyond the trees where at least two dozen Vietnamese soldiers were advancing through the mist. "Oh, my God," he whispered. "They're coming from both sides!"

Lyons rose to an elbow and squeezed off six more frantic rounds, but then found himself kissing mud again. Another veteran, a grizzled ex-mortar man named Klugg, took a bullet in the throat, whispered something about Gadgets Schwarz and then threw himself down beside Lyons. Lyons reached for a wad of dressing, then realized it was useless as a solid arc of blood shot out of the man's throat.

"Where the hell is Gadgets?" he whispered, cradling the dying man in his arms as he glanced out at the meadow at the twenty-five advancing soldiers.

Suddenly Lyons heard someone shout in a laughing rage, but he couldn't grasp what was happening until the first three Vietnamese fell.

He watched the scene unfold in quick muzzle-flashes as another two or three Vietnamese began twisting with impact. Although the enemy was finally returning the fire, their AKs didn't seem to count for very much in the face of the minigun.

"Six hundred rounds per minute!" Gadgets shouted as he stepped out from the line of oaks. "Six hundred rounds per minute!" he yelled as the fire poured from the revolving barrels.

From where Lyons lay the weapon sounded like a monstrous buzz saw. One moment there were five Vietnamese crouched among the tangled ferns. A split second later they were all shuddering under the impact of fire.

"Six hundred rounds per second!" Gadgets shouted as he advanced into the meadow. Then, shifting the massive barrel to his left hand and mowing down another three or four scrambling soldiers, he yelled, "Come and get it."

As Schwarz continued to advance and the fog began to enshroud his body, he hardly looked human. He was like some sort of robot hunched beneath the minigun, his arms mechanical extensions of the backpack, his eyes plugs of glass blinking with the electric surge every time another soldier crumpled in a rain of blood.

LYONS REGROUPED his men in a dark hollow surrounded by some of the largest oaks in the forest. In addition to the earlier casualties an ex-radio operator named Harcourt had taken a bullet in the thigh, and an ex-ranger named Willis had broken his left index finger. But scattered among the dogwood in the meadow below were at least a dozen Vietnamese who had fallen under the minigun.

"You know, we probably could have chased them right into the sea," Schwarz said as he slipped the ammo pack from his shoulders.

There were muffled cries from the deeper ends of the hollow and the sound of a ripping dressing pack. There were also sounds of hard breathing and exhausted moans from where the veterans rested.

"We've already pushed these men too hard," Lyons said. "I mean, they may have a lot of guts, but they're still about fifteen years out of shape."

"So what do you propose?" Schwarz asked.

Lyons gazed out at the far ends of the meadow, noting the occasional flickering lights in the distance. "I propose we make every step count."

There were sounds of movement in the brush behind them, then the chattering of a night bird. A moment later, however, Blancanales emerged from the leaves, his uniform caked with mud, his eyes peering out from his coal-blackened face. "Round one for the good guys, huh?" he said as he stepped into the clearing. "And how about a round of applause for the man with that minigun?" he said, turning to Schwarz with a quick, hard grin.

Schwarz, however, merely shrugged and glanced out at shadows beyond. "Question is, what do we do for an encore?"

Blancanales put down his M-16 and collapsed on the leaves. Although clearly exhausted, his smile hadn't faded entirely.

"Now I don't claim to have the whole thing figured out," he said, "but I definitely got a glimpse of something from that stream bed."

Lyons knelt down beside the man, his hands still faintly sticky from the blood of the man he'd held in his arms. "What are you talking about?"

"He's talking about a tunnel," Swann said as he stepped from the shadows of an oak. "He's talking about the fact that they've got themselves a tunnel out there, the same kind of tunnel they used in Nam."

Blancanales withdrew his knife, cleared the leaves from a patch of earth and sketched a rough circle in the dirt. "Way I figure it, the Bitch has got her tunnel about four clicks from the end of the valley. Now we can harass them from here to Sunday, but we're not going to hit the jackpot until we find a way into that dragon's lair."

"And how do you suggest we do that?" Lyons asked.

Blancanales shrugged, then grinned at Schwarz again. "I don't know, but with six hundred rounds per minutes I'm sure we'll think of something."

# 26

Reverberations of mortar rounds had sent clouds of gray dust billowing down from the rafters and loose earth had shaken from the walls. Then, for a long time, there were no sounds at all, except for the pounding of Kim Kiet's own frightened heart.

When the shooting had begun, Kim had lain down on the cot again and drawn the filthy blanket over her head. She had remained very still, recalling a song her mother used to sing whenever the rockets had sounded. It was an old song, probably something her mother had picked up from a French movie.

Although she had received no direct word about how the battle was progressing, she was fairly certain the Americans were at least holding their own. She was also fairly certain that Jackie was with them, waiting for her signal in the darkness.

There were soft moans from the passage, then what sounded like a weeping child. There were screams for bandages and morphine, and then hysterical laughter. Finally, after another ten or fifteen minutes of silence, she heard the general slip back into her chamber.

He knelt by the cot again and slipped the blanket from her head. Placing a warm hand on her forehead, he whispered her name. She managed another smile, but she still couldn't bring herself to look at him.

"It's all over," he told her. "There's nothing to be afraid of anymore. We've beaten them back, and that's the end of it."

She rose to a sitting position, her knees drawn to her chest, her arms linked around her shins. In addition to the dust and fragments of earth shaken loose in the attack, it looked as if one of the support beams had shifted. "Are they all dead?" she asked softly, knowing they weren't, knowing the general was lying.

He nodded with a slight smile. "Most of them."

"Then we'll be leaving soon?"

He nodded again with a broader smile. "Yes, very soon."

She returned his smile and sank back on the cot. "Then maybe I should sleep for a while."

He bent over and kissed her on the cheek. "Yes, you go to sleep." Then, after another kiss, he said, "Sweet, sweet dreams."

Although she continued to lie very still for at least another half hour, she naturally didn't sleep. She thought about the general, and about what he had done to Jackie. She thought about Jackie and tried to recall the feel of his arms around her. She thought about the White Bitch, remembering her cold, black eyes. Finally she thought about putting her plan into action.

JACKIE'S EYES were fixed on the far ranks of black oaks and the still farther clusters of pines. He jammed another magazine into his M-16 and slowly ran his eyes along the men to his left. Although he hadn't said more than a dozen words since arriving at the airstrip the day before, he supposed he couldn't have felt closer to these men. Lyons, Schwarz, Blancanales, Swann and the others—he simply couldn't have felt closer. He also felt very close to this forest, to the dark ferns spread out before him, to the tangled vines and damp leaves.

"When do you think we'll be moving out?" he asked softly.

The thin ex-machinist by his side shook his head. "Soon enough, I guess."

He shifted his gaze to the deeper shadows where Gadgets was conferring with Pol. He glanced back over his shoulder to where Sammy Vong crouched among the vines. Then, shifting his weapon, he returned his gaze to the far trees where Kim was undoubtedly waiting.

CARL LYONS ROSE from the shadows to address his men in the center of the clearing. "Listen up," he said quietly. "In a couple of minutes we're going to be moving out in one column. Me and Pol on point. Gadgets at the rear. Now I don't expect a whole lot of action until we enter those pines, but then I've got a feeling all hell's going to break loose. The important thing, however, is to stick together and follow orders. Any questions?"

No one actually said anything, so they quickly moved out in single file, following another deep path through the ferns. Now and again there were more sounds of animals scurrying out of their way. As predicted, however, there were no signs of human life until they entered the last grove of pines.

"You see what I see?" Blancanales whispered.

The column had stopped dead and was crouching in the ferns.

"I'm not sure," Lyons replied. "What do you think you see?"

Blancanales extended an arm, his index finger pointing at a cluster of shadows atop a mossy knoll. "There," he whispered. "Up there. See it?"

Lyons removed the Starlite scope from his satchel and scanned across the silent forest floor. Then, lifting the eyepiece another three degrees, he finally whispered, "Maybe."

"How about I take a couple of guys and see if I can shake the tree?" Blancanales suggested.

Lyons put down the scope. "What couple of guys?"

Blancanales shrugged. "I don't know. Billy and—"

"Me," Minh said from directly behind him. "Take me."

Blancanales turned to meet the young man's gaze. "Okay. You."

The three men moved in the direction of ground that sloped slightly toward the stream, then quite steeply from a leaf-strewn rise. Below the rise lay another silent stretch of ferns and damp hollows filled with decaying pine needles.

"I don't mean to upset you," Blancanales whispered, "but I get the feeling we're looking at a forward bunker and another .51."

Swann held up the Armscor grenade launcher he had borrowed from Lyons. "So?"

Blancanales peered out between the ghostly pines at the humped mound a hundred yards ahead. "Too far, buddy. You'll only piss them off."

"What if I sneak up there and throw in one of these pineapples?" Minh suggested.

Blancanales shook his head. "Might look nice on paper, Jackie, but they'll nail you before you get to first base."

"Then what?" Swann asked.

"Smoke them out," Blancanales replied. "Let's see if we can't smoke them out of there with a little old-fashioned deception."

Although Lyons had originally requested at least two dozen smoke grenades from Stony Man, they had finally ended up with only twelve—twelve M-18s with a sixty-second burn time and a forty-foot spread. But given how Blancanales intended to employ the device, he supposed the M-18 would be sufficient.

"Now this is how we're going to play it," he said as he pulled the M-18 from his vest. "I'm going to toss this little sucker out in the clearing and let them think we're on the move. But we're not going to be on the move. We're going to stay right here and wait for them."

"What if they don't buy it?" Swann said.

Blancanales smiled. "Watch," he said as he tossed the grenade in a long, slow arc past the trees. As the canister began to hiss and the smoke billowed out across the carpet of pine needles, there were agitated cries from night birds in the branches above. But it wasn't until at least another twenty minutes that they heard the first sounds of the approaching Vietnamese.

"Come to Daddy," Blancanales whispered from deep within the ferns. "Come and see what Daddy's got."

But initially there were only minute stirrings, soft whispers of swaying ferns.

"Maybe we just spooked them," Swann whispered. "Maybe they're just shifting in the line and waiting."

And then Blancanales caught glimpses of them—gray shapes in the green darkness. "Easy," he whispered, his left hand raised. "Take it real easy now." Then, as the first five or six Vietnamese stepped out of the shadows, Blancanales brought his hand down. "Show time," he whispered.

They fired in 3-round bursts, Blancanales squeezing off the first shots, followed by Swann and Minh. There were two distinct screams from the ferns and a brief glimpse of a figure whirling with an arc of blood. Blancanales fired another quick burst and caught a glimpse of a shredded torso, the flesh reduced to pulp and the wide eyes staring at the sky. A third figure stumbled out of the shadows, blood spewing from a blackened stump as Swann squeezed out three more rounds, shouting, "Eat it! Eat it!"

But by this time there were also incoming shots, three long bursts from an AK concealed on the higher ground. Minh and Blancanales felt the damp earth kick up into their faces and heard the ugly whine of slugs passing through the leaves above them. They scrambled deeper into the hollow while Swann rolled behind a rotting log.

Swann waited, left hand squeezing a spare magazine, face pressed hard against the damp pine needles. Four more shots had torn out chunks of the rotting log, exposing at least a hundred termites. And they were crawling on him, burrowing into the folds of his jacket. He shut his eyes, gritting his teeth. Forget about the termites, he told himself. The termites don't exist. All that matters is the moment.

There were more shots from the high ground, sending more chips of rotting wood into his face. "Well, forget this," he whispered to himself. "Forget this cold shit." He eased his left hand along his thigh until his fingers encountered the grenade launcher.

*All that matters is the moment.*

Another burst of AK fire slammed into the log and a fist-sized pinecone struck his left knee. There were also sounds of movement now—at least three Vietnamese closing in from the rise. Slowly he dragged up the Armscor and placed it on his shoulder.

He shut his eyes before he squeezed the trigger and got a last quick look at the war inside him. He saw the White Bitch's eyes, the eyes of a gunner from the

Screaming Eagles who had literally lost his head. He saw a hundred blackened bodies in a ditch, a thousand restless Marines in the Highlands. He also saw his own racked body trembling under massive voltage. Swann squeezed off the first three rounds.

He shot for the shivering ferns at what looked like three figures descending from another patch of dogweed. His shot was really fired blindly, but when the first three rounds exploded there was no mistaking the screams.

Two bodies were immediately thrown from the ferns. A third, the legs twisted at an impossible angle, rose at least four feet into the air. There were also screams from unseen men.

"Eat it!" Swann shouted again. "Eat it, damn you!" Then, rising to his feet and advancing forward, he squeezed off another round from the Armscor. This time he fired for the willows, fired from the hip at the muzzle-flash of another AK. The three ensuing explosions sent up clouds of pine needles, moist soil and fragments of bark. There were also two more bodies briefly outlined in the white blast and a quick glimpse of another pulverized torso.

"Give me cover!" Blancanales shouted back at Minh. "Give me some cover!"

Minh responded with a high scream, flipped his selector switch to full automatic and began pouring rounds into the ferns.

Blancanales had also switched to full-auto. Then, jamming in another magazine and rising to his feet, he started moving forward. At fifteen yards he squeezed off three rounds into a dark shape in the ferns, then another six rounds into the willows. A thin silhouette slid into the clearing, staggered a dozen paces and finally pitched forward into the stream bed.

"Two o'clock!" Swann shouted as another spray of AK fire raked the leaves above their head. "Two o'clock and closing!"

"Got it!" Blancanales acknowledged, sinking to his knees and squeezing off another burst from his M-16.

Then, amid the rain of shredded leaves and twigs, two more Vietnamese rose, fell and finally lay shivering on the ground.

Swann laughed. "We're doing it!" Then he jammed another four shells into the Armscor and followed Blancanales into the ferns.

They waited, signaling for Minh to join them. Although there were still agonized moans from deep within the forested area, it was suddenly very quiet again.

"Maybe we should call up the others," Minh said.

Swann shook his head. "Forget the reinforcements. Let's just keep going."

But as Blancanales rose above the foliage to scan the far knoll, a dozen heavy shells tore into the pines around them. "Definitely a .51," he whispered.

"Then let's give them another little taste of Mr. Armscor," Swann said. He flicked off the safety and rose to his haunches. "Now how about some of that smoke?"

Pol nodded and withdrew another M-18 canister. "Ready when you are."

Swann nodded, waited until Blancanales had tossed the smoke grenade and then eased out of the ferns. He kept to the denser pines, moving in a half crouch. There were more shots from the heavy Soviet machine gun, but they were blind shots, sprayed at random into the rising cloud of yellow smoke.

Swann paused in a narrow grotto where the pines converged. Beyond the pines lay another eighty yards of relatively open forest. He lifted the Armscor and sighted down the eyepiece, adjusting to a single spot. The .51 was sandbagged behind a timer barricade. But given the angle and a little bit of luck, Swann told himself, he just might be able to pop it.

He dropped to his belly and started crawling forward. Pausing again at the mouth of the grotto, he gently drew the leaves aside. From there he could see the machine gun nest quite clearly—a dark mound of matted earth and pine needles rising above the surrounding foliage. He let the leaves slip back around him and eased back down to the damp ground.

Swann shut his eyes, trying to form a clear vision of the nest, of the dark eyes peering out from behind the .51-caliber heavy machine gun. Supposedly there had been guys in Nam who could pop a grenade into a can at two hundred yards—did it by feel, a long, slow feel from the muzzle to the target.

But as Swann finally began to squeeze the trigger he wasn't so conscious of feeling the target as feeling the ghosts, the ghosts of at least a dozen guys he'd seen blown to pieces during the war.

"That's right," he heard them whisper. "We're all just ghosts. We're all just long-lost ghosts. But we're with you, Billy Boy. We're really with you."

And as Swann continued squeezing the trigger, he adjusted the barrel—up a little, down a little, over to the left—until he had it right on target.

He fired with his eyes still shut, fired even as the .51 opened up and the slugs began to kick up debris all around him. Then, grunting with the impact of a big shell in his shoulder, he squeezed off another two rounds.

After that, a lot of things happened at once. There were four white flashes from inside the bunker. There was blood on his shoulder and his arm went numb. There were two quick visions of a screaming face from behind the .51 and what might have been another shredded torso falling into the leaves. He heard Blancanales shouting his name, and the distant cheers of another dozen men from behind him. The Vietnam vet heard what might have been the awful crack of bone in his arm and the tearing of a ligament.

But there were no more shots from the machine gun nest.

THEY DRAGGED Swann onto a bed of matted leaves, lapped a battle dressing on his wound and gave him a little water. Then he was really conscious of nothing except the night sky through broken patches of leaves and the sound of his own exhausted breath.

"How is he?" Lyons asked.

An ex-medic named Thatcher wiped blood from his hands and shrugged. "Just a nick."

"What about the pain?"

The man shrugged again and adjusted his glasses. "The pain's another matter."

From where they now stood there was a clear view to the last dark grove of oaks some four hundred yards across a shallow glen. But although there was a suggestion of movement, of dark shapes shifting among the pines, it was still impossible to tell exactly where things stood.

"We're going to have to leave the badly wounded." Lyons said grimly. "Billy's all right, but we'll have to leave the others and push on."

"Which naturally assumes we know where we're pushing to," Schwarz said.

Blancanales nodded. "I think Gadgets has a point, Ironman. Trying to find an entrance to that tunnel will be like trying to find a needle in a haystack. If it's anything like the tunnels in Nam, they're going to have it bobby-trapped six ways to hell, not to mention the dead ends."

"So what are you saying?" Lyons asked.

"I'm saying that before we move out again, we'd better have some idea where we're going. If we start probing around in the dark out there, they could nail us right to the wall."

"So what are you saying?" Lyons asked again.

But before Blancanales could answer there was a soft shout from the edge of the glade.

"Hey, maybe you guys should see this," Vong said.

Lyons, Schwarz and Blancanales moved past the rank of resting veterans to the small knoll where Vong was sitting with Minh. Although the view across the flatlands was somewhat more oblique from there, it may have been longer. And as Able Team gazed out at the blackness, they couldn't help but notice the tiny blinking light in the distance.

"What do you make of that?" Schwarz asked.

Lyons shrugged. "Cutest little come-on I've ever seen."

Blancanales, however, shook his head. "I don't think so. I think it might be legit."

"Yeah?" Lyons countered. "How so?"

"As a signal. As an indication of where that tunnel might be located."

"And who out there would want to give us a signal?" Schwarz asked skeptically.

"Kim Kiet," Minh said softly from over their shoulders. "Kim would do it."

## 27

Kim Kiet lowered the flashlight and slipped it back into the folds of her jacket. Although reasonably certain that none of Phom-do's people had spotted her, she still couldn't seem to keep her hands from trembling, her heart from beating like a battery of mortars. She was also cold now that her clothing was drenched in perspiration.

Suddenly she heard footsteps in an adjacent tunnel and she pressed herself against the earthen wall of the firing post. There were also hushed voices from the conference chamber, and she crouched a little deeper into the shadows.

It had taken her more than two hours to work up the courage to attempt the signal, to kneel in the blackness with her tiny Mag-Lite extended to the eastern hills. And, of course, she had no idea whether or not the Americans would believe it, assuming, of course, they had even seen it.

Kim waited until the footsteps and the voices had faded, then began the long half crawl back to her chamber. Although she had only seen a very small part of the tunnel, she had already begun to grasp its size—

a vast, intricate network of passages extending beneath the forest floor. From above one saw almost
nothing except the mounds between the pines where
the firing posts had been placed. Below, however, it
was like a monstrous rabbit warren—a black, labryn-
thine dreamland where anything could happen.

She caught another scent of the pines from the ventilation shaft and the odor of boiling rice from the
"Dien Bien Phu" kitchen. She heard hushed whispers from the sleeping chamber and then her own
blood roaring in her ears, her heart pounding in her
breast. There were also rats to contend with in the
passage.

Kim passed another dark chamber and heard more
whispered voices in Vietnamese—something about a
tactical advantage, something else about sheer luck.
She caught a glimpse of a fleeting shadow where the
passage gave way to a narrow flight of wooden steps.
There were more voices—something about a de-
stroyed machine gun, and at least ten more fallen soldiers. Obviously, she thought, the Americans were
very close—at least close enough to have seen her signal.

Below the steps lay a network of secondary passages, a virtual spiderweb of connecting tunnels, gas
traps and blast walls. Although there were faint glim-
merings of lantern light in the distance, it was still very
dark and she had to feel her way along the walls,
which were slippery with seepage.

It must have been about midnight when she finally
managed to creep back into her sleeping chamber. Her

wristwatch had stopped, but she supposed it was at least midnight. Although she knew she had no hope of sleep, she again lay down on her cot. For a while she focused her thoughts on the view of the forest she had seen from the firing post. Then, for a time, she focused her attention on her body, the alternating waves of fever and chills that continued to leave her trembling.

Finally she let herself think about Jackie, about how he would respond to her blinking light, how he would convince the Americans that her signal hadn't been a trick. Then she thought about how he might also take a moment to send her his love before picking up his rifle and moving out into the night.

LYONS PUT DOWN the Starlite scope and turned to Jackie Minh. "Tell me about her. Tell me what kind of girl she is."

Minh scratched his head. "All I can say is that it's exactly the kind of thing she would do. Exactly."

"How do you know?"

"Because I know!" Then, very softly, hardly above a whisper, he added, "And because we love each other."

Lyons turned to Blancanales with a quizzical shrug. "What do you say, Pol? Do you want to put your faith in love?"

Blancanales also shrugged, still trying to figure the coordinates. "Sure, why not?"

It was nearly midnight when they moved out. Another blanket of fog had moved in from the lowlands.

There were also clouds obscuring the moon and a faint north wind that smelled of the deepest woodland groves. When the men had reassembled and Lyons slowly scanned their ranks, his eyes eventually fell on Swann. Although still obviously in pain, apparently the bleeding had stopped.

The ground fell away sharply from the cluster of pines to another long stretch of silent forest. They passed the blown machine gun nest and the fallen bodies. As they neared the rise above the meadow where Minh had seen the blinking light, they spread themselves into a fan and slowed their pace by half. All eyes remained fixed on the dark swell.

THE FIRST SHOT couldn't have sounded more remote—a distant and apparently insignificant pop from deep within the blackness. A moment later, however, an ex-corporal fell to his knees with a dark hole below his left eye. Hesitating a moment to examine the blood on his hands, he finally collapsed into a patch of skunk cabbage.

"Down!" Lyons shouted. "Get down!"

Two more shots cracked out of the night, then the shattering explosion of a mortar shell. There was a choked scream from the shivering vines, then someone shouted, "No, it's okay! I'm all right!"

Another mortar shell fell between two oaks. Blancanales scrambled out of the rising dust and clouds of leaves, threw himself beside Lyons and withdrew the Starlite scope.

"Anything?" Lyons asked.

"Maybe," Blancanales whispered. "Maybe."

A lean ex-rocket man named Hutch appeared with two LAWs on his back. Vong and Minh had also scrambled up from the rear amid the falling debris.

"Anybody got a fix on them?" Hutch whispered. "You give me a fix and I'll nail that slime to the mud faster than you can blink."

But before Blancanales could even lift the scope again another mortar-AK combination sent them scrambling back behind the pines.

"We ain't getting any cherry this way," Hutch whispered, a thin line of blood streaming from his thigh. "We ain't getting shit."

"Hutch is right," Blancanales said. "We're getting eaten alive out here. We can either pull back or ram it down their throats, but we sure as hell can't stay here."

"Then let's ram it down their throats," Lyons breathed. He rose to an elbow and cupped a hand to his mouth. "On three! Constructive load! Pass the word. Constructive load!"

For a while it was difficult to tell what was coming in and what was going out. Pure white flashes of light left the trees momentarily etched against the sky. Tracers divided the night into long triangles of blackness. Two 66 mm rockets left whole portions of the forest aglow.

Lyons rose to an elbow again and cupped a hand to his mouth. "All right, let's go. Go! Go! Go!"

They advanced at a half run, firing at anything that moved. There were screaming echoes of rocket-propelled grenades, then the higher screams of pain.

But by now Gadgets had moved in from the flank and had opened up with the minigun again. Four more distinct screams echoed from the vines as at least two hundred rounds chewed through the vegetation like a buzz saw.

"Get some!" Gadgets shouted. "Get some!"

Someone else, maybe Swann, kept shouting, "Vietnam! Vietnam! Vietnam!"

Return fire sliced above their heads, cut through branches behind them and ripped into the stomach of another ex-rifleman named Harrigan. "I'm hit!" he screamed, then tumbled into the bush with a second slug in his chest.

There were a dozen more rounds from a shallow trench below a row of mossy oaks. Another mortar shell burst above Sammy Vong's head, threw him to the pine needles and left him vomiting on his hands and knees. "Okay," he breathed to no one in particular. "I'm okay."

Another long burst of AK fire slammed into the pines above Swann's head. He scrambled into a hollow of ferns, noticed that his shoulder was bleeding again, but finally said, "Screw it! Screw it all!" and squeezed off four shells from the Armscor.

The ensuing blast sent at least one Vietnamese staggering from the shadows, blood pumping from a severed artery, AK firing pointlessly at the sky. In response to Swann's barrage, however, at least ten more AKs opened up from the adjacent hollows and left two men thrashing among the vines. Then, following another round of fire, Swann actually saw figures in the mist ahead—twenty, thirty, forty advancing Vietnamese charging to meet the attack. "Here they come!" he shouted as he squeezed off two more shells from the Armscor.

The exploding grenades sent at least another six Vietnamese staggering to the forest floor. Blancanales had also begun tossing grenades, while Lyons directed an awesome burst of fire from the left flank.

But it wasn't until Gadgets lumbered out from the tall ferns that the advancing shadows began to waver. Gadgets began firing from the high ground, with a long, sweeping burst and another maddened scream. He fired for the most obvious shadows first, then simply raked the entire field, the minigun screaming like a chainsaw, his own screams rising above the electric hum as the shadows reeled and scattered from the spray of death.

Gadgets fired his second, third and fourth bursts from a tiny hill above the stream bed. He fired at the long rank of shadows now exposed below the oaks. Dark shapes writhed, sagging to the ground. Black forms crumpled in the rain of lead. Then it seemed that he was firing at nothing, at the dead stillness that lay before him, at the silent columns of pines and oaks, at the swirling mass of memories from the war.

Leaves continued falling for at least five minutes after the shooting stopped, leaves from the bullet-riddled oaks and shattered dogwood. The birds, however, had fled, and there were no human sounds except for labored breathing.

"Maybe we should press them," Blancanales said. "Maybe we should just keep going with a full court press."

Lyons turned to Schwarz with a questioning glance. "Gadgets?"

But Gadgets just shook his head. "There ain't going to be nothing to press unless you're ready to crawl down into that tunnel."

They had paused in a tangle of mashed vines and shattered branches. At least two Vietnamese lay at their feet, two horribly mangled bodies that must have taken at least thirty rounds apiece. Another body, chewed into pulp, lay among the ferns.

Swann appeared, limping slightly, the blood still seeping from his shoulder. Behind Swann stood Vong, Minh and seven other exhausted veterans.

"We've got three down," Swann said. "Three down and two walking wounded."

Lyons glanced over his shoulder at the drawn faces and tired eyes. "What about the others?"

"The others," Swann said, "are fine."

Lyons turned back to Schwarz and Blancanales with another questioning glance. "And the tunnel?"

"Tunnels are a bitch," Blancanales said. "We know for a fact that tunnels are a real bitch."

"But assuming Minh was right, assuming Kim Kiet was actually showing us the way...?"

Blancanales glanced at Schwarz, and Gadgets nodded with a small shrug. "Assuming Kim Kiet was actually showing us the way," Schwarz finally said, "I think we should probably go for it."

Lyons turned to Blancanales. "And you, Pol?"

"Yeah," Blancanales breathed. "Assuming it really was the girl signaling from a firing post, then I agree we should go for it."

It was nearly two o'clock in the morning, however, before they finally started moving out. Again they moved slowly, cautiously, pausing every sixty or seventy yards so that Lyons could scan the terrain ahead. As they approached the dark mound between the pines where the light had flashed, Minh seemed to grow increasingly agitated. At first his complaints were unspecific, a nagging sense that something was very wrong. Then, by degrees, his fears began to focus on Kim Kiet. He claimed she was in danger, in pain, and that if they didn't hurry, the White Bitch would kill her.

# 28

Kim Kiet was lying on the cot when Sonny Trang and Phom-do entered her chamber, followed by two slender corporals in black pajamas and sandals.

The Woman in White picked up one of Kim's slippers and then knelt by the cot. The general watched nervously from the doorway as the corporals conducted a silent inspection of the room.

"Are you awake?" Phom-do whispered.

Kim opened her eyes and met the woman's gaze, but said nothing.

"Tell me something," Phom-do whispered. "What have you done to ruin your lovely slipper?"

Kim shook her head, still unable to escape the woman's gaze.

"The slipper," Phom-do repeated. "Look, your slippers are covered in mud. How did that happen? There's no mud in here. There's no mud in the passage. There's only mud in the firing ports. How did you get mud on your lovely slippers?"

Trang approached from the entrance and addressed Phom-do in a clearly frightened tone of voice. "Look, let me talk to her. She trusts me."

Phom-do merely smiled and turned her gaze back to Kim. "How did you manage to soil your lovely slippers? Surely you weren't wandering through the passages alone, were you? Surely you didn't wander into one of the firing posts, did you?"

One of the soldiers approached Phom-do, pressing something into the woman's hand that he had found while searching the room.

"And what have we here?" Phom-do cooed. "A flashlight?"

Kim responded with a silent shiver, cursing herself for neglecting to conceal the light.

"And what were you doing with a flashlight?" the woman persisted. "The use of flashlights has been forbidden. Did you signal your boyfriend?"

Trang approached again, this time virtually shouting. "Look, she's just a kid! This isn't her fight!"

Again Phom-do smiled. "Tell me, General, would you like to take her place?"

"Look, I'm just saying that she doesn't know anything."

But by this time the corporal had also found the diary.

"Take her to my chambers," Phom-do ordered.

"TELL ME ABOUT the tunnels again," Lyons requested.

He was kneeling in the tangled dogwood beside Swann, Blancanales, Schwarz and Vong. Although the question had been addressed to no one in particular, it was Swann who responded first, withdrawing his knife and sketching a diagram in the soil.

"The basic configuration—if they're anything like the ones in Nam—will look something like this," he said. "You've got two or three concealed trapdoors up top and a fairly random network below."

"What will the angles be like?" Lyons asked.

"One-twenty, one-sixty."

"And the crawl?"

"About a meter until you hit the lower levels and then they get pretty elaborate."

"What about the doors?"

Swann sketched two additional lines in the soil, then a third descending at a steep right angle. "The doors look like this: planks of wood sealed with nylon and wax, then covered with bushes. But you can blow 'em if you know where to place the charges."

Another ex-rifleman appeared, a thin man named Hooper who had spent the past fifteen years selling Hondas in Pasadena. "Looks like they've got a couple more .51s guarding the perimeter," he said. "Could be mortars, too."

Lyons turned to Blancanales. "How many rockets we got?"

"Six, but one of them took a slug. Could be out of whack."

"And grenades?"

"Grenades are plentiful," Blancanales replied.

Minh appeared, slipping out of the ferns from where he had been scanning the terrain.

"Look, I'd like to say something."

Lyons and the others exchanged quick looks, but said nothing.

"Kim Kiet has told us where the tunnel entrance is," Minh continued. "She risked her life to signal us. Now I think she's probably in extreme danger. We can't just sit here talking anymore, okay? We have to get moving."

Although both Swann and Schwarz started to protest, Lyons finally cut them off with a glance. "Jackie's right," he said. "We have to get moving."

IN MANY WAYS it felt like a dream. From her sleeping chamber they had led her down a narrow ladder to a dank, unlit air raid shelter. Then they dragged her along a narrow passage and through a long, winding crawl space, until at last they came to the White Bitch's lair.

It was a vast, circular room, far larger than Kim could have possibly imagined. The ceiling was high-beamed and coffered with what looked like dragons cut into the woodwork. The walls had been paneled with varnished pine, which set off the collection of watercolors from the homeland: landscapes of water orchids, temples laced with vines, and rice paddies. The furniture was dark: burgundy velvet and black teak. Only the bed and its canopy of mosquito netting was white. The chains and manacles dangling from the ceiling were silver.

The corporal attached the manacles to Kim's wrists and slowly drew the chains taut until she was standing on tiptoe. He then withdrew a broad leather strap from a teak chest, placed it on a table and stepped back into the shadows. There may have been other instruments on the table, but Kim couldn't bring herself to look.

"You know, I've been dreaming of this moment for some time," Phom-do whispered from behind Kim's line of sight. She stepped to Kim's side and began to toy absently with Kim's hair. Then, tugging a little harder so that Kim found herself arched like a bow, she added, "And now we're about to play a little game."

A knife appeared, a long, slender instrument that cut away Kim's blouse as if it were paper and left her naked to the waist. Kim shut her eyes, but she couldn't control her trembling at the sound of leather sliding off the table.

There was no whispered word of warning, nothing at all to prepare her. There was merely the whistle of leather through the air and the explosion of hot pain on her back. Kim bit her lip to keep from screaming, but she couldn't suppress a slight whimper.

"Smarts, doesn't it?" Phom-do rasped.

LYONS AND THE OTHERS approached the dark mound from the east. When they reached the rise above the mound, Lyons gathered his men around him for a few last words. "Listen up. There's something I want to say. Now I don't pretend to know what you boys went through in the war, but I know this much—for some reason we've been given a second chance to even the score with the enemy. And this time it's on our ground. So let's just nut up and do it!''

Although no one actually said anything, the response was fairly evident in their eyes—a cool hunger and a slow-burning resolve.

They moved out slowly, softly, easing through the ferns until they reached the edge of the circular glade. The vantage point gave them a fairly clear view of the mound and two more bunkers wedged into the side of the hill. It was also evident—thanks to the Starlite scope—that there was a sentry watching from behind a fallen pine.

"Any ideas?" Lyons whispered.

He was resting on his elbows between Blancanales and Schwarz. Swann and a dozen others lay to the left. Hutch, Vong and Minh lay to the right.

"How about giving them another little taste of the LAW?" Schwarz suggested.

Blancanales shook his head. "The angle isn't right. You'll never score."

"So?" Lyons asked.

"So how about I just crawl on up there, stick it to that sentry and then slam-dunk the bunker with a couple of grenades?"

"And how the hell do you think you're going to reach the sentry without being seen?" Schwarz countered.

Blancanales grinned. "I'll show you," he said as he slid into the tangles of ferns.

Pol took the sentry from behind, rising out of the darkness, engulfing the man in blackness and then dragging him back to the ferns. It was as clean and perfect a kill as any Schwarz had witnessed. When the body was safely out of sight, Blancanales withdrew the grenade and Lyons extended an arm into the air as a signal to the others to start moving out.

PHOM-DO PUT DOWN the strap and pressed a cold hand on Kim's burning back. Kim responded with an involuntary shiver and a slight jerk of the head, but otherwise continued to remain silent. Her body was drenched in perspiration. Her hair hung in damp ringlets around her shoulders. Although the lashing hadn't broken the skin yet, the welts had begun to blister.

Phom-do smiled. "Hurts, doesn't it?"

Kim responded with another involuntary shiver and attempted to bury her face in her arm. In addition to the salt from her tears, there was the faintly metallic taste of fear.

"But to be quite honest, this has only been the introduction, the necessary introduction of pain and stress," the Woman in White informed her. She ran a finger along Kim's spine, smiling again at the trembling response and the sharp intake of breath. "You see, it's necessary to open the pores and to excite the nerves. That's the reason I haven't begun to question you concerning your act of treason. The questions will come later. The questions come when you've been reduced to a quivering mess of raw flesh."

Phom-do withdrew to a corner of the room, and then the sound of squealing wheels across the planked floor broke the silence. Kim shifted her head a fraction of an inch and caught a glimpse of an automobile battery and dangling electrical cables.

The Woman in White wasted no time connecting the cables to the fleshy areas of Kim's thighs. The last thing Kim saw before shutting her eyes was the quick spark of the hot volts dancing between the electrodes. Then she became aware only of the sounds of her own blood rushing through her ears, of her heart pounding in her chest, and finally of the explosion that rocked the whole room.

Phom-do dropped the electrical cables and turned to the door. There were two distinct shouts from the passage above, four rapid shots, then the breathless voice of a soldier in the doorway.

"They've attacked the bunkers," the soldier screamed in Vietnamese. "And now they're going for the firing posts."

ABOVE GROUND automatic weapons flashed in the blackness. Tracers cut the night sky and resulted in screams of agony and terror. Two Vietnamese soldiers, shredded from the blast of the first grenades, moaned from beneath the dark mound of pine needles.

Lyons jammed another magazine into his rifle and rose from the ferns. "Let's go!" he shouted. "Go! Go! Go!"

The veterans followed with enraged cries, spraying lead at anything even faintly human-shaped. Another grenade sent up a spray of leaves and soil. Another dark shape staggered from the mound between the pines and unleashed a blind burst of AK fire before sagging back into the shadows.

Lyons jammed in yet another magazine while Schwarz and Swann scanned the glade for enemy movement.

"Pol's found the entrance," Schwarz panted. "It's just to the left of that mound."

"One entrance ain't enough," Swann countered. "We've got to get them in a pincer."

More AK-47 fire flashed from a knoll at the edge of the glade. There was also the heavier thump of a larger weapon.

"How about we blow that .51?" Schwarz suggested. "How about we blow that sucker and expose the tunnel under it?"

Lyons exchanged a quick glance with Swann, then nodded. "All right, where are those LAWs?"

Hutch appeared, lugging two of the antitank weapons in collapsible, discardable firing tubes. He laid one of the LAWs at his feet, then hefted the second one onto his shoulder and peered out from behind the oak. Although the night was still alive with flashing muzzles and arcing tracers, it seemed to Hutch as if he had entered a very quiet place of awesome concentration and perfectly controlled fury.

"Put that guy to bed," he whispered to himself as his finger eased onto the trigger and his eye descended to the sight.

There was a trailing streak as the rocket left the tube, then a muffled thump and shower of orange sparks. A thin scream lingered for a moment in the aftershock, then nothing.

There were a few isolated shots as Lyons and the others moved out, but finally it was very quiet. Although Lyons and Schwarz were the first to reach the blown firing post and peer into the tunnel, the first to actually make the descent was Blancanales followed by Minh, Swann and the remaining veterans.

# 29

Two passages diverged from the entrance below the blown machine gun nest. The first was relatively straight and had been meticulously laid with timber. The second was crude and fell almost vertically into blackness.

"What's your preference?" Blancanales whispered to Swann.

The Vietnam vet shrugged, then said, "Makes no difference to me."

By now four more veterans had scrambled down behind them. They carried knives, pistols, flashlights and grenades. Their rifles, however, were pointless— too loud and too bulky.

Blancanales held up two fingers and pointed to his left to indicate the darker passage. Swann nodded, turned to the men behind him and repeated the gesture. Then they started moving again: Blancanales, Minh and a wiry ex-tunnel rat named Tragg to the lower passage; Swann and three more veterans along the higher route. Somewhere beyond sight and sound Lyons and Schwarz led a six-man team into the primary passage below the dark mound.

FIRST CONTACT CAME after only thirty meters. Blancanales paused where the passage turned sharply to the north. He transferred his pistol to his left hand and withdrew his knife to probe for booby traps. His attention was mainly focused on a patch of soft earth that he knew might conceal a bed of sharpened stakes or possibly a claymore. Then, out of the corner of his eye, he saw it—the telltale glint of steel.

He pressed himself against the passage wall as two silenced shots sliced past his left ear and thudded into the earth. Signaling to the men behind him, he replaced his knife and cocked his handgun. Although the .45 had long been Blancanales's weapon of choice, it had never been used by the tunnel rats. It had always been considered too bulky and loud. But Blancanales rarely let others influence his decision and so he quickly flicked off the safety and fired.

He squeezed off three rapid shots that rolled like cannon fire through the dark passage. But even with the deafening explosion, he was still able to hear the scream as his slugs impacted with muscle and bone.

The Able Team warrior hesitated, waiting for the roar in his ears to subside and the after-flash to fade from his vision. He felt something cool and dry slide across his left wrist and prayed it wasn't a snake. Then, finally signaling to the others, he started crawling forward again.

Beyond the point where the passage curved lay a narrow drop to a larger passage. There were also steps and another concealed door. Pol replaced the .45 in his left hand, withdrew his knife and began to probe the earth.

"Check for wires," Trang whispered softly over his shoulder.

Just as he said it, Blancanales felt the blade of his knife encounter something hard, possibly a steel spring. Then, suddenly rolling forward and flattening himself on the ground, he shouted, "Get down!"

Although Tragg responded instantly, he still couldn't escape the spring-driven spike that shot from the ceiling—fifteen inches of tempered steel pierced his left eye.

Tragg screamed and groped blindly for the cylindrical steel protruding from his eye. Blood and ocular fluid sprayed in every direction as the man's head whipped from side to side. He fell back into Minh's arms, shuddering in pain and shock. Then, finally letting his hands fall and arching his back with another long spasm, he became still.

No one spoke. No one even exhanged glances. The body was simply laid aside and the slow crawl continued. Thirty yards farther on they passed the Vietnamese Blancanales had shot earlier. The man had curled into a fetal position before dying.

LYONS FROZE at the sound of shots, glanced back at the team behind him and withdrew his weapon. He carried a modified Smith & Wesson .44 Magnum. Weighing only thirty-eight ounces and fitted with a silencer, it fired a 15-pellet bullet with a two-foot shot pattern. Although not necessarily a killing weapon, it was well suited for close-quarter work in the darkness.

He eased himself forward, then paused again and waited for the others to follow. Among his party were two former tunnel rats—a wiry Puerto Rican named Guitterez and a stocky little Irishman named Flanagan.

Beyond the point where Lyons lay the passage veered sharply down and to the left. He flicked off the safety on the Smith & Wesson and switched on his Mag-Lite, easing the beam along the passage walls until his eye encountered what looked like a firing ledge. Then, switching off the light and putting it back in his belt, he slowly inched forward again.

A bat squealed from the blackness beyond the ledge, and a hammer, probably on a Soviet pistol, eased back into the firing position. Lyons shot before he actually saw anything, shot for the center of the blackness ahead, knowing that the spread of pellets couldn't possibly miss. He heard a muffled groan, shot again and heard what must have been a body slumping to the ground. Then, finally moving past the ledge and leveling his weapon at the shadows below, he squeezed off three more rounds.

A shrill scream broke from the passage, and a face virtually shredded by the pellets briefly appeared in the glow of a tumbling flashlight. A second scream broke from the darkness as Lyons squeezed off another round. But there were also incoming shots now, four or five quick rounds from a Tokarev.

Lyons flattened himself on the floor of the passage, squeezed off his last round, then dropped his head as another six or seven slugs whistled above him. "Gadgets!" he whispered as fragments of the walls rained down on his back. "Gadgets!"

"Right here," Schwarz answered, leaning out with a .44.

The .44 fired a highly potent segmented shell. Although technically illegal under the Geneva Convention, the bullet had proven to be extremely effective in the tunnels. And moments after Schwarz fired that effectiveness was obvious.

Two Vietnamese screamed at the impact of the shells as the bullets tore into their midsections. Lyons caught the fragmented impression of a wide-eyed face with a mouthful of blood. Then, hearing the .44 blasting again, he heard a third scream and caught another glimpse of a crumpling form and a spray of blood.

Four shots cracked out in reply to Schwarz's .44, but by now both Flanagan and Guitterez had also opened up with handguns. They shot rapidly, bracing themselves against the cold wall and squinting into the darkness. Then, taking four seconds to reload, they squeezed off another sixteen rounds between them. Silence then fell over the tunnel.

THE MOMENT THE SHOOTING stopped Blancanales began easing forward again. Swann's team had joined them, and together the two teams moved forward.

Beyond the point where Blancanales had found his first kill lay a narrow drop that served as a blast wall. They then passed another passage before reaching the first sleeping chamber.

Blancanales paused again, resting on his haunches, his back against the rough wall. The door to the chamber consisted of a rectangular sheet of sailcloth suspended from the ceiling of the passage. Lantern light threw a dim rectangle on the opposite wall, but there were no other signs of life.

The Able Team warrior extended the .45 until the muzzle of the weapon reached the sailcloth. Then, slowly easing the cloth back, he peered into the chamber. Apart from the narrow cot, a tin cup and a soft drink bottle, the only indication of human habitation was a pair of woman's shoes.

"Kim!" whispered Minh from over Blancanales's shoulder. "Those are Kim's shoes!"

Blancanales eased the sailcloth back until his eyes encompassed the entire room. Minh's eyes, however, remained fixed on the shoes.

"Those belong to Kim Kiet," Minh whispered again. Then, turning back to Swann and the others, he said, "Kim's here! Just as I said, she's here!"

Blancanales let the sailcloth fall back into place, then turned to Swann. "All right then, Jackie boy, let's go find her."

Two more passages led from the sleeping chamber. Blancanales looked down one as far as he could until it faded into the shadows. Then, peering along the lower passage, he finally started forward again. He moved on his hands and knees, his knuckles scraping against exposed rocks. He moved slowly, his eyes continually scanning for trip wires, punji stakes and claymores. Now and again he paused, listening for the sound of a cocking weapon or the quiet echo of boots.

Suddenly Blancanales froze, lifting a hand and extending his fingers. The passage seemed to fall away to nothing, to a black hole that might extend for miles. He turned to his left and saw Minh's eager eyes peering over his shoulder. He turned to his right and exchanged a quick glance with Swann.

"What?" Swann mouthed silently.

Blancanales tapped his finger against his ear, then pointed at the inky blackness below. In addition to the sounds of a dozen breathing men, Pol had heard fingers anxiously tapping rifle barrels, the soft rustle of uniforms and even a suppressed cough.

Swann held up two fingers, but Blancanales shook his head and mouthed the word, "More." Swann nodded and withdrew a four-gauge riot gun, a weapon that had been a favorite of the tunnel rats. Blancanales, however, shook his head and withdrew a grenade. Then, pulling out his knife and transferring the .45 to his left hand, he started forward. By the time he reached the mouth of the hole, his body was drenched in sweat and his knees had begun to bleed.

Pol paused again at the mouth of the hole, transferred his knife to his left hand, placed his .45 between his knees and pulled the pin on the grenade. Although there was always the possibility that a blast might cause the walls to collapse, grenades had always had their place in tunnel warfare. He paused once more before actually pulling the pin, his ears fixed on what sounded like another tapping finger. Then, counting to three, he lobbed the grenade into the hole.

The explosion, echoing off the walls, left him momentarily deaf, and the dust and blown fragments left him temporarily sightless. But finally springing off the wall and leaping into the blackness, it seemed that sight and sound no longer really mattered. All that counted was the feel of his blade against flesh and bone.

Blancanales landed on something soft and damp, heard an agonized moan and then actually felt his hand slide into what seemed like a gouged chest. Then, spinning at the sound of a second moan, he brought his knife down in a long arc and felt another spray of blood on his face. After that, silence reigned.

Although the blackness was still impenetrable, it was obvious that he had landed in some sort of storage room. Extending his hand, his fingers encountered what felt like steel shelves packed with canned food. His boot touched a filing cabinet. When he finally switched on the Mag-Lite, he saw the bodies—at least a dozen mangled corpses thrown against the wall by the blast.

Blancanales rose to his feet, extending the light through the drop and flashed it on and off. He shifted the beam back down to his feet, then along the walls until he found a circular trapdoor. Hearing another bat flap beyond the door, he switched off the light and crouched in the corner. As the whisper of wings drew closer, he once again transferred his .45 to his left hand and gripped the knife in his right.

The trapdoor was a fairly massive affair constructed of pine and rubber sealing as a precaution against gas. There had apparently been two locks fitted to the door, a crude bolt and a complicated spring. When Blancanales heard the bolt slide away on the opposite side of the door, he rose to a half crouch. Then, as the spring sounded and the door eased back, he lifted the knife level with his waist.

He fixed his attention on the sounds: on the scrape of another boot on the floor, on a whispered question in Vietnamese and the softly grunted reply. Then, finally extending a hand, he made contact with a shoulder and struck with a quick slice to the throat. Then, grabbing hold of an arm and drawing the body closer, he struck again—this time the chest. He saw the wide eyes briefly lock onto his own, felt the weight of the man working against the blade and the hot blood on his wrist. Then, finally wrenching the blade free, he tossed the body aside.

There were confused shouts from the passage. A flashlight streaked across the ceiling. The Able Team warrior felt another shoulder brush past his fingers, and he lashed out with the blade again. More blood sprayed across his face. A frantic scream reverberated off the walls. Three wild shots sent bullets singing into the blackness. And then more soldiers poured through the door.

Blancanales slashed like a madman, plunging the knife into backs and bellies, drenching himself in their blood. An unseen hand closed like a vise around his ankle, and he brought his boot down hard on the wrist. He heard another agonized scream as the bone cracked, and then he dropped to one knee and began frantically stabbing and slicing.

LYONS SWITCHED on the Mag-Lite and trained the beam down the length of the passage and through the trapdoor where the bodies lay. "Pol?" he whispered softly. "Pol, that you?"

Blancanales rose slowly from the gore, glanced over his shoulder at the anxious faces of Swann, Minh and the others. Then, finally turning again to the passage beyond the door, he breathed, "Yeah, it's me."

There were sounds of boots hitting the earthen floor and a quick glimpse of a falling flashlight. Then, as more flashlights cut the darkness, the whole group became visible. At their feet lay at least six more bodies.

"So where are the rest of them?" Blancanales asked, his arm drenched in blood.

Lyons nodded at the passage behind him. "Down there."

"Well, what are we waiting for?" Blancanales questioned.

Schwarz stepped forward, letting the beam of his flashlight briefly play on Blancanales's blood-soaked form. "I don't think they're going anywhere. I've got

Hutch up there with the minigun, and he's *definitely* got the exits covered."

"So what are you telling me?" Blancanales asked. "This is it?"

"Yeah," Lyons sighed. "This is just about it."

As the two teams formed into a single column and moved off down the passage, however, Jackie Minh made himself heard. "But where's Kim?"

## 30

Although the shooting had subsided, there were still frantic voices in the passage and the acrid scent of cordite in the air. There were also traces of blood on Phom-do's cheek, and her white silk tunic had been torn at the shoulder.

A pair of footsteps echoed from the passage and then the general's agitated voice drew Phom-do's attention away from Kim Kiet. "We can't wait any longer! Do you hear me? We can't wait any longer!" he yelled.

But Phom-do just smiled.

A second man entered the chamber with further news of the situation. "The survivors have been deployed in the station above, Colonel, but there's no way to secure the secondary passages," he informed the Woman in White.

"Listen to him, Colonel. He says there's no way to secure the secondary passages," the general pleaded. "That means they could begin shooting at us any moment."

Phom-do frowned. "Very well," she finally agreed.

In the corner of the chamber, beneath a print showing cranes in a pond, lay a cleverly concealed door. Beyond the door lay another passage that eventually led to an escape hatch in the forest. When the hidden spring was activated and a passage revealed, Phom-do moved slowly to the tiny door and slipped inside. But as Trang made a move to follow, she glanced back over her shoulder. "I'm sorry, General, but it seems you've served your purpose." She then turned to the young soldier. "Kill them both!"

JACKIE MINH HESITATED at the mouth of the passage. Having slipped away from the others, he had let his instincts guide him—first along a tunnel to the forward aid station, then still deeper past the sleeping chambers. Although there had been moments when he felt himself hopelessly lost, he never entirely lost a sense of Kim. He felt that she was silently calling out his name from the blackness below.

Minh withdrew his Mag-Lite, switched it on and peered out from an alcove. In contrast to the network above, the tunnels here were large enough to accommodate a small truck. The walls were smooth, as if they had been bored by machine. The floors had been lined with shaved planks and the ventilation shafts fitted with gas traps. There was also a scent he hadn't encountered before—an oddly sweet blend of jasmine and roses.

He switched off the Mag-Lite and picked up his weapon—a .25 Beretta he had borrowed from one of the more experienced tunnel fighters. Checking the chamber, he started forward again. When he heard the frantic whispers at the end of the passage, he increased his pace to a half run. And when he heard Kim's muffled cry, he broke into a sprint.

AT FIRST KIM could do nothing but stare. The young soldier who had been ordered to kill her had withdrawn a serrated bayonet—a weapon that had been a favorite of the Vietnamese tunnel rats. The White Bitch had vanished into the secret tunnel, leaving nothing but the scent of her perfume. The general had backed up against the far wall, shaking his head and repeatedly mouthing the word, "No." It wasn't hard for Kim to tell what the soldier was thinking as he slowly ran his gaze along her naked body.

"Listen to me," Trang finally pleaded, realizing the peril of the situation. "I'm not without resources. Spare me and I'll make you rich beyond your wildest dreams."

The boy, however, ignored him, his eyes still glued to Kim's helpless body.

"Oh, I see," Trang added desperately. "So it's the girl you want. Very well, you can have her. I give her to you. But just spare me. Do you understand? Spare me and I'll make you rich."

The soldier may have hesitated, actually pondering the general's words for a moment, but he still didn't take his eyes off Kim, which was his first and last mistake.

The general lunged like an enraged bear, clamped his hands around the soldier's wrist and used his weight to press the boy against the wall. The soldier grunted, straining to escape Trang's grip, and bringing his knee up into the general's groin. Trang brought his shoulder into play, yanked the bayonet free and plunged it into the soldier's stomach. The young man screamed with horror and pain as Trang drove the blade still deeper into his flesh. Then he grunted again with a mouthful of blood, and his eyes rolled grotesquely back into his skull as he dropped.

A lot of things went through Kim's mind as she watched the general approach with the bayonet still in his hand. She thought about how it was one thing to stand chained and naked in front of Phom-do, but quite another to stand in front of a man who now knew she had betrayed his love. She thought about the first time she and the general had met, the first time he had made love to her. She thought about the ache in her arms, and the burning sensation across her back from the strap.

And then she heard another footstep behind her, a cocking pistol and a half-familiar voice...and she also found herself thinking about Jackie Minh.

MINH FACED the general at the entrance to the chamber. His back was straight, his eyes fixed on Trang's and his left hand clamped to his right wrist in order to steady the pistol.

The general immediately shielded himself behind Kim, holding the bayonet at her throat. And then the two men just looked at each other... waiting, planning, calculating the odds.

"You!" Trang finally breathed.

"That's right," Minh whispered. "I've returned."

"I'll cut her throat, boy," Trang threatened. "You hear me? Pull the trigger and I'll cut her throat from ear to ear."

Minh shook his head. "That won't be necessary, General." Then, tossing the Beretta onto the floor and moving to the center of the room, he said, "Now come and get me. Come on, you bastard, make your move!"

At least three seconds passed before the general finally lowered the bayonet from Kim's throat, three taut seconds during which Kim couldn't prevent herself from whispering Minh's name.

But although Minh may have heard her, he didn't take his eyes off Trang. "Come on, General. It's just you and me now. It's right back where it all began—just you and me."

Trang approached slowly, the bayonet weaving in his hand like a cobra. Although Minh seemed to withdraw, in actual fact, he delivered a springing rear kick. He struck for the groin and then clamped his arm over the general's wrist. Trang screamed as his elbow cracked, and at least four inches of bone slid through the bloody flesh.

"Bastard!" Minh growled, his face only inches from Trang's. The young man suddenly increased the pressure so that the bayonet clattered to the floor, and the general's body arched in agony. Minh brought his left hand down to the man's throat in a classic killing

blow—the fingers slightly bent for tension, ready for
that last little snap that would intensify the impact.

Trang sank to his knees in pain, clutching his shattered windpipe and shaking his head in disbelief.
When he fell, his eyes were still fixed on Minh, his lips
whispering something over and over again.

Minh only returned the gaze for a moment. Then,
slowly rising to his feet, he released Kim's wrists from
the manacles and gathered her up in his arms.

## 31

Carl Lyons assembled his men in the darkness, then turned to face Billy Swann in the glow of a Mag-Lite. "I want you to get your boys out of here," he said quietly. "Get them on top and tell them to open up on anything that comes crawling out of the ground."

Swann responded with a frown. "You know, this tunnel ain't made from the same shit they had in Nam. You try to blow it and you could bring the whole damn thing down on your head."

"That's why I want you to get your boys out of here," Lyons said.

Swann seemed to hesitate for a moment, then finally nodded and slipped back down the passage. Although he knew there might be one or two complaints, he didn't think anyone would be upset about the prospect of daylight and fresh air.

Lyons waited until the passage had grown quiet again before rejoining Schwarz and Blancanales. From where they now crouched the tunnel extended about thirty yards before plunging into blackness again. Although there were no specific signs that men waited below, the odors couldn't have been more evident—sweat, urine and rotting rice.

"Ever seen a cornered rat?" Blancanales whispered. "Damn thing will go right for your throat. And if you cut off its head, you'll still need a crowbar to pry its jaws apart."

Lyons switched on the Mag-Lite and eased the beam along the passage until the tunnel bent out of sight. "You got any better ideas?"

Blancanales shrugged. "Not really. But there ain't nothing the three of us can do that I can't do alone."

"No way," Schwarz put in. "No way am I going to allow that."

But Blancanales had his response ready. "Look at it this way. Only reason they're holed up in there is because they think we've got an army up here. Now I go down there alone and they're not going to be ready for it. And that can work to my advantage. Know what I mean?"

"All right," Lyons finally said. "But at the first sign of real trouble—"

Blancanales cut him off with a quick grin. "Do you think I'm some kind of hero or something?"

THERE WERE FRAGMENTS of broken pottery, spent cartridges and even a discarded boot along the passage. There were also traces of blood and wads of bandages. They were definitely hurting, Blancanales told himself as he inched through the blackness. Maybe not down for the count, but definitely hurting.

He paused where the passage gave way to another fire wall, then withdrew his knife and began to probe the floor. If this were Nam, he thought, they'd be long gone by now. But here they've got no place to run. Here it's do or die.

The blade of his knife struck something metallic, and after another five minutes of probing, he found four more eighteen-inch spikes embedded in the earth.

He paused again where the passage gave way to a pool of black water. And then the soft sigh of someone waiting just beyond the bend sent a chill up his spine.

Blancanales stopped, waited and listened, holding his breath. He heard the faint rustle of a uniform and the gentle muffled crack of a leather boot. Carefully transferring his knife from the left hand to the right, he eased himself forward another foot. Silence, he thought vaguely, wasn't just the absence of sound; it was a state of mind, a state of becoming nothing.

He stopped again at the sound of air sucking through clenched teeth. Although the figure was now hardly more than a patch of clotted darkness, the Able Team warrior was close—very close. There was a faint echo of dripping moisture, and suddenly Blancanales could feel the enemy.

Pol struck when the fingers of his left hand encountered the hairless arm. He struck for the throat, severing the vocal cords so that there were only sounds of escaping air and the soft crack of bone. Then, for a moment, he just sat and listened to his own sweat dripping onto the passage floor.

Pol didn't really hear them as much as sense them—fifteen, maybe twenty silent soldiers waiting for him in the blackness. Ahead, the passage zigzagged for at least thirty yards. Then came another fire wall, then another thirty twisting yards.

He pressed himself against the wall, feeling the cool moisture of underground water. A tough spot for a last stand, he thought, recalling one of the first maxims of tunnel design: water means pressure and pressure means collapse. He withdrew his Mag-Lite, switched it on and inched the beam along the passage until he heard the snap of a bullet entering a chamber.

Bingo.

He switched off the light, withdrew a grenade and sank to his belly. Twenty yards farther along the passage he found a second booby trap—a claymore wired to the ceiling. He also found another carpet of stainless-steel spikes, just as he became the target of gunfire.

Four slugs glanced off the walls beyond the next turn. Blancanales plastered himself to the floor, then realized that his caution was pointless. Given the zigzagging design of the passage, the line of fire didn't extend more than ten yards. The shots had merely been a warning, an announcement of the stalemate.

The Able Team warrior rose to his knees. His clothing was now drenched with moisture, and it vaguely crossed his mind that the tunnel walls must have been under tremendous pressure because water was actually trickling through the cracks. Another four or five shots rang out, but this time he hardly blinked. A Mexican standoff, he told himself.

He eased himself forward to the last bend in the tunnel, then slowly peered around the wall. Six more shots immediately cracked out from between two steel sheets, whining off into the blackness.

He withdrew a grenade and took another quick look around the corner. Although he had little hope of tossing the explosive through the firing slits of the steel sheets, he was fairly certain the blast would at least rattle them a little, maybe shake the plates loose so that a second or third grenade would drop into their laps. But as he extended a finger to pull the ring, an entirely new thought struck him. Why not tell them the war was over?

He waited almost ten minutes before he finally tossed the first grenade—ten minutes just sitting in the blackness and trying to decide if he should tell them the damn war was over. But when he tried to peer around the corner again, at least eight more shots rang out from the steel barricade. At that point he pulled the pin and tossed the grenade without further thought.

The blast sent shock waves all along the passage, leaving him briefly deaf again and coughing with the rolling dust. There were also sounds of spurting water now, and chunks of rock like the size of watermelons fell from the ceiling.

"You in there!" he shouted. "This is pointless! Do you understand? Pointless!"

But when they let loose with another round of fire, he couldn't stop himself from tossing a second grenade.

He followed it with a third and a fourth...until whole sections of the passage began to collapse as blackness folded in on blackness and underground pools of water began pouring from the fissures.

Blancanales actually found himself swimming for a thin shaft of light and the echo of his name called out through the darkness.

PHOM-DO HEARD the screaming rats, hundreds of them fleeing the collapsing sections of her tunnel. When she glanced behind her, however, she saw nothing in the darkness. Although she had been crawling for the better part of thirty minutes, she had actually traveled less than a hundred yards. And she was tired—tired, cold and utterly alone.

She rose to her haunches in order to relieve her bleeding knees. Then, draining the last bit of water from a plastic canteen, she sank back to the floor. It wasn't so much that she was afraid to die. It was just that she was afraid to die alone and in the blackness where all her tortured victims might come back to haunt her.

She paused where the tunnel rose toward a narrow shaft of light that filtered through a hidden grate. Although there may have been a safer exit deeper in the woods, the shaft and the scent of pines that came through it were too tempting.

She hesitated again three feet from the mouth of the exit, taking in deep breaths of air and fixing her gaze on the shadows of foliage above. She glanced back down the passage into the blackness and then, hearing what was probably another section of the tunnel collapsing, she finally started climbing up to the light.

She eased away the grate and slid her head and shoulders through the opening. But when she finally dragged herself out of the hole and onto the forest floor, all she saw were the ghosts—ten, fifteen, twenty grim faces that had come back from the dead to haunt her.

BILLY SWANN HESITATED before giving the order to fire. He hesitated long enough to let the Woman in White look into his eyes and remember. Then, dropping the safety and nodding his head, he squeezed the trigger with the rest of the veterans.

They fired from a ragged semicircle above the tunnel door. They fired with long, simultaneous bursts that lifted the White Bitch into the air, left her briefly shuddering on tiptoe and then virtually cut her in two.

IT WAS NEARLY six in the morning before the last of the seriously wounded were evacuated and the last of the bodies were dragged from the ferns. A fine mist had replaced the night fog, spreading from the hollows in undulating waves. The pines were alive with birds, and it was cold.

"So what happens now?" Swann asked.

Carl Lyons looked skyward at a circling hawk. "We go home, Billy. That's what happens. We get the hell out of here and go home."

Gadgets Schwarz appeared, stepping out of the trees with at least six dog tags dangling from his fingers. "These are the last of our own. Bagged, tagged and accounted for."

Lyons nodded, took the dog tags and handed them to Swann. "I don't know what you're going to tell their families, but officially last night never happened. Do you understand?"

Pol Blancanales appeared, still shivering with the chill, still covered with filth from the tunnel. "We've got a dozen more Commies by the stream. You just want us to leave them?"

Lyons nodded and sighed. "Yeah, just leave them there for now."

"And what about our wives and kids?" Swann asked. "What are we supposed to tell them?"

Lyons turned again to watch the gray forms of the veterans wandering through the mist—some scouring for souvenirs, some just resting among the pines. "Tell them the same thing you're going to tell yourselves. Tell them the war's over."

# Epilogue

Detective Sam Vong pulled out a pack of cigarettes, lit one and took a long draw. Among the jingling change in his pocket were two shells from an AK-47. Among the debris on his coffee table were two notices from local newspapers concerning the death, by natural causes, of Sonny Trang.

"Something tells me that people around here are going to be celebrating a wedding pretty soon," he said.

He tapped on the windowpane. Below, Jackie Minh and Kim Kiet were still locked in each other's arms.

It was six o'clock in the evening. The breeze from the bay smelled faintly of canneries and noodle houses. The darkening sky was filled with at least a dozen newspaper kites. Lyons, Schwarz and Blanca-nales lay sprawled across Vong's shabby furniture. The radio was tuned to one of the underground stations that mostly played Irving Berlin and Cole Porter.

"So where do you guys go from here?" Vong asked.

Lyons responded with a slow sigh, then took another sip of beer. "Does it matter?"

Vong shrugged. "Not really."

Also among the papers on the coffee table was a reprimand from the Orange County police chief and a notice to appear before an Internal Affairs board.

Blancanales picked up the notice, examined the signature and tossed it back onto the table. "What about you, Sammy? What are you going to do when they start asking questions about what's been going on around here?"

Vong grinned slyly, his cigarette drooping from his lower lip and his fingers still toying with the change in his pocket. "I guess I'll just tell them it's Gook Town." He smiled. "I'll tell them it's Gook Town and leave it at that."

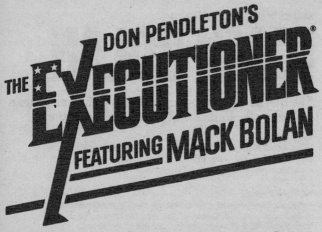

# DON PENDLETON'S
## THE EXECUTIONER®
### FEATURING MACK BOLAN

Baptized in the fire and blood of Vietnam, Mack Bolan has become America's supreme hero. Fiercely patriotic and compassionate, he's a man with a high moral code whose sense of right and wrong sometimes violates society's rules. In adventures filled with heart-stopping action, Bolan has thrilled readers around the world. Experience the high-voltage charge as Bolan rallies to the call of his own conscience in daring exploits that place him in peril with virtually every heartbeat.

"Anyone who stands against the civilized forces of truth and justice will sooner or later have to face the piercing blue eyes and cold Beretta steel of Mack Bolan...civilization's avenging angel."
—*San Francisco Examiner*

GOLD EAGLE

**Available wherever paperbacks are sold.**

MB-2RR

**Vietnam: Ground Zero is written by men who saw it all, did it all and lived to tell it all**

**"Some of the most riveting war fiction written . . ."**
— Ed Gorman, *Cedar Rapids Gazette*

# DEATHLANDS

## A different world—a different war

**RED EQUINOX**            $3.95 ☐
Ryan Cawdor and his band of postnuclear survivors enter a
malfunctioning gateway and are transported to Moscow, where
Americans are hated with an almost religious fervor and blamed
for the destruction of the world.

**DECTRA CHAIN**            $3.95 ☐
A gateway that is part of a rambling underwater complex brings
Ryan Cawdor and the group off the coast of what was once
Maine, where they are confronted with mutant creatures and
primitive inhabitants.

**ICE & FIRE**            $3.95 ☐
A startling discovery changes the lives of Ryan Cawdor and his
band of postholocaust survivors when they encounter several
cryogenically preserved bodies.

| | |
|---|---|
| Total Amount | $ _____ |
| Plus 75¢ Postage | .75 |
| Payment enclosed | $ _____ |

**Please Print**

Name: _____

Address: _____

City: _____

State/Prov: _____

Zip/Postal Code: _____

DL-B1

## by GAR WILSON

The battle-hardened five-man commando unit known as Phoenix Force continues its onslaught against the hard realities of global terrorism in an endless crusade for freedom, justice and the rights of the individual. Schooled in guerrilla warfare, equipped with the latest in lethal weapons, Phoenix Force's adventures have made them a legend in their own time. Phoenix Force is the free world's foreign legion!

"Gar Wilson is excellent! Raw action attacks the reader on every page."
—Don Pendleton

Phoenix Force titles are available wherever paperbacks are sold.

PF-1R

PHOENIX FORCE

GOLD EAGLE